LANDSLIDE
1988

"A fast-moving, entertaining first novel with an intriguing plot and some interesting insights into back-room and fast-frame presidential politics."
—*Dallas Morning News*

"Lamm and Grossman have created a compelling story with realistic characters. Their keen insights into the rough and tumble arena of presidential politics keep the reader engrossed."
—Morris K. Udall, member of congress

"Firsthand political and media insight...A behind-the-scenes look at the political system in contemporary America." —*Library Journal*

"Dick Lamm and Arnie Grossman know politics and public policy from the inside. They recognize the promise and the danger—*1988* is a compelling tale of one at the expense of the other."
—Timothy Wirth, member of congress

"The narrative is skillfully put together, with all-too-credible characters who use unscrupulous methods in the Presidential campaign. All sorts of skullduggery is brought to bear from simple bribery to attempted assassination...Mark this up as a banner year for Author-Governor Lamm." —*John Barkham Reviews*

1988

GOV. RICHARD LAMM
★★★★★★★★★★★★&★★★★★★★★★★★★★
ARNOLD GROSSMAN

St. Martin's
Press

1988
Copyright © 1985 by Richard Lamm and Arnold Grossman

First St. Martin's Press Mass market edition/ August 1986

ISBN: 0-312-90287-5
Can. ISBN: 0-312-90288-3

10   9   8   7   6   5   4   3   2   1

For our children: Scott and Heather Lamm;
Alex, Rachel, and Daniel Grossman.

ACKNOWLEDGMENTS

The authors wish to acknowledge Clarus Backes, book editor of the *Denver Post,* for his generous counsel and encouragement, and Dan Buck, administrative assistant to Congresswoman Patricia Schroeder, for his assistance and guidance. We also wish to thank Charles Bartholomew, president of Evans and Bartholomew Advertising, for his many contributions to this effort.

1

SO THIS IS WHAT IT'S LIKE, GETTING SHOT BY someone who wants you dead. A maniac walks up to you and points something black and shiny at your midsection. He doesn't say a word. You hear a popping sound. See a flash of light. And somewhere in your midsection, you feel like you've run into the corner of a table. Things start to spin, just like in all those second-rate movies. You're lying on the floor. It doesn't hurt much. Your legs are going to sleep. Everything seems to echo. The screams. The people shouting for police, for a doctor.

Do you really lose control of your bodily functions? I can't tell if I have. Am I going to wet my pants? My life isn't flashing past me. Time doesn't seem altered. A second is a second. I don't feel euphoric. I don't see any bright lights on some approaching horizon, just people staring down at me, looking worried. Or uncomfortable. They must know I'm dying. They keep looking at the spot where the pain is getting worse. Right around my navel, I think.

Everyone is talking at once. It sounds like a religious gathering. There's a girl saying "Oh, God, oh, God." Over and over. Some man I've never seen says "Jesus Christ." Do I look that awful? Are they actually praying? For me?

Someone asks who I am, anyway. And that's the crushing injustice of it all. Nobody had to ask who Bobby Kennedy was when he lay dying on the floor. Or his brother, John. Or Reverend King. But this crowd doesn't know me. Just somebody who walked out of a hotel ballroom, following some kind of press conference, and got shot. At close range. By a crazed gunman. No one's crying for me. They're all concerned that I might die on their hands and ruin their evenings. Their appetites. Maybe that girl who keeps saying "Oh, God!" has an important dinner date and has lost her interest in food. Or maybe she'll be detained as a witness by the police.

Where are the police? Never around when you need them. My father always used to say that when we got stuck in traffic jams. My father. He didn't die this way. No one ever wanted to shoot him in the belly. People who knew him liked him. Some loved him. People who didn't know him had no reason to shoot him. He died all alone, in a hospital. A heart attack. No one hovering over him saying "Oh, God," or "Jesus Christ." Some nurse just watched him stop breathing and efficiently told someone to do whatever is done in hospitals when people die.

Something tastes terrible in my mouth. Blood. Up from my stomach. It must be bad. People only bleed internally when it's bad.

There's a face staring into mine. I can smell garlic. Maybe it's not all that serious, if I can still smell someone's breath. He must be a doctor since he's not frightened like the others. A good floorside manner. Looking concerned about my well-being, while he gently pokes at the area that feels sore and wet.

"Are you in pain?"

Not really. But I can't tell him that. My lips refuse to form the words. My mouth won't open on command. A mute, now, I just stare at the man. Why doesn't he try one of those code routines? It's done all the time on television. *"Don't try to speak. Just blink your eyes once if your answer is yes, twice if it's no."* Maybe this doctor doesn't watch television.

Insurance. Think about insurance. How much do I have? A couple hundred thousand, at least. My dull cousin, who sells the stuff, took care of that for me. Cover the eventualities, he used to say. What kind of eventuality is getting a hole punched in your belly by a bullet, in some dark corridor of a plastic hotel? Why didn't my cousin hike up his double-knit slacks, look me in the eye, and say, "Look, someday some crazed asshole is going to run up to you and shoot you so bad, you won't even know if you're wetting your pants"?

It's absurd. My life should be rushing by me, cinematically. Instead, I'm trying to count up how much life insurance I have. If I die from this encounter, as I suspect I will, I'll never know how much I had, will I? But I can feel good while I'm waiting to die, realizing that I provided for the eventualities.

Dead leaves and bits of lint and paper swirl round and round on the gray concrete of the alley. The wind is wet and cold on my cheeks. I have to pee, but I keep watching the debris swirl around on the concrete. It's too much bother to go inside the house and take off my leggings, unbutton the fly of my corduroy knickers, fish out my little weenie and let myself go. Why bother with all that? A five-year-old kid has the right to wet his pants. My mother didn't think so. She threatened to tell all my friends that I wet my pants out in the alley. She warned me I'd never grow up and amount to anything at all if I couldn't control myself better. Prophetic, she was. Here I am, about to lose control again. At age forty-four. Still not grown up. And amounting to what? But I'm sure she'll forgive me this time. After all, a bullet in the belly is a pretty good excuse. You see, Mom, I couldn't walk to the toilet if I wanted to. I'm just lying here.

Okay, okay, what's next?

Only a moron would fail first-year Latin. Well, if not a moron, what then? Maybe just a lazy, good-for-nothing kid, with no sense of appreciation for what his parents are trying to do for him. Go be a brain surgeon—the first one in history to have failed Latin. Maybe they'll let you work on morons' brains. Thank you. Thank you very much for slapping your mother and me in the face. That's what you did, slapped us across the face. By failing Latin.

Here are two young men in uniforms. Cops. They both have neatly trimmed mustaches. They say sir and ma'am to everyone. Somebody's shot and close to dead, and they still don't forget their manners. There's a badge right over me. LAPD TO PROTECT AND SERVE. A name. PTL. ESPINOSA. So Ptl. Espinosa of the LAPD has responded to the call for help.

"Did you see the man who shot you, sir?"

Of course I saw him. How could I miss him, any more than he was able to miss me? Hey, Ptl. Espinosa, what difference does it make right now? I'd rather you and the other cop see about that bullet in my belly. The doctor with garlic on his breath must have read my thoughts. He gently moves the cop aside and is back in front of my face again. This time he has a stethoscope stuck in his ears. His eyes don't say a damn thing as he listens to whatever is coming through from my chest. He might just as well be listening to the Melachrino Strings on an airplane headset. Maybe he isn't hearing anything. No, that's not possible. Even if I'm very nearly dead, something would have to be coming through on the headset. At least a weak beat. A slow thump. Otherwise I couldn't see badges or mustaches or cops. Come on, heart, make some noise for the man. Do something. Make him smile. Or even shake his head.

Making midnight love on a float out on Lake Kameesha is one of those things you simply can't leave out of a lifetime that's flashing by. How can I ever forget the painful abrasions I inflicted on my elbows from the woven hemp that covered the wooden deck of the float? We swam out there without our bathing suits. We had taken them off on the shore, after an hour or so of sweet, but painful petting. Somehow, the beer I had drunk gave me the courage I needed to suggest we swim nude to the raft. The cool water helped ease the aching that an hour of writhing with Linda Stern had produced. I'm only doing this because I really care for you. Really. How could she? I'd never seen her in my life before the dance we had just sneaked away from, the senior-counselor mixer for the young men and women of Camp Tomahawk for Boys and Camp Wigwam for Girls. Yes, I know you really care. And I'm the same way. I care for you. Jesus Christ, it hurts, rolling around on this matting. But the moonlight is nice, revealing the wonderful breasts I knew just had to be poised beneath the white Camp Wigwam blouse. She smelled so clean. She breathed so hard. How many other girls have you had before me? A few. Of course I couldn't admit that I had never done it before, that it was, therefore, a deflowering of sorts for me. I didn't want to know how many times she had had it before, but I knew I wasn't her first. Probably not even in the first five, the way she knew what to do and when to do it. Well, it's not all that shameful, getting your first piece at age sixteen. When we reached that glorious, suspended moment—together—I actually thought as much about telling my fellow senior counselors of my triumph as I did about the joy of the moment itself. Tell me you care, tell me you care. Of course I care. I'm tearing the skin off my elbows for you.

How did I all of a sudden get inside this thing? It's an ambulance. It's moving. The doctor isn't here anymore. Nor are the two cops. Now it's a disinterested-looking guy in a white suit. He's barely paying any attention to me. It's as though he's delivering a bread route. One more goddamn stop, one more store and he's through for the day. He can go home and watch the six o'clock news and hear about some guy who got shot by a crazy in a hotel. Some guy in politics. Did he put that tube in my arm? Where was I when he did it? Where was I when they wheeled me in here? I must have been on the raft with Linda Stern. No siren. Don't I rate one? Maybe people who aren't going to make it don't get sirens. Maybe they figure, what's the rush? This guy isn't going anywhere, except to one of those subterranean vaults. Do they really put a tag on your toe?

I wonder if this guy in the white suit knows I have a record. I mean, if he had any idea that I was busted in the sixties—three times, as a matter of fact—would he even bother putting a tube in my arm? I was probably in the slammer in Washington right about the time he was getting that dragon, and the USMC, tattooed on his forearm in San Diego. I could have been lying limp on the sidewalk in Chicago while he was lying, scared shitless, in a mud puddle in Vietnam. If he knew that, he'd pull out that tube, for certain. He might even tell the driver of this thing to pull into a Jack-in-the-Box for a coffee break. A long one. Imagine dying in an ambulance parked next to a talking clown that asks for your hamburger order. Hell no, I won't go; hell no, I won't go.

Jesus, did I look stupid the day I reported for my new job as a copywriter at the world's largest advertising agency. A tie. A suit. A goddamn vest, no less. The old radical. The peace freak. The doer of dope. The Latin failure. The float fucker. Sitting in a creative director's office overlooking the street we used to make sneering jokes about. Madison Avenue. (I'm wearing a three-piece suit again tonight. And someone made a hell of a mess out of the vest, didn't they?)

Sure, I knew I was selling out. But I thought I looked pretty cool, anyway. I actually looked like someone even the guys on the inside would laugh at. The other sell-outs were all dressed like I used to when I was out on the streets. Work shirts. Jeans. Sneakers. My first assignment: a TV commercial for a beer made by some fascists in Milwaukee. It was about as successful as my first-day appearance on the job. Nobody laughed when I sat down. It was supposed to be a funny commercial. They said I mentioned the name of the beer only three times. You never do that. I did, and I fell on my ass. Someone said I was too much of an idealist to succeed at beer. Instead of firing me the first week, why not send me up to the fourteenth floor, to the weirdos and fags who were doing the "freebies"? The "freebies," I found out, were public-service commercials, done as a contribution to causes by the agency. They worked for groups like the Inner-City League, which was trying to rebuild the city neighborhoods that the advertising agency's clients were destroying. I did better with the weirdos and fags on the freebies. Even won an award, for the best public-service TV commercial of the year, category of 60 seconds or less. It had a talking rat in it, telling folks how much it was enjoying its new home, which happened to be a South Bronx apartment.

I didn't even know who Hattie Lewis was when she called me and asked me to do some commercials for her congressional campaign. She knew about me and my talking rat. But I didn't know her any more than I know the ambulance attendant who's sitting next to me. Or the girl who must have thrown up by now. No one knows me. But Hattie

Lewis did. And she's still in Congress. Where am I? Somewhere in Los Angeles. Melrose Avenue? Santa Monica Boulevard? Fairfax?

I'm losing it. The spinning is starting. Backward. And with a sideways roll, too. Like a very slow fade-out. The credits ought to start rolling right about here. Pins and needles, on my tongue. That time they took out my appendix a nurse with enormous boobs leaned over me and told me to count backward from one hundred while I sucked in the ether.

No ether now. No nurse. No boobs. One hundred. Ninety-nine. Ninety-eight. Will they find out who I am? Ninety . . . ninety . . . what? Ninety-two? Eighty-six. Fifty-two. Seventy. Where does seventy go? Twenty-four. Breathe deeply. It's only an appendix. Nobody needs an appendix. Nobody needs a bullet, either. They don't give ether anymore. They give needles. Do you still count backward? I do. Ninety-four. Ninety-three. Why fight it? It's nice and warm, anyway. Eleven. Ten. Hattie Lewis has moved up in the world. So have I. Hey, ambulance man, see my show tonight? On the networks. All three. I'm not kidding. That was me. Holding a press conference. Jerry Bloom, media consultant. Don't you know that, you, with the white suit and the tattoo? Jerry Bloom. Creator of the talking rat. Of would-be presidents. You probably don't even know what a media consultant is. Want to be in a commercial? Want to be famous? I can get you elected. Just don't let me die and I'll take care of it. Eighteen. Nineteen. Twenty. Wrong way. There are worse things than dying.

2

SOMETHING ABOUT AN AUDIENCE OF college students made the juices start flowing for Jerry Bloom. Speaking on politics and the media to a group of young people excited him even more than appearances before more auspicious gatherings, like Senate campaign committees. Maybe it was the enthusiasm of the younger people. Or the mystique of respectful, if not admiring, young women, who managed to fit right into some of his more intriguing fantasies.

"Mr. Bloom?" It was a soft, pleasant voice.

"Yes. The young lady in the back."

Seated in one of the last rows of the large lecture hall was an attractive young student with sun-streaked blond hair and makeup that wasn't really makeup. She wore jeans and a temptingly translucent blouse. She was soft. And clean. And very desirable.

"Just how much power do media manipulators really hold over the voters?"

"Manipulators? Thanks a lot."

"Okay. How much power do, ah . . ." A facetious pause.

"Media consultants will do," he offered.

"Media consultants. Okay. What about your power?" She still smiled. And Bloom felt a warmth moving through his body.

"Let me put it this way: Given a large enough budget and enough creative genius, Colonel Qaddafi could get himself elected president of the United States."

The Qaddafi nonsense always managed to get a laugh for Bloom, especially on campuses. It didn't let him down today at Arizona State University, where he was a guest speaker at a seminar on "Politics and the Media." Five hundred dollars plus expenses. The five hundred would be contributed back to the university's political-science scholarship fund, a standard practice for Bloom. An income of $200,000 a year for being one of the country's more successful political advertising specialists permitted that kind of generosity.

"Don't you think that's an awesome power that could easily get into the wrong hands?" The soft-spoken student was less baiting now. Almost seductive.

"Of course it is. We're seeing the results of a communications revolution. The age of television has brought right along with it a frightening new power. Put it in the wrong hands, and—"

"It's never been in the right hands!" was the explosive interruption from somewhere in the room. A strong, angry male voice.

"Perhaps," Bloom replied. He searched for the

11

source of the interruption. His eyes caught an angry, challenging face. The young man was glaring at Bloom, waiting for a response, daring him to pick up the challenge.

"Sounds like you don't like the revolution." Bloom was staring down his young antagonist. He paused. "The one in communications."

"You're goddamn right I don't. That fucking television tube put Richard Nixon and a third-rate actor in the White House."

Dr. Frey, the seminar leader, rose quickly.

"That'll do, Mr. Peters. We can get along without the obscenities." He turned to Bloom. "I'm sorry."

Bloom raised his hands in mock self-defense.

"Oh, no, that's fine, Dr. Frey. I've heard a lot worse. I should tell you where the nice wife of a Senate candidate once told me to put my campaign ideas, and what to tamp them with."

Bloom got an even bigger laugh this time than he had with his Qaddafi story. He was still in control.

Frey was holding a magazine in his hand. He raised it as he addressed the baiting student.

"Perhaps you ought to read this article on Mr. Bloom."

Bloom winced. "I don't think he'd believe it."

"Perhaps not. But I think it's worth noting that our guest speaker is considered something of a maverick among his peers." He read from the magazine. " 'Jerry Bloom, one of the rising stars in the field of political media work, isn't in it for money alone. He frequently works for underdog candidates and unpopular causes, sometimes without pay. Perhaps it's a throwback to the days when he led antiwar marches in Washington, and to his involvement in the protests at the Democratic Convention in Chicago. Although he won't discuss it publicly, it's reported he created Congresswoman Hattie Lewis's successful media campaign with no fee at all because he wanted to see another black woman in Congress. He also produced the television commercials for nuclear safeguards initiatives in three states with no payment for his services. As a result, Bloom is frequently held in disfavor by his fellow media consultants, who feel his altruism hurts their business. One of his competitors said, "Bloom forgets this is a business we're in. If he wants to change the world and live humbly, he ought to join the Peace Corps and let us get on with our work."'"

Bloom looked uncomfortably at his feet. He could almost see his face in his expensive loafers. The room was silent. Frey lowered the magazine, smiling slightly, as he spoke.

"Perhaps this tells us something of our guest today."

The interruptive student was right back again. "Or about his press agent."

The laughter that broke out stung Bloom. That particular article had meant more to him than anything else written about his rise to success. It had also given him occasional pause to reflect, to wonder if he had, in fact, sold out. The thought occurred to him with more frequency these days, as he achieved more success. What was once a thrill— scoring a political upset on a shoestring budget— had become a profitable business. He now received a minimum of $50,000 in consulting fees for his work, instead of a few hundred dollars to cover his expenses and the gratitude of his fellow committed liberals.

Bloom was still studying his $180 shoes when the next question came.

"Do you think it's wrong for media consultants from our country to get involved in the campaigns of other countries, like the ones that Henry Devin has handled in South America?"

"Obviously I don't think it's wrong. I've done some consulting work with Devin on some of his overseas campaigns. It's perfectly legal."

"But is it moral?"

"It's no more or less moral than any American business having activity abroad."

"That's crazy!" shouted Bloom's tormentor. "You're not talking about selling soda pop in foreign countries. You're meddling in the governments of other nations. You promote the campaigns of dictators, you might as well sell them guns to shoot people with."

"Sure. But I don't seem to recall any fascists that Henry Devin has worked for. Unless you're privy to something that I don't know."

"You don't think Manuel Puentes is a fascist?"

Bloom's voice was soft and controlled. "The last I heard, he was still a member of the People's Labor Party. But, of course, I don't have access to the same information you seem to have."

A whistle came from the corner of the room, and a few students turned and smiled at the taunting student, who merely flipped up a middle finger in response.

A little relief came from another side of the hall,

14

where a young man was patiently holding his hand in the air. He, at least, didn't appear to be hostile.

"Sir, do you think some new federal restraints on media campaigns for political office are in order?"

"I'm afraid it's inevitable. And I'm not really all that opposed to regulation of our business. When you have excess, in any industry or profession, it's an invitation to regulation by government agencies."

The soft blonde was back for more. Which pleased Bloom. "Then you'd agree that people who run some of these campaigns have already gone too far?"

"No, *you're* agreeing. I haven't yet. At the risk of sounding more professorial than I should, it looks like we have a semantics problem here. You say I agree that things have gone too far, when I say I acknowledge they *could* go too far. The gentleman talks of Manuel Puentes, the fascist; I think of him as Manuel Puentes, the liberal. What I call involvement, you call meddling. Maybe we all ought to get into a good seminar on the semantics of politics." He turned to Dr. Frey. "Know any good ones going on today?"

The blond girl continued. "But you yourself said things have gotten to the point where we could see a Qaddafi elected president."

"I was merely trying to point out the power that can be held by people who know how to use media effectively. And I worry about what might happen, just as you do. Look what a man like Richard Nixon was able to do with his media. He somehow convinced the electorate that he was a decent and honest enough person to be president."

"A good case for controls of what you do," said still another skeptical student.

"Or is it a case for remedial education of the voters?" Bloom replied. "Maybe we ought to be talking about screening. Do you realize there are virtually no qualifying processes that a political candidate must face before he can be elected? A White House waiter has to prove he's honest, emotionally stable, physically sound, and of good character before he can carry a tray to the dining room. But a president doesn't have to prove any of those qualities before he carries the destiny of two hundred million people in his hands. He just needs enough votes."

The blonde turned to the girl next to her and smiled. Was Bloom actually getting through?

"Thomas Jefferson once said," he continued, "the people will only get the kind and quality of government they deserve. Did the people deserve anything better than a Nixon at a time when they were condoning Vietnam and cheering for police who were brutalizing dissidents?"

Bloom knew he could count on disarming a skeptical, if not hostile, young audience when he got into some of his own social or political views. Students were usually stopped by such liberal notions coming from a man who wore expensive suits and an equally expensive suntan. Bloom enjoyed his ability to frustrate the angry young men and women.

He wanted to press his point further.

"Look, media people are no more responsible for

the sins of politicians than defense lawyers are responsible for their clients' wrongs."

The hostile student was back again. "As long as they get paid their fees, everybody's happy, right?"

"Wrong!" Bloom wasn't going to let this kid get by him. "If you get caught red-handed selling a bag of heroin to a ten-year-old kid, you're still entitled to a good legal defense. You may be scum for what you did, but that doesn't make your lawyer one for defending you in court. . . ."

"Presidents can do a lot more damage than any dealer can. They've got bombs and armies. Besides, media heavies *help* tyrants get the power they need to succeed. Lawyers don't help dealers do their thing. They only defend them afterward."

Maybe the lawyer analogy wasn't so terrific. Score one for indignant youth. But don't let the little bastard know about it.

Dr. Frey stepped to the podium again. "I'm afraid I'll have to sound the bell." He smiled, somewhat apologetically.

"Well, at least I went the distance," Bloom quipped. "Now, who renders the decision?"

"We only spar in our seminars, Mr. Bloom. Nobody loses, we hope. We come away with some new insights into this business of choosing our leaders, and you go away with some notions of what's going on in the classroom these days."

"Plus a check and expenses," was the taunting student's parting shot.

As Bloom was walking down the hallway of the classroom building, accompanied by the seductive blond girl, who still had a question or two, he heard someone call his name.

"Mr. Bloom?"

He turned to see Dr. Frey's secretary coming toward him holding out a note.

"Phone message for you, sir."

He took the small piece of pink paper and stopped to read the message: CALL BACK OPERATOR #6, DALLAS, TEXAS. CALLING PARTY: MR. DAVIS.

He wondered who this Mr. Davis was, and why he was in Dallas, calling him in Arizona. Christ, he thought, not another race to handle. In Texas yet.

"Well, pardon me, but Texas calls, Miss——?"

"Walker. Lenore Walker." The soft-spoken young student seemed to want him to remember the name.

"Nice talking to you, Lenore. Hope to run into you again."

She smiled and did a little unnerving thing with her tongue and her upper lip. "I hope so, too. But ring a bell before you do. I'm in the student phone book."

Come-ons like this one still had their reassuring effect on Bloom. He appreciated them, even though he didn't pursue them.

"I'll be sure to remember. Excuse me."

He smiled and stepped into the political science office and asked the receptionist if he might use a telephone.

Bloom heard a southern female voice answer a phone in Dallas. "Good afternoon, Davis, Andrews, and Sutherland."

"Ready on your call to Mr. Bloom," said the disinterested operator.

"Thank you, ma'am. We're expecting his call."

After the briefest of pauses another southern

18

female voice came on. "Mr. Davis is coming on, sir. Thank you for returning our call."

"Hello, Mr. Bloom. This is Harrison Davis."

"What can I do for you, Mr. Davis?"

"I trust you had a pleasant session with those graduate students." His voice was cordial and educated. The accent made Bloom uncomfortable, though. Texas drawls reminded him of those terrible days in Dallas.

"My seminar was fine, just fine."

"Good. Mr. Bloom, I'd like to open a friendly discussion of politics with you, at your earliest convenience."

"Just a discussion?"

Davis laughed. "No, it *does* involve a business proposition, too, since politics is your business—and mine."

"Are you running for office?"

"No, sir, I prefer to leave that to people of more durable constitution than I."

"Who's your candidate?"

"I really hate to discuss this over the phone. As you can imagine, confidentiality is important in these things."

"I guess it is. But I really can't tell you if it makes sense for us to talk if I don't even know who we're talking about. Is this a congressional race?"

"Bigger."

"Oh, a Senate seat."

"Mr. Bloom, I'm talking about a campaign for the presidency of the United States."

Blood rushed into Bloom's head. When that happened, a headache usually followed. But he tried to remain cool. No sense letting on that he didn't really believe he was that big yet. A presidential race. For Jerry Bloom?

"I'm afraid I don't quite understand, Mr. Davis. Both candidates have had their media people on board for months."

"Mr. Bloom, there are *three* major candidates for president."

Some more blood went up to his head. Suddenly Dallas, Texas, made sense.

"You're talking about Stephen Wendell." He was both puzzled and angered by his revelation.

"My lifelong friend and former law partner."

"Mr. Davis, at the risk of offending you, I have to point out where I happen to stand, politically and philosophically."

"I'm well aware of your background, Mr. Bloom."

"Then why are you interested in me?"

"Because you're a winner. And because we need someone with your record to help make *us* a winner. You've performed remarkably well for your candidates. Two years ago you handled five winning congressional campaigns, correct?"

"That's right."

"Including Miss Lewis."

"*Congresswoman* Lewis," he corrected.

"I know. The first black *and* the first woman ever elected from the state of Arizona. In a conservative district. An unusual feat, Mr. Bloom."

"She won because she's a beautiful human being, and one hell of a campaigner."

Davis's voice stayed at the same patient level. "Yes, well, Stephen Wendell is 'one hell of a campaigner' as well."

Bloom couldn't resist. "Is he also a beautiful human being?"

"The people of this great nation will decide that on November the first."

"I'm not so sure. All we know is they'll choose a president."

"Mr. Bloom, there's a first-class ticket to Dallas waiting for you at the Phoenix airport. May we look forward to the pleasure of your visit?"

"This is my first inquiry from a presidential campaign, Mr. Davis. I'm flattered. But I have a pretty strong loyalty to my party, plus some definite feelings about Stephen Wendell. I'd be dishonest if I tried to hide that from you."

"And I'd be a fool not to realize you feel as you do."

"Yet you still want to talk with me?"

"Yes. And what's more important, Mr. Wendell still wants to speak to you. You see, he may possess more tolerance than you give him credit for, after all."

"I'm sorry, Mr. Davis, but I have a problem with politicians who want to seal off our borders to immigrants." Bloom, the son of immigrant parents, disliked the growing American trend toward immigration reform. And he disliked any politician who might profit from the trend.

"I had hoped you might be prepared to begin showing a little tolerance toward us. After all, we are merely trying to offer the people needed alternatives. By the way, speaking of Congresswoman Lewis, she'd like to have a word with you."

Bloom could not hide his irritation, nor did he especially want to. "What's the joke?"

"Joke? I said she'd like a word with you."

"If she would, I don't imagine she'd leave a message for me at Wendell-for-President headquarters."

Bloom heard a woman laughing in the background at the other end of the line. He also heard the rustling sound of the phone being handed to someone, followed by a very familiar voice.

"How's my imagemaker?"

Bloom was unable to speak. He stared at a blank wall as he realized he had just heard the voice of Hattie Lewis, a black congresswoman, a loyal, liberal Democrat and civil rights activist, a dear and special friend. And she was sitting in the offices of a conservative Democrat now turned independent, a man who appealed, most of all, to that part of middle America that opposed everything Hattie had stood and fought for.

She spoke again. "Jerry? Are you there?"

"Yes, I'm here. But I can't believe you're where you are." His shock subsided and he began to find the situation humorous, in an absurd way.

"You've been kidnapped."

Hattie laughed that deep laugh that already had become famous. "I just walked right in and made myself at home. And nobody even thought I was the cleaning lady."

"What gives, Hattie? What the hell are you doing with those people?"

"Stephen Wendell wants my advice on his campaign."

"I'm sure he does. But is he prepared to shove it where I presume you told him to shove it?"

"Hey, times are changing. And so are people, imageman."

"They ain't changin' that much, missy," Bloom drawled in his best Uncle Tom imitation.

"Seriously, Jerry, I think you ought to listen to what this man has to say. I know how you feel, but give me a little credit for remembering where we're all coming from."

"I think you're serious about this."

Now it was Hattie's turn to recall the in jokes of the old days. "Land sakes," she imitated, "the man ain't asking for to marry my sister. He just wants to talk to my imagemaker."

"Are you supporting him?"

"I'm listening to him. That's all, for the time being."

"And you want me to do the same—just listen?"

"That's all."

"If I do, will you explain how in hell you could justify even setting foot inside his office?"

"You can count on it."

Bloom wondered how Davis was reacting to the end of the conversation he was obviously hearing in his office in Dallas. He surely must be enjoying sitting in his big chair and hearing Hattie Lewis convincing her old friend to show enough tolerance to talk to Stephen Wendell about the presidency.

"Mr. Bloom?" It was the smooth voice of Davis again. He wasn't sure, but Bloom thought he might have heard a giggle in the background. The knot in his stomach was getting tighter.

"I'm still here," he replied.

"I trust it was good speaking to your old friend again."

Bloom thought Davis overused the word *trust*. Earlier, he had *trusted* Bloom had had a good session with the students. What was he going to trust next?

"Well, Mr. Bloom?" The man had a smooth way of letting you know you were keeping him waiting.

"I was thinking about my schedule."

Actually, Bloom was thinking about other things. In addition to trying to figure out Hattie's motives, he was also thinking about his family. He had been looking forward to spending a few days back in Los Angeles with his wife and children. It was time for one of those let's-get-to-know-each-other sessions again. Too many days spent away in too many cities. Not enough time to ask the children what they had been doing lately, or to hear from their mother about what they had not been doing. And then there was that painful issue to confront, the breakdown of what had once been a successful, fulfilling marriage.

"There's an excellent connection leaving Phoenix in just two and a half hours. That should give you ample time to phone home and apologize to your wife for the change in plans. I trust that's satisfactory?" That word again.

This Davis had all the answers. It was as though he knew just how frustrated Anne had become lately, never knowing when her husband would appear or how long he would stay.

"We'll have a driver meet you at the airport and bring you directly to our office," Davis continued.

"I *trust* the congresswoman will be joining us." Bloom wondered if Davis caught the mockery. Apparently he had, because he chuckled ever so slightly.

"Yes, Miss Lewis plans to join us. May we look forward to seeing you?"

"Just as long as we understand one another—about where we stand."

"I think we do, Mr. Bloom. Rather clearly, in fact."

"Thank you." Thank you for what? he wondered.

"Until this evening, Mr. Bloom?"

As Bloom hung up the phone, he looked at his watch and bumped into the secretary who had given him the message. She was smiling at him.

"Sorry," he said.

"Would you like me to call a cab to take you to the airport?"

"I have to make a phone call first."

"You have two and a half hours before your flight to Dallas," she said, looking at the clock on the wall.

What the hell was going on? How did she know what he had just agreed to do?

"Is there something wrong?" she asked.

"No, I guess not. Except I'm curious. I was going to fly back to Los Angeles. How did you know about my change in plans?"

"Easy. The gentleman who called you asked me if I thought you could make a five-thirty flight."

"And you knew I'd be taking it?"

"The gentleman told me you would."

"Figures. I suppose he even told you to get my wife on the phone for me."

She smiled mechanically, and pointed to the phone on her desk. "Mrs. Bloom is holding on line two."

He stared at the blinking light, took a deep breath, and picked up the phone.

"Anne? Hi. I'm afraid I've got another detour."

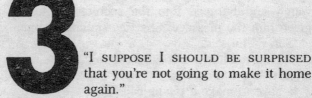**3** "I SUPPOSE I SHOULD BE SURPRISED that you're not going to make it home again."

By now Anne Bloom had become cynically resigned to phone calls from just about anywhere in the United States. Now, on occasion, the calls even came from other countries. "The price of success" was the cliché she had been using to explain to friends Jerry's continued and prolonged absences.

"Where are you going this time?"

Her husband's voice had the usual apologetic tone to it. "Dallas."

"What on earth is in Dallas?"

"A man running for office."

"Oh, they'll love you down there."

"I know." The headache was getting worse as he waited for Anne to ask who the new candidate was.

"Find yourself a Texas liberal?"

"Not quite."

"A misunderstood moderate?"

Anne was obviously in a fencing mood. Must have been another bad day, with their children demonstrating just how much they could misbehave when their father was gone for too long. It seemed to be their punishment plan: Make their mother miserable enough to come down on their father. And he, of course, would respond with predictable guilt.

"Look, I'm sorry I can't get home tonight. And, no, he's not a misunderstood moderate. He just happens to be a candidate for president."

"President of what?"

"Cut the crap, will you?"

Bloom caught the receptionist looking up at him. He flushed, thinking how dumb he must appear, having an argument with his wife long-distance at a time and in a place like this.

"My God! I don't believe this. You're not trying to tell me you're going to work for Stephen Wendell, are you?"

"I'm trying to tell you I'm going to Dallas to meet with him. He wants to talk. I'd be a fool not to at least hear him out."

"I certainly wouldn't want you to be a fool, dear." The sarcasm was oozing through the phone.

Bloom tried to lower his voice. "Now wait a goddamn minute. I'm not going out to march for Stephen Wendell, I'm going to listen to what he has to say. I'm also going to see an old and dear friend who happens to be with the Wendell people right now."

"Who could that be?" she taunted. "George Wallace?"

"Hattie Lewis. She's agreed to listen to what he has to say."

Bloom couldn't help but enjoy the silence, the

small victory of Anne's speechlessness. "Did you say something?" he asked patiently.

"Well," she finally answered, "I suppose nothing in politics should surprise me anymore. Jesus—even Hattie."

"Tell the kids I miss them, will you?"

He winced at Anne's shrill voice, as she shouted across the room, "Kids, your father misses you!"

"Thanks," said Bloom, his head throbbing.

"Don't mention it."

"Good-bye."

Anne hung up the phone and turned on the small television set in the kitchen, then began to prepare the evening meal. Her attractive, youthful face was flushed with anger. She unconsciously brushed at her prematurely gray hair. She was, at forty-two, every bit as handsome a woman as she had been at twenty, when she had fallen in love with an angry young radical named Jerry Bloom. Danny, with his insatiable fifteen-year-old appetite, was munching from a box of pretzels. He got a dirty look from his mother, but he kept right on munching. Beth, twelve, blond, and slender, and looking very much the shiksa, as her paternal grandfather called her, was engrossed in a book. She seemed oblivious to the argument Anne had been engaged in with her father.

From the television set, America's favorite network newsman, William Cronin, smiled at Anne, Danny, and Beth, and said, "Good evening. The race for the presidency took another unpredictable turn today, as independent candidate Stephen Wendell pulled the biggest coup of his campaign. Helen Dumont has the story in Pittsburgh."

Anne shook her head and held an imaginary microphone in her hand. "Jerry Bloom today swung his support to Mr. Wendell," she replied, imitating an intense newswoman.

"Huh?" It was more of a grunt than a question from Danny, through a mouthful of pretzels.

Helen Dumont, bundled up against a chilly Pittsburgh wind and holding a microphone in her hand, stood in front of the entrance to the Hancock Hotel. A crowd of rugged-looking men, most of whom seemed happy, stood behind her.

"The leadership of the Teamsters Union today gave Stephen Wendell his biggest boost yet in his dark-horse race for the presidency. After the third straight day of debate and deliberation and, very nearly, an outright brawl, the executive council announced its support of Wendell. This is the largest union yet to commit to the independent candidate. And the move clearly spells trouble for both the Republican and Democratic candidates. It was expected that the Teamsters would either go with the Democratic ticket this time or stay neutral. But no one was predicting a swing to Wendell, who, as a Democratic governor of Texas, called for a national right-to-work bill, which would have been a near fatal blow to unionism."

Anne threw down a saucepan and glared at the woman on the screen.

"Great. That's just great. Unions throwing in with union-busters."

"Don't worry," said Danny. "That Texan can't win."

"Please be sure to tell your father that—the next time you happen to see him."

A few of the men gathered behind Helen Dumont, most of whom wore WENDELL FOR AMERICA buttons on their coats, began mugging for the camera, holding their hands up in Churchillian victory signs. Some whistled. Some shouted "Wendell for America!"

The television camera pulled back to reveal a stone-faced man. He wore a more expensive coat than any of the others. He was graying, in his late fifties. Anne immediately recognized him.

"Standing next to me," said Helen Dumont, "is Louis W. Forest, president of the Teamsters. Mr. Forest, what convinced your union to endorse the candidacy of Stephen Wendell?"

Forest looked as though he really didn't want to be interviewed about Stephen Wendell, or about anyone or anything else. He always had a look about him that seemed to say he'd just as soon be left alone. But he spoke to the reporter anyway.

"Our brotherhood of workers has come to realize that neither major party has offered us what we need to survive."

"And what is that?" asked Ms. Dumont.

"Hope. We're hearing the liberal Democrats telling us we've got to settle for lower wage demands, and the Republicans are making it clear they want to break up unionism, allowing corporations to use bankruptcy laws to do it. So we've got one party telling us we're going to have to settle for low wages and the other one telling us we're going to have scab labor to take away what jobs we have left."

"And what does Stephen Wendell offer as an alternative?"

"What does he offer? Some straight talk about the

30

working men and women of America. He's willing to stand up and fight the corporations *and* the elitist liberals."

"But haven't many of your members walked out of this meeting over the Wendell endorsement—particularly minority members?"

"There's always going to be some disagreement over something like this."

"We've been told that a Hispanic caucus of Teamsters is preparing an announcement of a massive walkout from the union. They point to Wendell's position on immigration. They disapprove of his support of immigration quotas."

Forest's stone face cracked just a little.

"Look, you newspeople keep trying to connect new immigration policies—and Governor Wendell—to racism. That's a bunch of baloney, and you know it. These new quotas are designed to protect American working men and women."

"Including minority working men and women?"

"Especially minorities. Who do you think are the first to lose their jobs to immigrants? It's the people on the bottom of the labor ladder. And most of them are minorities."

The camera moved in tight on the reporter again, as she wrapped up the interview. "So, it looks as though Stephen Wendell's campaign, one that started out to be a minor-party challenge, is well on its way to finishing with him as a major candidate. This is Helen Dumont, in Pittsburgh."

Anne began slicing a carrot, almost with a vengeance, as the face of anchorman Cronin reappeared on the screen. Anne thought she saw just the slightest hint of disdain, a not quite perceptible

31

shake of the head, as Cronin resumed speaking. Or maybe she hoped she saw it.

"Not only has the candidacy of Stephen Wendell moved from minor status to major, but some important staffing changes are apparently forthcoming from his Dallas headquarters. A reporter for *The New York Times*, which, incidentally, only began covering the Wendell campaign last week, wrote today that Wendell has fired his longtime friend and media consultant, David Mattson, and is about to replace him with one of the nation's more prominent and successful political advertising specialists. No name has been mentioned yet, but speculation is growing that it will be a surprise choice—very possibly someone previously connected with one of the major parties, perhaps even someone who has served important liberal candidates."

"Shit," barked Anne, as she put her hand to her mouth and sucked on the end of her left index finger.

"What did you say?" asked Beth, displaying surprising hearing ability from the distance of the next room.

"She said *shit*," was Danny's helpful reply.

"I cut my finger slicing this carrot," said Anne.

Danny smiled. "She cut her finger when she heard that Wendell is going to hire a liberal advertising guy. Maybe it's Dad, huh?"

Anne could barely contain herself. She wanted to blurt out how ironically correct her son's notion was. But she thought better of it, deciding to spare her husband the wrath of his children. After all, she reasoned with herself, he was only going to hear the man out. He was only going to listen to what kind of syrup Stephen Wendell was pouring these days.

An inane commercial for a mouthwash concluded, and a warm, friendly face appeared on the television screen. It was Grant Chase, the elder statesman of the network, the man who had grown to be hated by those politicians who had reason to fear him and to be respected by those few who understood the wit, the homespun candor—the genius—he possessed.

"Good evening," said Chase, begrudgingly offering the only smile he had to give, the one that always preceded his evening commentary.

The departing birds and the purposefully busy ground squirrels are telling us autumn is here, although not officially for another week. It is the fifteenth of September. The children have returned to their schools, the psychiatrists are back in their offices, and the campaign for the presidency of the United States is entering its final forty-five days, the most crucial days of all. The political pollsters are scurrying about as frantically as are the squirrels. But they're not planning for a lean, hard winter. Instead, they're getting ready for the luxurious vacations their lavish fees will buy them after November the first. What they're storing away is data . . . changing and surprising data . . . on the trends that are developing in this critical election year.

Anne felt very close to the kindly looking man on

the screen who could be so justifiably unkind to people who incurred his soft-spoken wrath—the politicians, the hypocrites whose words and actions were rendered suddenly transparent by this wise man.

And while the squirrels and pollsters chase after their rewards in the northeast, another species is chasing something very, very big in the southwest. In Texas. The Stephen Wendell organization is moving with a purpose, and, it seems, with a knowledge of something that the rest of us have not yet discovered. We won't learn it from the squirrels of autumn. We'll undoubtedly hear all about it from the pollsters. And what that discovery will be is becoming increasingly, and uncomfortably, clear: Stephen Wendell, who was not being taken very seriously by the political experts only a few months ago, is now making the presidential campaign a real three-way race. He could, in fact, be the next man to occupy the same oval office that was occupied by Franklin Roosevelt, that was denied to Hubert Humphrey, and that was desecrated by Richard Nixon. But I, for one, do not think he has shown the inspiration of a Roosevelt, the integrity of a Humphrey, or the cunning of a Nixon.

Here in our studios, the switchboard is about to be crammed by incoming phone calls, not just from Texas, but from the northern industrial cities as well, demanding that I be fired. Or committed. Or shot. For I am treading upon the character of Stephen Wendell, a man who is particularly skilled at arousing people to such phone calls. But I would reassure the indignant listeners who would like my image to disappear from their living rooms and kitchens that nothing I can say will diminish the speed, or the force, with which the fast-moving freight train of the Wendell organization is moving through this country.

And what is wrong with that? Should a man be denied a chance at the presidency merely because of his independence? Because he offers an alternative to America's political parties? On paper, no, he should not. Nor should the people be denied the chance for a new option of leadership offered by a man of strong principle with an enviable record of public service.

The problem lies not with the notion of an independent candidacy, but with the way in which Stephen Wendell is exploiting that notion. People are fearful of the flood of humanity sent to our shores by unrest in Caribbean nations and Stephen Wendell is exploiting that fear with ideas that, if carried to extremes, could extinguish the flame of welcome that has always burned so proudly in the hand of the Statue of Liberty.

He is also exploiting the fear of an uncertain economic future that justifiably haunts all of us. During the eight years of the Reagan reign, we have seen deficits swell to the bursting point, while interest rates have soared to the point of disbelief. Along comes Stephen Wendell to blame the Republican party for allowing the economy to get so out of hand and the Democratic party for offering nothing in the way of sound solutions. He indicts both parties for their economic failures and promises success with nothing more substantive than anger and indignation. He warns America of the dangers of the political right and left and promises us Utopia in the middle. That is the stuff of which pleasant dreams are made. But what does it do for the reality of our plight in 1988?

Speaking of reality, the two major political parties have brought upon themselves the confusion and the disaffection that have created Stephen Wendell's golden opportunity. Both the Democrats and Republicans have been existing in a massive state of flux in this election year. The battle they have been waging is over both personalities and ideologies. The question is not only who shall lead, but also what the parties shall stand for.

The conflict has been intense, and only partly visible to the voting public. Small groups are determined to capture and keep control of their respective parties, not on behalf of broad constituencies, but of narrow extremes. The fighting has been over both platforms and personalities, over who and what will better serve the interests of the far right and the far left—instead of who and what will better serve America. And now, as we approach the final weeks of this stormy campaign year, there are already winners and losers to declare. In both parties the extremes have won out, while moderation has been shut out.

The Republican battle between George Bush, Howard Baker, Robert Dole, and Jack Kemp ground to a predictable conclusion with the nomination of Mr. Kemp. Bush, Baker, and Dole fragmented the moderate vote, while Kemp out-Reaganed Reagan and walked off with the prize. The addition of Elizabeth Dole to the ticket, while politically appealing, does not temper the reality that the right wing of the Republican party has gained even stronger control. That result, however, would not mean a great deal to voters, considering the conservative failures of the last four years, if the Democrats had not moved, at the same time, so dramatically to the left.

In that party, the fight was even more divisive. Bradley, Bumpers, Biden, Hart, and Cuomo all would appear to have come from the political center. But the party's problem was not with the candidates. Indeed, the problem was with its nominating process. The Democrats have become a party of special pleaders. Their platform has not offered an objective vision of what America needs in these troubled times. Instead, it has offered the sum total of all the subgroups within the Democratic party—teachers, unions, gays, minorities, environmentalists—they all scored victories for their interests in the primaries. Gary Hart won the nomination not because he waged the best campaign, but because he endorsed the largest number of extreme positions. Senator Hart showed us that the way to the Democratic nomination is not what is good for America, but what is good for three thousand nine hundred thirty-four delegates.

Thus, America is presented with a choice of extremes. It is what some would call a real choice. But others would call it a real dilemma. Voters are asked to pick one of two extremes. Gone, now, is the flexibility and pragmatism of the American political process. In its place we have two adversaries facing each other across a political battlefield already strewn with the bodies of fallen moderates. And into this polarized political landscape steps a new factor— Governor Stephen Wendell. He is rubbing his hands as he surveys the damage to a good system of American political choices. He is confident the damage is heavy enough to give him his golden opportunity—an opportunity created by men and women who became too inflexible, too passionately committed to their narrow view of the world. In the past, a natural system of checks and balances has always brought our two parties back to reason. But it has not worked this time. Stephen Wendell knows it. And he is turning the chaos and the disaffection to his advantage. He is still a registered Democrat, calling himself a "progressive conservative." He thus is forming the most unlikely political coalition in history. And who knows what may come of it.

Now came that familiar, powerful pause of Grant Chase's, that staring confrontation with his millions of viewers, during which he said nothing. Then, with no expression at all, he said softly, but devastatingly, "Good night, and pleasant dreams, America."

Anne felt herself on the verge of tears as she heard the familiar network disclaimer, reminding viewers that the opinions of Grant Chase were his own, and not those of the network, the local station, or the sponsors of the newscast. She gently pressed the television's on/off button and watched the image of a car commercial shrink back to a tiny white dot, which seemed to provide one last period to Chase's editorial. She thought of her husband. And of the man who wanted to meet with him, Stephen Wendell. And she wanted to cry.

In a waiting area at the Phoenix airport, Jerry Bloom also stood staring at a television screen. The car commercial was still playing. He, too, had heard Grant Chase deliver his views on the candidacy of Stephen Wendell. Two men in leisure suits were standing next to him. One spoke to the other in a rural, southern accent. "What do you expect from someone like Chase? Shit, he's just another smart-ass Jewboy who runs the TV networks."

"Chase? Ain't Jewish-sounding to me," answered his companion.

The first man snickered. "They don't keep their old names anymore."

Jerome Bloom, who had always kept his name just the way it was now, wondered what would happen if he hauled off and punched either one of the two slobs next to him. He felt something burning and foul come up in his throat. His arm muscles trembled as he clenched his fists. His forehead and upper lip broke out in a sweat. He stared at the two men. Perhaps all that stopped him from even making a remark was the announcement on the public address system:

"U.S. Airlines flight one-fifty-two, service to Dallas is now in the final boarding stage."

Bloom reassured himself that the men weren't the first two bigoted assholes he'd encountered in his life, nor would they be, by any stretch, the last. But he still wanted to strike out at them, to bloody a nose, or, at least, to insult them, to make them regret their stupidity. But he did nothing except walk, heavily, toward the gate to board his flight. He felt shame and anger, while, four hundred miles away, his wife stood in their kitchen feeling a similar shame and anger. It was directed toward Stephen Wendell. Toward the American people. And toward Jerome Bloom.

4 SUNSET OVER THE PHOENIX AREA WAS
nearly always an impressive sight.
Purples and oranges commingled in
vivid streaks over the mountains bordering the city.
They bounced off the mirrorlike glass of the new
high-rise office buildings in the downtown area.
They illuminated the surrounding desert.

But the sunset didn't move Jerry Bloom as he
stared out the window of the airliner that was
climbing into the Arizona sky, taking him to meet
Stephen Wendell. He stared down at Camelback
Mountain, where the very wealthy and the very
conservative went to play golf, to sit in the sun, or
to retire, away from the cold and the cares of the
cities of the north. Somewhere down there was Arizona's liberal young governor, an exciting new politician whose campaign Bloom had worked on two
years earlier. Also down there was Barry Goldwater,
Arizona's aging conservative, who still held stead-
fastly to his rightist views. He was no longer the
threat he used to be to people like Bloom. He was
now merely an aging antagonist who had to be ad-

mired for his conviction, and, perhaps, even forgiven for his inability to understand the social and moral change he so vigorously opposed in the 1960s.

Change. That's what everything had been all about for people in the "movement." That enormous army of young people, and some who were not so young, who had rallied behind the banners of peace, of civil rights, of freedom for the human spirit. God, what an unforgettable sight it had been in Washington. The largest group of people ever to assemble in the nation's capital to speak out for a cause. The Moratorium. It was both a culmination and a beginning. It was the result of a massive effort to bring together every individual voice that had shouted out in protest of the shameful war in Vietnam. This was where it had all ended. In one enormous showing of determination, of solidarity. And Jerry Bloom had been part of it. He had been a few years older than most of the other protesters and the principal organizers. But they were still his peers. What a beautiful conclusion to all the work, all the humiliation of being denounced as traitors, all the threats, all the insults.

But what a beautiful beginning, as well. It had been the start of the new course the United States would take. All those voices had been heard. But more than that, they had had an effect. An enormous one. This was a country whose citizenry had rarely questioned their leaders' decisions to wage war. Now it was becoming one whose leaders were being constrained from entering armed conflicts. Not for tactical reasons, but for reasons of conscience. It was a country that, for the first time in its history, was willing to be viewed as the loser of a war, if the war was considered an unjust one by its people. That's change. Change that most Americans, just a decade earlier, would have said never could have been achieved. And to have been a part of it was something that made Jerry Bloom feel he had been blessed to have been born into this time in history, rather than any other.

A voice from nowhere in particular jolted Bloom out of his reflections. It was one of the cockpit crew, coming through the public address system.

"The, ah, captain has turned off the seat-belt sign. We're expecting a pretty smooth flight to Dallas, but we do recommend you keep your seat belt loosely fastened while you're seated, just in case of unexpected turbulence. And thanks again for flying with us this evening."

Bloom wondered if there were any pilots in the airline industry who didn't speak with southern or western drawls. How come he had never heard a New York or Boston accent? Must be part of their training.

He looked to his left and saw, for the first time, the woman sitting across from him in the window seat. He also realized that he and she were the only passengers in the first-class cabin. Which meant it would be a quiet, relaxing trip. He couldn't help but notice the woman's attractive legs, crossed quite properly. She wore a tailored skirt and blouse, not one of those manly blue suits that working women everywhere had been wearing ever since the dress-for-success code for females had appeared in magazines. She had the look of a successful, confident woman. And she was deeply engrossed in a thick computer printout. Bloom surmised she was a programmer, or, possibly, the head of an accounting department. Her face was turned away from him, revealing only a small portion of her profile and her medium-brown hair. She reminded him of Anne. Most attractive women did. His wife formed a matrix against which Bloom compared other women. When he noticed a particularly attractive one, he would admire her, not as an alternative to his wife, but as a complement, for when Bloom felt lustful stirrings over women, he was, in fact, lusting for Anne.

"What would you like to drink, Mr. Bloom?"

This voice was from somewhere directly above him.

A tidy, businesslike flight attendant smiled cordially at Bloom.

"I'd like a glass of orange juice, if you have it."

"Are you sure you wouldn't like a cocktail? Or perhaps some champagne? It's complimentary."

Bloom returned the efficient smile. "Thanks just the same, but orange juice would be just fine."

The flight attendant smiled and shrugged, as though she had someone strange on board.

Bloom turned to his left and saw the attractive woman smiling across at him.

"They don't know what to make of it when a man doesn't order a drink," said the stranger. "Funny, though, I don't think they find it strange when a woman declines."

Bloom was now twice embarrassed—first by the flight attendant, who had trouble accepting orange juice for an answer, and now by the woman across the aisle, whose friendliness caught him by surprise. He was at a loss to continue the conversation. He certainly couldn't carry on the discussion of men and women ordering orange juice on airplanes. He simply put something between a grimace and a smile on his face and self-consciously looked out his window at the white, puffy clouds that slid by, tinted deep orange by the sinking sun.

Bloom picked up a *Newsweek* that a previous passenger had left in the seat pocket. He began thumbing through the pages, unaware of what was on them, thinking, instead, about the woman across the aisle. He wanted to talk to her, to pass the time, to get his mind off things that had disturbed him in Phoenix and continued to trouble him at home in Los Angeles. He didn't even notice the prominent photograph of his dear friend, Hattie Lewis, on the magazine page.

"She's remarkable, isn't she?" The voice came again from his left.

Bloom was startled. He looked up at the woman, puzzled.

"Hattie Lewis," she said, pointing toward the magazine.

Bloom looked down at the page his hand was holding open. He nodded.

"Yes. She is remarkable." She *does* want to talk. He looked at the full-color picture of Congresswoman Hattie Lewis. She was at the rostrum of the National Women's Rights Convention in Atlantic City. The photo showed her leaning into the microphone, with a determined—almost angry—look, making what surely must have been a forceful point. Beneath the picture was a caption written with more than a little preciousness: NOBEL PRIZE FOR NOBLE WOMAN?

Bloom had missed the rumor that was reported in the story, but he wasn't surprised. Because of her worldwide work on behalf of women's rights, her continuing civil rights activities, and, more recently, her efforts to help bring peace between two warring African nations, Hattie Lewis was being considered a leading contender for the Nobel Peace prize.

He stared at the photo of his old friend and client, remembering how sweet her latest reelection victory had been, how easy it had been to create a media campaign to give her a broad margin for a clear third-term mandate from her constituents. He thought of Hattie's meteoric rise to national prominence, and of the leadership role she had taken in the Democratic party. What would her partisan colleagues think if they knew she was, right now, in Stephen Wendell's office? At least it could not jeopardize her chance of winning the Nobel prize. Or could it? Perhaps the selection committee did not take kindly to Wendell.

"Are you a Hattie Lewis fan?" he finally asked.

"I wouldn't call myself a fan. But I admire her intelligence, if not her ideology."

"Sounds like you're a Republican," Bloom joked, good-naturedly.

"Sounds like you put labels on people," she retorted. Her smile was just a bit mocking.

"Your orange juice, sir." It was the efficient voice of the flight attendant again.

"Thanks," said Bloom, taking the glass.

"If you change your mind, we'll keep the champagne chilled for you."

Bloom turned back to the woman across the aisle. He watched her as she studied the printout on her lap. She seemed to be about thirty-five. She had a pale, almost delicate complexion. The way she spoke, her total demeanor, bespoke strength, an interesting contrast to her features, which seemed to be those of a more passive woman.

"It looks like you have a real job," Bloom said to her.

She didn't look up from her work, but smiled and shook her head. Then she spoke into her papers. "I'm afraid I don't. I'm a consultant."

"Guess we can't pick each other out in public."

"You consult also?" She still did not look up.

"Of course. That's how I get to ride up front here. It all gets billed to clients."

She finally looked up at him and smiled. It was a becoming, if not warm, smile.

"I don't want to keep you from your work," he said. Actually, he wanted to keep her from her printout, if he could.

"I appreciate that. So would my client," she answered, turning back to her work.

Well, Bloom thought, you didn't exactly sweep her off her feet.

Bloom was restless. He checked his watch and saw he had nearly two hours before the plane would land in Dallas. He wanted to get his mind off what lay ahead of him. The meeting with Wendell. The confrontation with Hattie Lewis. He also thought of the problems that were going unresolved at home. Work was the answer, as usual. The Braun campaign needed more television commercials. It was time to get going on a new pool of thirties. Braun was seeking his second term as the Democratic senator from California and was facing heavy opposition from his conservative opponent, Neimeir, who was still milking the tax revolt in California for all it was worth.

Braun had achieved a great deal in six years, particularly in areas of environmental protection and consumer advocacy. But these were times when people were finding issues like protecting wilderness areas and keeping corporations honest far less important than their own financial plight. The wealthy were crying poor now, faced with paying the piper for the monumental federal deficit. Yet people in California, and just about everywhere else, were still spending more money on more vacations and bigger homes and cars than ever before. Candidates like Braun found themselves defending the social programs they espoused strictly in terms of dollars and cents. It was no longer a question of need, or of correcting wrongs. Now it was a matter of how much it all would cost. And nothing more. Braun's brilliant record as a congressman before going to the Senate, particularly his efforts on behalf of medical care for the aging, seemed of little importance to constituents in this election.

The polls still showed Braun running ahead of the challenger, but the gap was narrowing enough to make the campaign staff edgy. They were urging Braun to sound more and more like an antigovernment, tax-cutting conservative. They were reading all the columns that were sounding the death knell of the old liberalism in America. They were telling Bloom to move with the times and the temper of the electorate, toward Gary Hart and his new liberalism. Bloom was telling them to stop trying to present a new Senator Braun, because voters weren't so naive as to think the man who helped bring national health insurance to America was now a man who wanted to throw out useful social programs just because they cost money. If the people wanted a Neimeir for their senator, they could get the real thing. They weren't going to settle for an imitation by Braun, an imitation that wouldn't be plausible to begin with.

Finally, Bloom had forced a confrontation. He had demanded a meeting with the candidate and his key advisers, and insisted they agree on what Braun really stood for. If he no longer represented the views he had held during his previous six years as senator, then a new media strategy would be in order. But if he had not changed—which he obviously had not—and it was only the mood of the voters that was changing, then the campaign must continue to present the real man. It was a long and painful meeting. Braun tried to keep peace between his staff and his trusted consultant and friend, Bloom. At one point, his campaign manager offered to resign, rather than watch the campaign "go down the tubes" with the wrong strategy. Braun talked him out of it, and the campaign manager was obviously grateful, having made his point in front of his peers and still kept his job. Then the issues chairman had had *his* tantrum. He stood in the middle of the room and tore up a stack of issue papers he had been working on for six months. He was trying to show what the campaign was doing to his carefully framed issue positions. Senator Braun calmed him down, as well. He even made the gesture of humbly crouching down and picking up all the torn pieces of paper, as though he might help glue them together again.

When it was all over, everyone agreed that Senator Braun was still the same man the people had elected six years earlier, and that he, indeed, could be proud of his achievements; and that, yes, the voters *did* have a clear choice: between a record of remarkable progress and integrity and a stream of hollow promises and negativism. Bloom's assignment remained the same: Let the people of California know what progress had been made on their behalf and how important it was to all interests in the state to continue the work that had been begun under Braun's leadership. It was the kind of meeting that Bloom was becoming increasingly accustomed to, in these days of changing voter moods. In most cases, he won his battles. He was generally able to protect his candidates from themselves and their staffs. On occasion, he would fail. And then he would be faced with the choice of bowing out of the campaign or going ahead with a strategy he knew would be wrong. If he offered to bow out, chances were still good he would stay in. Because his candidates knew his value. They also knew the dangers of changing media consultants late in the campaign. It was frequently like a game of poker, and few people wanted to risk calling Bloom's bluff.

With the latest Braun confrontation behind him, he now had to produce quickly the next, and probably final, pool of thirty-second commercials. The messages had to be about pride in achievement, as well as hope for the future, at a time when people were questioning more and more what their elected representatives were achieving and what effect they could actually have on the future. There was no longer a silent majority to worry about out there, Bloom had concluded. It was the *skeptical* majority that concerned him. Voters were listening to the people who called for tax revolution. They were nodding with the demagogues who spoke out for an end to virtually all forms of welfare. But still, there had to be a way for people like Braun to maintain their integrity and still win at the polls.

Bloom had his yellow legal pad in front of him. In the upper right-hand corner was the familiar identification:

> Braun for Senate
> 30-sec. TV
> # 18-A
> "CARING ABOUT SENIORS"

This was to be a commercial that talked about the need for decent health care for senior citizens, the kind provided by Braun's comprehensive health insurance bill, which had narrowly passed both houses and become law. It was a "credentials" commercial. Proof of performance.

On the left-hand side of the page, at the top, Bloom wrote in the heading: "Video." Halfway across, on the same line, he wrote "Audio," and drew a line down the middle of the page, to form two columns. He first described the situation in the video column:

Medium shot of elderly couple, sixty-five or seventy, sitting on a park bench in an urban setting. They are posed, looking into the camera, almost motionless, as though waiting to hear something. Camera begins ever so slow move-in to closer framing.

He skipped a space and began writing another instruction.

A middle-aged man, dressed like a carnival pitchman, walks into frame. He stops, looks at the elderly couple, and turns to camera. He opens a suitcase he's carrying, and it becomes a portable pitchman's table, which he sets up in front of him. He holds a kitchen knife, and begins to speak.

Bloom moved over to the audio column. He paused. He thought about what the sounds should be, and what the man should say. He had conceived the spot earlier in the day, while waiting to speak to the students at the seminar in Phoenix. God, he wondered, had that been today? It seemed so distant. He began to write.

SFX: Natural presence that would be found in an urban park. Birds, children's voices in the distance, some very slight traffic sounds. Establish sound presence for three seconds, to time with entry of the pitchman.

PITCHMAN: (played broadly) All right, folks, tell you what I'm gonna do. You say you don't like your taxes. I'm gonna cut 'em. That's right. I said cut 'em.

Back in the video column, Bloom wrote some more instructions, then more audio to match.

Pitchman takes the shiny knife, which looks like a gadget sold on a television commercial, and holds it up to be seen. As he's doing that, the old man behind him leans forward to interrupt.

OLD MAN: How you going to do that?

Pitchman is annoyed, talks over his shoulder.

PITCHMAN: Don't bother me, son. (back to camera) We're gonna cut welfare. We're gonna cut programs like health insurance.

OLD MAN: What happens when folks get sick?

PITCHMAN: (dismissing the man) There's one in every crowd . . . all right, folks, just watch me cut (trailing off) your taxes. . . .

Camera moves in past the pitchman to close-up of the older couple on the bench. Lock in on close-up two-shot.

ANNOUNCER (voice-over): If we start cutting off programs like health care, we start cutting off people. Senator Braun made full medical care possible for all Americans. Because he cares. Do you?

Freeze frame on E.C.U. of older couple, pull back image and add black frame. BRAUN FOR SENATE logo pops on. WE'RE GETTING THERE. KEEP SENATOR BRAUN.

Bloom stared at his completed rough script. He

read it to himself, his lips actually forming the words of the dialogue, to get an accurate timing, using the stopwatch he wore on his wrist.

Thirty-three seconds, he calculated. But it didn't worry him. His scripts always came in a few seconds long in early drafts. He could tighten up some of the action and pull a few words from the pitchman's spiel. But he was more concerned about the appropriateness of the commercial. He was intrigued by the device of the pitchman, which turned the issue of tax-cutting back on Braun's conservative opponent, making him look like a carnival-type who could hardly be believed, let alone entrusted with the job of a United States senator.

But was it too hokey? he wondered. Not if it's well executed, he reassured himself. In fact, it's just the kind of spot his friend and associate, Chuck Hanselman, would love to direct. He had a good understanding of whimsy in political commercials. There was a very fine line in such approaches, a line separating disaster and success. Treat a humorous political commercial too heavy-handedly and you're in big trouble. Stay on the proper side of that thin line and you can have a message that's far more persuasive than any "straight" commercial. Bloom always called it "high-risk" advertising. But he was also quick to add that the chance for high return went right along with it. And that's what the Braun campaign needed right now.

Bloom turned and looked out the window. The sky outside was nearly dark now. Only a faint streak of reddish light to the west was visible. He stared out at the void and saw his wife's pretty face. He pictured her on the phone, standing in the kitchen, when he had called her from Phoenix. He imagined she had been shaking her head while she spoke to him. The same kind of head-shaking that went with her frequent reminders that he was too wrapped up in his work. "Sorry, children," she would say at the breakfast table, "but your father isn't with us today."

"Yeah," one of the children would chime in, "Dad's staring into the sugar bowl again."

It was true. Bloom was somewhere else a good deal of the time these days. Off filming a commercial or reassuring a nervous candidate. He seemed to be trying to cram two days into each single one that remained before an election. He couldn't say no to a good, liberal candidate. Especially one who could pay his fee. He was guided by principle, but driven by money. The more he believed, the better was his work and, therefore, the more people were willing to pay him. He had sometimes thought it was the best of both worlds—working for what he believed in and getting rich on those beliefs. But he wondered if he hadn't been lying to himself. And to Anne. Especially now, when he was en route to Dallas to talk to a man he did not believe in, but one who could undoubtedly pay him, and pay him very handsomely. Bloom reassured himself that he was only going to hear the man out. And he was only doing that much because a dear friend had asked him to. He again saw Anne's face. And he heard her voice: "Come on, Jerry." It was her way of saying "You're full of shit, Bloom." And he knew he was.

Questions were coming so easily these days. It was the answers that were getting so difficult.

Are you a sellout, Bloom? What would John McGuire think of you now? Your dear friend, who lost his job in Chicago because you talked him into taking off to march in Washington. You told him to choose between conviction and "all that fucking money." He chose conviction. How about you?

The barely perceptible motion of flight was relaxing Bloom, almost lulling him. He was drifting toward sleep. He had found, lately, a pleasant little escape from the pressures of reality. As difficult as it was to sleep in bed at night, he could, at almost any time of day, drift into a state that was nearly sleep. He would dream in that state and become rested. He was just slightly conscious of sounds around him. Maybe it was what people called a cat-nap. Whatever it was, it had a soothing escapist quality that Bloom enjoyed and appreciated.

He now drifted into that dreamlike state and found himself standing in a large room that resembled a courtroom. Seated high above him, on something like a judge's bench, was his high-school Latin teacher, Mrs. Laffer. Liverlips, he and his friends had called her. She was scolding him, as she had done for most of the three years of Latin class he had suffered through. "Jerome, you have not finished your final term paper. In fact, I suspect you have not even begun it. And this is the last day of school. Jerome, I am going to fail you, unless, of course, you can research and write a fifty-page paper by tomorrow morning. Now I know what your parents will do if you fail Latin. And I'm sure you know, as well. It would be a remarkable achievement if you were to somehow complete the paper. But I know you are not superhuman. So I suppose we'll simply have to set a conference with your mother and father. But we will wait until tomorrow, just in case you prove me wrong and become super-human."

She smiled at him. A broad smile. With those purple liver lips. Twenty-four hours then melted away. Bloom was still standing beneath the judge's bench. Mrs. Laffer was still smiling. And he held a pathetic, lone sheet of paper in his hand. He looked down at it. It said only: CAESAR'S MOST IMPORTANT SPEECH, BY JEROME BLOOM, LATIN II, MRS. LAFFER. That was all. And the deadline had arrived. He experienced a kind of vertigo, his body growing weaker as his panic heightened. He wanted to run out of the room, but his legs wouldn't move. He tried to shout at Mrs. Laffer, but the words were stuck in his throat. Only a brief, muffled grunt came forth. At the instant he felt the sound jump out of his throat, he awoke from his dream state, startled, and looked across the aisle. The woman was looking back at him.

"Did you say something?" she asked.

He pointed to his throat, shaking his head. "Must be getting a cold." And he felt like a fool, wondering what she must have thought, hearing him utter some subhuman noise.

The flight attendant brought Bloom and the woman passenger their dinner. It was the usual first-class airline fare, made to appear far better than it could possibly taste, served on white linen, with decent china and flatware. Bloom was not very hungry. He was too tense to find food appetizing. When the flight attendant came around with champagne and wine, he decided he needed something to drink more than he needed food. He had three glasses of wine during the twenty minutes or so that followed. He didn't speak to the woman across from him, but the wine helped lower his inhibitions, and he felt like talking to her. He was actually too shy to get up and move to a seat next to her and begin a conversation. He smiled to himself as he stared into the wineglass he twirled in his fingers. He imagined himself getting up, stepping across the aisle, and saying something perfectly natural to the woman, such as commenting on dinner. And he then imagined her asking him to return to his seat, because she had work to do and didn't really want to talk to anyone.

"Excuse me," said the woman.

Bloom turned to her.

"Do you know anything about these things?" She was holding a pocket-size calculator in her hand and pointing to it. "It's gone dead."

Bloom was quite pleased to move across the aisle and offer his help.

"I'm not exactly an electronics engineer," he said, "but I sometimes use one just like it."

He pressed a few buttons and came up with nothing on the small display screen. The only thing he could think of was to check the battery. He opened the compartment and fished out the small cell, wondering how in the world he was supposed to tell if it was dead. But then it dawned on him that his portable dictating machine used the same size battery.

"Be right back," he said and went over to his seat to get his recorder from his briefcase. He found it and moved back across to the woman.

"Let's try this." He slipped the battery from his machine into the calculator, closed the compart-

58

ment, and pressed some keys. Numbers flashed onto the screen. He felt, in some absurd, small way, heroic.

"Wonderful," said the woman. "But I can't let you do that. You'll probably want to use your dictating machine."

"No, no, that's fine. I really have no reason to use it. I especially don't like to use it on airplanes."

She laughed. "I know. It's always embarrassing when someone stares at you while you're talking out loud into your hand."

Bloom slid the dead battery into his dictating machine and flicked on the power switch. He was startled to see the recording light go on.

"I'll be damned," said the woman. "It isn't dead. Only in my calculator."

"Here, we can, uh, switch them back again, to see—"

The woman interrupted him with a laugh. She placed her hand on his arm. "No, please. We'll end up taking both machines apart and dropping some critical, tiny screw on the floor, which we'd never find. Let's both put our machines away. I don't want to do any more calculating, anyway."

The little encounter was enjoyable for Bloom. He agreed to a mutual withdrawal of battery-operated devices and tossed his dictating machine across to his seat.

"What kind of consulting do you do?" she asked.

"Mostly political," he answered.

"This must be your busy time of year."

"It's what my kids call 'crazy-time.'" Bloom no longer wore a wedding band and, therefore, felt obligated to admit to being married (or at least to being a father) early on in any conversation with a woman.

"Nine weeks until election day. And it's frantic?" She obviously didn't care whether he had children. Why should she?

"Too much time on these things," he said, gesturing around him.

"I fly a lot too. By the way, my name's Jeanette Wells."

"Jerry Bloom. Nice to meet you, Jeanette. What kind of consulting do you do?"

"Research."

"Any political?"

"Some," she replied. "I do mostly motivational research. Only recently, I've become interested in political polling."

"I don't know many people in your business. I seem to work with only two these days."

"Don't tell me," she said. "Let me guess. Philip Howe."

"Not bad."

"And the other one, let's see, it must be the young genius, Paul Crowell."

She knows her politics, he thought. She picked the two pollsters he most frequently worked with on his campaigns. Both Democrats, and both very good at what they did.

"It must be written all over me. I'm a liberal Democrat who likes Hattie Lewis, so I must work with Phil Howe, the solid, methodical one, and Paul Crowell, the bright young brat of liberal polling."

"Is he all that bright?" she asked.

"Of course. Ask him."

"Well, he did something right for Gary Hart."

"Perhaps he did. But I think the reason Hart is the nominee goes well beyond his choice of pollsters. He was ready, and the party was ready for him. Crowell has excellent instincts. But he also has an inflated view of his work, and what it can do to change the outcome of elections."

"You don't sound too crazy about him." She had a very warm smile, which Bloom found inviting.

He shrugged. "He's not my favorite person. But he's good. And he's worked for good people."

"Are you a political junkie?"

"I suppose so. I've tried to kick the habit cold turkey more than once. But it doesn't work. If I just walk past a campaign office, I can't stop myself from dropping in."

"But only if it's a Democratic office, right?"

"Are there any other kind?"

"Do you mean to say you wouldn't get involved in a race other than for a Democrat?"

"No, I'm not saying I wouldn't. It's just that I haven't worked for a Republican yet. Unlike other business, politics demands partisan loyalty from the people who work at it. I guess it's because most of us get into it for ideological reasons."

"But what happens when you change? Or when the ideologies change?" she asked.

"Then it's a different story." Bloom enjoyed talking with Jeanette, but he was uncomfortable with the subject. "I suppose that's when you decide to change parties."

"Or walk away from both of them," said Jeanette.

"But where does that get you?" He didn't give her a chance to answer. "You're proving a point, maybe, but without the apparatus for change. The parties will always have that." He realized he was not arguing with Jeanette nearly as much as he was with Stephen Wendell.

"What do you make of Wendell?" asked Jeanette.

Bloom was not surprised that the name came up. Millions of people were asking the same question about him. But it was, nonetheless, unsettling.

"I'm not sure what to make of him. He's obviously very smart. And he's already gone farther than any independent candidate ever has. But he still can't go all the way. The two-party system isn't dead. It's just in poor health for now. And I don't see much hope for a Democrat calling himself a progressive-conservative."

"I've seen some data that just might prove you wrong," she said. There was a challenge in her tone, albeit a nonthreatening one.

"So, you really *are* getting into politics," he answered. "But the question is, on whose behalf?"

"Sorry," she shrugged. "Client privilege."

"Maybe. But you'll show up, sooner or later, in a mandatory disclosure. Believe me, I know."

"Can I look forward to any disclosures about you in the near future?"

"Only in five states for now," said Bloom.

"You're not working on the presidential race?"

"Sorry. No one's invited me yet," he lied. But, he thought, it wasn't really a lie. Wendell had only invited him to a discussion so far, he told himself.

"Do you want to handle a presidential campaign?"

"Are you offering me one?"

She ignored his playfulness. "I should think that would be a logical step for you. Especially with a win—loss record like yours."

Bloom was flattered. But he was also troubled. The woman had not so much as hinted that she knew anything about him.

"How could you know about my record?"

"All right, I confess, I know who you are. As would anyone who's done any serious work in politics. In fact, I read about you last month. It was quite a complimentary piece."

Bloom recalled the article the political science professor had read, earlier in the day, to his class. And he realized that anyone involved in campaign work would probably know something of him and of his work. But he was still uneasy. Why didn't she admit earlier that she knew who he was? Jeanette must have anticipated the question.

"I wasn't about to say 'Oh, you must be Jerry Bloom, the famous media man.'"

"That's fine. Notoriety is not, thankfully, one of the rewards of what I do." It was not that Bloom was opposed to celebrity status; he preferred to wait until he could one day become Bloom, the famous filmmaker, rather than Bloom, the famous media consultant.

"Would you handle a presidential candidate if you *were* invited?" Jeanette asked.

"Of course, for the right man." He paused. "Or woman. After all, as one of my favorite politicians once said, 'You have to want to go to the top of the mountain, if you believe in what you do, whether you're an athlete or a politician.'"

"Mo Udall?"

"For someone only peripherally involved in politics, you know a lot about it." Bloom was impressed with her knowledge. Morris Udall's comment about his presidential aspirations was not one of the more familiar quotations.

"The truth is, I volunteered for Mo in seventy-six."

"Did Democratic politics appeal to you then?" asked Bloom.

"Not nearly so much as its candidate did."

"I get the feeling that something happened to move you away from liberal politics. Was it the Carter presidency? Or did you get rich?"

Jeanette did not, apparently, find his remark humorous. "Can't it ever be something honest? Like discovering the hypocrisy of it all?" Something had angered her.

"Of course it can be. But I think you'd have a hard time convincing many people that what was wrong with the party of Roosevelt and Kennedy was hypocrisy. Perhaps a temporary attack of ineffectiveness in recent years, or even irrelevance. But sorry, I don't see hypocrisy."

"Well, maybe you and I view things from different vantage points," said Jeanette, somewhat aggressively. Bloom could see he had touched a nerve.

"Maybe we do. But I hope you'll agree that the things the Democratic party has stood for over the years are things that brought change to this country—change very much for the better."

"I'm sure you're talking about civil rights, and about peace."

"And about women's rights, too," said Bloom, smiling.

"Of course. But the effectiveness of Roosevelt, and the commitment of Kennedy and Humphrey, are quite different from the duplicity of a Johnson or a Carter."

"Duplicity? Come on now, don't you think you're overstating things?"

"As a matter of fact, I might find duplicity an understatement."

"How on earth can you arrive at that?" asked Bloom. He could see Jeanette was angry. Her face was flushed. She was no longer playfully debating him.

"I can very easily arrive there. Especially when I watch someone die at the hands of criminals who were cordially invited to our streets from Cuba by a so-called liberal and humane president."

"You're blaming the crimes of aliens on Jimmy Carter? He didn't bring criminals here. Castro *sent* them, as a perverse joke. And who did you actually see die on the streets?"

Jeanette stared at him. "My husband," she said quietly, but with unmistakable bitterness, if not hatred, in her voice.

Bloom was stunned by her words. He felt foolish, not knowing whether to say he was sorry or to ask what had happened, and who her husband had been. She finally spoke again.

"Have you ever heard of Jeff Wells?"

"The film producer?"

Jeanette nodded.

"He was very gifted," said Bloom, his voice lowered. "I'm sorry."

Bloom was familiar with Jeanette's late husband, the successful young filmmaker who was killed just weeks after receiving an Academy Award for his documentary on illegal aliens living in Southern California. Ironically, he had died of injuries sustained while he was filming a riot in the barrio of Los Angeles. No one was charged with his murder, but police were certain the gunshot that had killed him came from the weapon of a rioting alien.

"He was trying to tell the story of injustices he thought the immigrants were suffering," said Jeanette, her eyes becoming clouded, her voice shaky. "And he suffered the only real injustice—the taking of an honest, meaningful life."

Bloom would ordinarily have challenged the notion that an alien's life was not meaningful; but he chose not to. He could sense the pain with which Jeanette spoke of the tragedy, and he understood her need to be bitter, to lay blame. He smiled weakly at Jeanette, trying silently to let her know he, too, felt a sense of loss.

For what seemed like a long time, they both remained silent. Then Bloom cleared his throat and spoke. "I think I'll get back to my seat now."

Jeanette placed her hand on his arm. "It's not necessary. In fact, I'd rather you stayed here and continued talking, if you don't mind."

"Of course." He nodded, and he felt a welcome warmth in her light touch.

"But you were nice to offer to let me be alone." She smiled now.

"Well," said Bloom, breathing a deep sigh, "it's hard to say anything that wouldn't be inappropriate. No one has come up with words that can make someone feel better when they're grieving."

"I'm not so sure. I think you just did."

Bloom gradually eased the conversation back to

more pleasant things. He and Jeanette discussed current films. They discovered a mutual reverence for Woody Allen, and for Robert Altman. They disagreed on the brilliance of Wim Wenders, but agreed completely on Wertmüller. They discussed books and restaurants, music, and even football. And they deftly avoided any further talk of politics.

As the jet began its descent into Dallas–Fort Worth, Bloom surprised himself by suggesting he and Jeanette see one another again.

"We should get together and chat again," he said, thinking he, a married man, was making a pass.

"I agree. How long will you be in Dallas?"

"Oh, I imagine only until tomorrow night, or the following day."

"I'm free tomorrow evening, if you're still here," she said. "Perhaps we could have dinner."

Bloom felt an exciting sense of anticipation at the suggestion, mixed with a gnawing guilt.

"That would be nice," he said, an understatement. "You *do* know I'm married, don't you?" He felt absurd saying it.

"I assumed you were. But I only suggested dinner, if you'll recall," she reprimanded.

Bloom could feel the crimson overtake his face, and he was certain Jeanette could see it. She smiled knowingly and reached into her large leather purse. She pulled out a business card and wrote something on it, then handed it to Bloom. HASTINGS HOTEL, it said, written beneath Jeanette's printed name and title, RESEARCH COUNSELOR.

"You can reach me there," she said. "If you can make it, just leave word, with a time and place. Okay?"

"Sounds fine. Have you been to Dallas before?"

"Several times."

"Good. I'll let you choose a place, since I've never been here before," he said.

"Fair enough. And if you can't make it, perhaps you can give me a call next time you're in Phoenix."

Bloom had a very strong feeling he would be able to make it for dinner.

"Ladies and gentlemen," came the efficient voice over the intercom, "the captain has turned on the no-smoking sign in preparation for landing. Please extinguish all cigarettes and see that your tray table is secured and your seat in its full upright position."

Bloom glanced at Jeanette, with particular appreciation of her understated beauty, as he thought of dinner with her and, perhaps, even more. The jarring of the plane's wheels on the runway interrupted his musings and reminded him he first had some troubling business to deal with in Dallas.

He was anxious to leave the plane, even though he would have preferred, under other circumstances, to linger and continue talking to Jeanette, perhaps even to share a cab. But he didn't want his new acquaintance to know the nature of his visit to Dallas. He was relieved when she waved good-bye, telling him she was going to remain behind the other passengers because she had stored some oversize luggage in the rear closet.

When Jeanette went to the rear of the plane to retrieve her garment bag, she noticed a man who looked very familiar sitting in a window seat in the last row. He wore dark glasses. He seemed engrossed in some paperwork he was trying to finish before deplaning. Jeanette couldn't help but stare at him. She was sure she knew who he was. She had, in fact, met him once, but she couldn't be sure where or when. It possibly had something to do with a film. The sunglasses he wore made it difficult to identify Aram Saraf, who had also flown from Phoenix to Dallas.

Few people would have recognized Saraf, who looked like a successful young businessman, perhaps of Italian or Latin American descent. Certainly no one would imagine that this Palestinian refugee was being watched very closely by FBI agents, who had obtained information linking him to various terrorist acts against Israel, including everything from kidnapping to hijacking to murder. Even if Jeanette had figured out Saraf's identity, she would have had no way of knowing the reason for his presence on the same flight she and Bloom had taken; nor would she have known that he was about to telephone Harrison Davis to report that she and Bloom had met and gotten along rather well.

5 AS HE STRODE INTO THE STERILE, gray-walled concourse of the Dallas airport, Bloom looked around, wondering how he was supposed to know who would be meeting him.

"Hi, Mr. Bloom." The voice of a man with a southern drawl came from behind him. Bloom turned to see a young man—no more than twenty-five—in neat, casual dress, smiling broadly, holding out his hand in greeting. He was clean-cut, somewhat studious-looking, not at all unlike the many earnest young workers so common in political campaigns.

"I'm Alex Hyman, of the Wendell campaign." It always startled Bloom to hear a Jew speak with a southern accent. And he was further startled to hear a Jew, no matter what his accent, announce he was part of the Stephen Wendell campaign.

"Glad to meet you, Alex," said Bloom, shaking the young man's hand.

"Have any baggage checked, Mr. Bloom?"

Hyman asked as they began walking toward the main lobby.

"Nope," he said, slapping the underseat leather bag he was carrying. "I travel light. Especially when I'm not planning to make detours to Dallas. You may have to find me a place to buy a shirt, though."

"No problem," Hyman replied cheerfully.

Young Hyman said they would be going directly to Wendell's ranch, where Bloom was to join the candidate for dinner. Bloom explained he had already eaten. Hyman acted as though he hadn't heard him, and simply continued to be the gracious, cheerful guide.

"Is Dallas your home?" Bloom asked.

"Yes, sir. I was born here," Hyman answered, sounding proud.

"Are you a student?" asked Bloom, looking out the window into the night, seeing only blurring streetlights and neon.

"No. I finished law school last year. I'm clerking part-time, and working on the governor's campaign."

"How did you get into politics?"

"I heard Governor Wendell speak last year, when he addressed the graduating class. I knew right then that this man ought to be president, and I wanted to help him."

"Why?" Bloom asked, almost as a challenge.

Hyman seemed stumped by the unexpected question. He laughed nervously. "Well, Mr. Bloom, I guess I feel he gives us answers. The other people, they just keep raising more questions."

"You think he can beat the two parties?"

"Yes, sir, I do. Things are moving in the governor's direction. This country is ready for him."

"Tell me," said Bloom, "were you alive in November 1963?"

"No. I was born six months after John Kennedy was killed."

And that, perhaps, as much as the Wendell candidacy, was what made Bloom so uncomfortable about being in Dallas. It was a city that he had never forgiven for being the scene of the assassination of John Kennedy. Like many other sixties liberals, Bloom held Dallas culpable for providing too fertile a bed in which violence could root and nourish. His mind went back again, as it had hundreds of times, to that tragic time, that four days of nationally televised nightmares. He saw himself sitting in front of the television set, watching the morning news with live reports from Dallas. He had shouted to his wife in another room, "He's been shot. They shot Oswald. Right here on TV." Anne hadn't believed him. Bloom had questioned his own sanity. Had he gone over the edge and imagined everything? He then saw himself making love to Anne two days later, right after they had both tearfully watched the funeral. They had made love not out of lust or for pleasure, but to ease their fear of the future, to hide from the reality of a world going mad around them.

"Where's the Texas School Book Depository?" he asked.

"Just a few miles from here. We come pretty close to it going through the city to the governor's ranch."

"Would you mind a little detour?"

Hyman seemed at a loss for words. He finally shrugged. "I don't see any problem, Mr. Bloom, as long as we don't keep the governor waiting."

Fuck the governor, Bloom thought. He looked at his watch. "We're a little early," he said. "I'm sure he has plenty to do. I just want to see the place."

"Not much to see at night, sir. But I'll take you by," said Hyman, glancing at his watch. "Besides, it might throw the reporters off."

"Reporters?"

"Yes, sir. They're always around. I'm sure there'll be someone at the house, just checking to see who's coming to visit."

Bloom smiled to himself. He thought he might just end up in a newspaper story. Which would give him some explaining to do to his liberal friends.

As the car slowed down to exit the freeway, Hyman pointed to a darkened brick building off to the right. "There it is, Mr. Bloom. I'll double back and take you in front of it."

The car slowed to a stop. Bloom looked out the window and tried to place the building in all the newspaper and television images he had seen. Then he opened the car door.

"Just give me a couple of minutes," he said, and stepped out onto the sidewalk.

It was an ordinary brick building, devoid of any design or style. It was just a box. Bloom searched for some familiar detail, but in the darkness he could find none. He looked up to the fourth-floor windows and tried to picture Lee Harvey Oswald taking aim from one of them. He turned and walked back to the curb, looking out on the freeway beneath the grassy knoll. A chill came over him as he saw the grainy 8 mm film that had been shown over and over, depicting John Kennedy's last moments as a living human being, then his head being shattered by the bullet, his wife, in pink hat and suit, reaching for him. Last year Bloom had stood on the steps of the Senate building in Rome's Forum while a guide pointed out for him and Anne the very spot on which Caesar had been stabbed. That had been an interesting, exhilarating experience. Tonight was a sad, chilling one. Maybe time does heal, and even forgive, but Bloom hoped it would not do so in Dallas, Texas, or anywhere else. Not yet, at least not while the country still drifted about in search of ideas and people to believe in again.

"There's a monument here now." It was Hyman's voice, and it startled him. He had not heard the young man approach.

"I've heard," said Bloom.

"I'm not sure what purpose it serves," said Hyman, "except maybe to remind us—the people who live here—what kind of violence we're capable of."

Bloom walked to the stone tablet that commemorated the assassination. Hyman walked with him.

"It's funny," Hyman continued. "Governor Wendell asked me to drive him by here once. He kind of did what you did. Just got out and walked around, staring up at the building. And when he came back to the car, he had tears in his eyes. He was all choked up. The next day he delivered the most successful speech of his campaign."

74

"The 'Back to Greatness' speech?" Bloom remembered it well.

"Yes, sir. 'The man who asked not what his country could do for him, but what he could do for his country gave his life for a vision of greatness. Let us return to that quest, here in Texas, where it was brutally interrupted.'"

"You have a good memory," said Bloom.

"Especially for eloquence, sir."

"Well, let's get out of here," said Bloom. He wanted to be somewhere else. Not necessarily at the ranch of Stephen Wendell. Just somewhere else.

Bloom got out of the car, took a deep breath, and looked over the enormous house and grounds. There was a sweet smell in the air. He guessed it might be magnolia. Not because he was sure what magnolia smelled like, but because he had the notion that it was what you found in Texas. The air was pleasant, with just a slight chill and a light breeze. He looked up at the house, which, as far as he could tell in the dim evening light, was constructed of brick, with white wooden trim and shutters. The porch had traditional columns extending up to the second story. The driveway he stood on was brick. He couldn't help but feel he was at least going to be treated to an interesting look into southwestern wealth and comfort. Bloom saw two young men, standing in the driveway, talking. One looked up at him and shrugged. Reporters, he thought.

The front door opened, and instead of a black man in a white jacket, a black woman in a gray business suit stepped out. And Jerry Bloom was struck speechless.

"You going to stand out in the driveway all night, imagemaker?"

It was Hattie Lewis. The knot in Bloom's stomach came back again. He was always exhilarated to see his old friend—anytime, anywhere. Except here, and now. Her phone call from Wendell's campaign office earlier in the day had been hard enough to fathom, but now she was coming out the front door of the man's home. She looked as though she belonged there, and was even comfortable about it.

Bloom stared at Hattie for a moment. Then he laughed and looked down at the ground. He looked up again as Alex Hyman excused himself and took Bloom's bag up the steps and inside the house.

Bloom finally spoke, shaking his head. "Hattie, what the hell are you doing here?" He walked up the steps. He gave her the customary hug and kiss on the cheek. She returned his hug and laughed deeply.

"Good to see you." She held him off at arm's length and looked him over. "Lordy, lordy, you're looking flush. Get much more of a tan and you're going to start looking like you really *are* my brother."

Hattie Lewis was the kind of person who could immediately set anyone at ease. She turned an awkward situation into one that was as cozy as sitting home in front of your own fireplace. She was a tall woman. Her face was attractive, unmistakably Negroid in its features. She looked younger than her forty-two years. Her cheekbones were on the high side, her eyes large and round. And she wore very little makeup, just a slight touch of lipstick. Her hair was jet black, worn in the style of a middle-class, white housewife. She had once told Bloom she'd tried an Afro when she was working on her master's degree, but laughed herself right out of the beauty shop when she saw how she looked.

"Well, Congresslady," Bloom said, "I hope you have an explanation or two ready for me."

"Hey, I don't have to explain what I do," she chided. "I have the mandate of the people to do whatever I want, remember? Thanks to the slick campaign you did for me."

"You'll get some mandate when this gets out. By the way, are those reporters over there?"

Hattie nodded. "They're like flies around sugar. Come on inside. Our host and his dinner are both awaiting your arrival."

As they stepped across the threshold into the foyer, Bloom whispered, "Is there such a thing as an Auntie Tom?"

"Fuck off, whitey," she whispered back, smiling properly.

They walked into the large, marble-tiled entryway. A great stained-glass window cast a church-like aura over the winding stairway. A few fine examples of period furniture had been placed around the foyer. A large portrait of an aristocratic matron hung over an elegantly upholstered love seat. Bloom gazed around, smiling.

"Not too shabby, huh?" asked Hattie.

"When does Scarlett O'Hara come down the stairs?"

From behind Bloom came a startling answer. "Sorry, Mr. Bloom, but I'm afraid you've got the wrong state." It was a familiar voice, the one he had heard on the telephone earlier in the day, that of Harrison Davis, Wendell's law partner and campaign manager.

Davis wore a smile that was slightly more arrogant than cordial. He was a large man, about six-foot-two and stocky in build. He was partly bald; what hair remained was silver. Dressed in a three-piece pin-striped suit, he looked to be very much the prominent lawyer he was.

"Harrison Davis," he said, extending a pale hand. "Welcome to Dallas. We're all grateful for your cooperation." His voice was as smooth and genteel as it had been on the phone.

Hattie joined the conversation, speaking to Bloom. "The governor's been on the phone with the president." Bloom had the feeling he was supposed to be impressed. He felt a little annoyed with his friend. It wouldn't be at all unusual for the president to be calling Wendell. After all, Wendell had helped sell the president's tax program in Texas, especially to wary Democrats. And the president had made it clear that he saw Wendell's candidacy as a denunciation of the Democrats and, therefore, a de facto approval of the Republicans. Of course, Wendell dismissed the president's conclusions as just another heavy-handed attempt to counter the effects of his campaign.

"Well," cracked Bloom, "maybe the president wants to get a spot on the ticket." There was nothing subtle about his sarcasm, which Davis seemed to accept without so much as a blink.

"Sorry," said Davis, with a perfect deadpan, "but I'm afraid that position has already been filled."

Hattie shot a glance toward Davis, then nervously looked back to Bloom. Bloom remembered that Hattie had always had a clear and open dislike for Wendell's running mate, Senator Henry Blandemann of Florida. Davis returned her look with his arrogantly cordial smile.

"I would imagine a cocktail might be in order after your rather full day, Mr. Bloom. May I interest you in one?"

"If there's room on the agenda, I think I *would* like one."

Davis led the way through a sliding door. A large parlor was beyond the door. Bloom noticed a grand piano in the corner and an enormous marble fireplace, over which hung a painting of a seascape. The painting looked familiar to him, as though he had seen a copy of it in an art book. It struck Bloom that this room, which was much larger than his living room at home, was merely a spacious sitting room. Maybe these houses don't have living rooms. Just parlors and libraries, perhaps.

"Please make yourself comfortable, Mr. Bloom. What may I get for you?"

Bloom chose an overstuffed chair and sat down in it as he spoke. "Scotch and water, please."

Davis smiled and turned to Hattie. "Miss Lewis, what may I offer you?"

"Wild Turkey on the rocks, please."

A servant appeared through a doorway at the other end of the parlor. It was the black man in the white jacket whom Bloom had expected on the front porch. Perhaps not as old, nor as subservient as he had imagined, though. The butler addressed Davis.

"Something from the bar, Mr. Davis?"

Davis placed orders for Bloom and Hattie and added a request for a glass of sherry for himself. The black man nodded and left.

Davis looked at his wristwatch. "Alex, your driver, tells me you dined on the plane, Mr. Bloom. Could we still convince you to join us for dinner?"

"Sure. I might not do much justice to the meal, though." He was not hungry. He was tired and edgy. He was also apprehensive, as he tried to imagine himself involved in a quest for the presidency.

There was no mistaking the man who swiftly entered the room. Bloom had seen his picture dozens of times, in black and white in newspapers, in full color on magazine covers. He had also seen television news film of him many times, including the time he had held his famous press conference, vowing to stem the immigration tide that, in his view, had become the nation's most serious domestic problem. Now, former governor Stephen Wendell stood in the same room with Bloom, smiling warmly and needlessly identifying himself.

"I'm Stephen Wendell, Mr. Bloom. It's a pleasure to have you in my home."

Bloom reached out and accepted Wendell's hand. He noticed the same look on Wendell's face that he had seen on his now famous television appearance in the final year of his second term in office as governor of Texas. It was a look of intense confidence, tempered by the hint of a smile. Not necessarily a warm, soft smile. But a smile that told you, in no uncertain terms, that this was a man to be reckoned with, never to be underestimated. Bloom was reminded of Lyndon Johnson. Only Wendell had more charm, more poise.

The television appearance had launched Wendell into national politics. It was Wendell's own version of George Wallace's infamous performance at the University of Alabama, when he had confronted federal marshals and tried to block the entire United States government from integrating his state's campuses.

Wendell had chosen a more current and complex issue with which to confront the United States government: immigration. An issue for the eighties. It was an increasingly emotional issue, one that made for strange alliances between liberals and conservatives, between minorities and middle-class America.

The federal government had, in late 1986, set up enormous settlement camps in Texas to house nearly one hundred thousand refugees fleeing from Latin American countries. Part of the government program, which had been an embarrassment to the Reagan administration, included attempts to find jobs for the refugees on the oil fields and farms of Texas.

The plan had not worked. Riots had broken out in the largest camp. Wendell had seized the opportunity to take a hard line against the refugees. He was applauded everywhere when he called for removal of all aliens from Texas. At the same time, he demanded that Congress enact far more stringent immigration quotas, even shut the gates of the nation completely to new émigrés. He appealed for support from labor: "Every job given to a criminal alien is one taken away from a law-abiding American working man or woman." Labor loved it.

He also appealed to minorities: "The black and Hispanic members of our great society worked hard for what they have today. When unemployment hits, it is they who are hit first and hardest. When urban crime erupts, it is the inner city—and minority—American who is the first victim." And the minorities loved it—to a cautious point.

The rhetoric worked. So did Wendell's theatrics. When it appeared things were at the breaking point in the camp riots, Wendell went on national television and stood at the gate of the facility just outside Fort Worth.

"My fellow Americans," he began, sounding like an outraged Lyndon Johnson, "the time has come to take appropriate action to protect the people of the state of Texas and the people of the rest of this great nation from a growing threat of violence, crime, and loss of jobs. The federal government has chosen to unload its tragic immigration errors on the people of my state. We will not accept the consequences of Washington's folly. I am here today to say we are giving the problem back to the White House and to the bureaucracy of Washington."

Wendell proceeded to outline his plan to place one thousand refugees aboard school buses and National Guard trucks and send them in a caravan, to Washington. The crowd that had gathered—or, perhaps, been carefully assembled—to hear Wendell went wild in its approval. Millions of Americans watched the carefully orchestrated performance on their television screens, during prime time.

And Stephen Wendell, a relatively obscure politician, took a giant step toward the impossible dream—the capturing of the White House by a candidate of an independent third party.

Now Jerome Bloom was face to face with the man who had exploited so successfully an explosive political issue, the man who was determined to break every rule in every campaign and history book.

Like him or not, Bloom had to feel some respect for someone with such uncanny political instinct. But he worried where that instinct might take the man. And the country.

Harrison Davis had quietly slipped out of the room. He was on the telephone, behind the closed door of Wendell's library.

"What's your reading of him?"

Four miles away in a downtown hotel, the attractive widow Bloom had met on the airplane, Jeanette Wells, was looking at a *Newsweek* photo of Bloom.

"He's what we need. But he's also very strong-willed. Still, very much the naive idealist."

"I have every confidence in your persuasive powers."

"I'll call you later," she said.

"No. Wait for me to call you," said Davis.

6

THE DINING ROOM WAS PREDICTABLY spacious. The table was long and sturdy, of solid oak. The chairs, twelve of them, were high backed. The group of four people at one end of the table threw things out of scale. This kind of table should be fully occupied, Bloom mused. As it was, it looked like Wendell had been insulted by eight no-shows. Too bad.

Bloom was studying Wendell as the former governor spoke. He was trim and athletic-looking. He had recently celebrated his fiftieth birthday, and as Bloom had read in a newsmagazine, his friends and well-wishers had thrown a big party, to which they had managed to attract one fairly visible political figure from each of the fifty states—one for each year of Wendell's illustrious life. Bloom had found the whole idea so self-serving that it was probably one of the more successful public relations coups Wendell had yet pulled off. Bloom studied the man's eyes. They were gray, the color of a midwinter Chicago sky. And equally cold-looking. He had a good tan and a carefully attended-to head of hair, which was dark brown, with distinguished, graying side-burns. He was addressing Hattie Lewis, reminiscing about her most recent campaign, his voice soft and purposefully warm. This man, who lived in such predictable surroundings, was himself far from a cliché. He had no paunch; he would never wear a rumpled suit or a shoestring tie. This was a man who appeared convincing in his role of seeker of the presidency. He had confidence. He looked strong and powerful. Bloom caught himself imagining how good he would look in professionally shot political commercials.

"That was a brilliant campaign you did for Hattie," Wendell said, turning his attention to Bloom.

"Thank you. It seemed to work," he said gratuitously.

"Do you prefer to be called Jerome or Jerry?"

"Either's fine." He tried his best to warm up to the man. "My mother calls me Jerome. My friends mostly call me Jerry."

Wendell leaned toward him with a penetrating smile. "What does the president call you?"

Bloom was jarred by the question. "Probably 'that guy from California—what's-his-name.'"

Hattie spoke up. "He doesn't like to admit it, Governor, but the president is completely familiar with him and with his work. In fact, he probably has lost a little sleep over Jerry already, wondering who he might work for in the election."

"I doubt it," said Bloom. "He knows all the teams and consultants are in place and that I don't number among them."

"At least not so far," Wendell said with a very confident smile.

Davis joined the conversation. "Perhaps you might tell us what your assessment is of the national race at this point, Mr. Bloom."

"Yes, Jerome, I'd enjoy hearing that," added Wendell.

Jerome. Bloom laughed to himself. Had Wendell chosen to be a mother rather than one of his friends?

Bloom took a deep breath. How could he sum up what had transpired in the last three months of this, the most unusual presidential campaign in years—perhaps in history?

"To begin with, it's so mercurial, like the mood of those voters out there, that I really find it hard to say just where things are headed."

The three of them had their eyes fixed intently on Bloom, waiting for him to continue, as he began to drum a dessert fork lightly on the tablecloth.

He looked up at Wendell. "What's made things change so dramatically is, obviously, your candidacy, Governor." Wendell smiled and nodded slowly, encouraging Bloom to continue.

"And there's no sense in pulling punches. You know my party allegiance. I've worked exclusively for Democratic candidates."

"We won't hold that against you, Jerome," said Wendell. "After all, Texas is rather proud of its successful Democrats."

"I just want to remind you that my assessment of things might be colored by my own bias."

Davis chimed in. "We accept the caveat, Mr. Bloom."

"Your campaign," said Bloom, staring hard at

Wendell, "has taken advantage, rather adroitly, of the new phenomenon of the land."

"What phenomenon?" asked Wendell, staring back at him.

"The dissatisfaction. The cynicism with which the people are viewing electoral politics. The new values that are being applied to the process of choosing leaders."

"If you're talking about alienation, we've been through that before," Wendell answered. "Not so long ago, in fact. Vietnam and the peace movement—remember?"

Bloom disliked the barb. "Yes, Governor, I remember, but that was a different kind of alienation. We—" He corrected himself. "The people who were turning away from the system were doing so out of principle . . . out of a commitment to a cause that they placed above everything else."

"Isn't that what people are doing today?"

"Are you kidding?" Bloom snapped. Hattie leaned forward in her seat, as if to speak. But then she stopped and watched. "Do you call trickle-down economics and destruction of public assistance commitments to a higher purpose?"

"Why not?" Wendell asked, his eyes staying cool, but not showing any anger.

"Because the real commitment in those notions is to greed. And that's what's happening all over the country today. People are making judgments based on their checkbooks, not on their conscience. They'll vote for a candidate solely on the basis of the money he'll save them."

"Is that such a bad notion?" asked Davis, glancing toward Wendell.

Bloom turned to Davis. "You're damned right it is, when the money's saved by destroying a program that has been feeding hungry children or educating their parents."

"The people have spoken," Davis said. "They want runaway welfare brought under control."

Bloom glared at the campaign manager. "Do they really? Or do they want blacks and browns brought under control?"

This time Hattie didn't stop herself. "Hey, Jerry, it's not always racism when someone wants to clean up welfare. When the program is mismanaged, our people are the first ones who get hurt. And don't tell me our Democratic party is out to save minorities from the ravages of budget cuts. If it is, why didn't its House members stand up to the White House?"

Hattie's defense of Davis put Bloom even more on the defensive. It also made him realize he was getting himself into a trap. He was, after all, a media consultant, not a candidate for office, something of which he frequently had to remind himself.

"Sorry," Bloom said. "I know you didn't ask me down here to listen to my views on welfare and Reaganomics. Besides," he said to Hattie, "our party gave the nomination to Gary Hart this time. And that's got to be good for minorities."

Wendell became warmer than he had been so far. "Please be assured, I have a great deal of respect for the conviction with which you approach politics. It's the kind of thing that has kept your work so far above that of your colleagues."

"Thank you." Bloom stared down at his empty

coffee cup, embarrassed by what he realized was unprofessional behavior.

"Do you think it's possible, Jerome, for an independent candidate to be elected in November?" Wendell asked. There it was. Flat-out and direct. No more games. The big question. Could Wendell win?

Bloom stared down again, trying to frame an answer. The silence in the room heightened the tension. Finally, he looked up at Wendell. "Governor, we've got a lot of disenchanted Republicans who think Reagan took their Grand Old Party too far to the right, creating a government by and for the very rich. There are equally large numbers of Democrats who think their party lost touch with mainstream America. We have black voters who feel they were abandoned by the president *and* by the party opposing the president. Labor is mad at their traditional friends, the Democrats. Wall Street is mad at *their* old pals, the Republicans. Seventy percent of the American public says it no longer identifies with, or is represented by, either major party, according to the latest Harris poll.

"Now, with that kind of alienation, coupled with a virtual Balkanization of the country, I would say almost anything is possible in November."

"Including the election of an independent president?" Wendell asked, his eyes showing, for the first time, a glint of fire.

Bloom paused. "I must say I find it possible. But very unlikely."

Now Davis leaned forward to bore in on Bloom. "Mr. Bloom, not only is it possible for an independent to win this year, but it is most likely to happen."

Bloom challenged him. "Look at the history that runs against you."

"Fine. Let's look at history. Because it's clearly on our side."

"It wasn't on John Anderson's side," Bloom replied.

"No, it wasn't. But it was waiting to be properly used to advantage by someone who understood it," he continued, sounding as though he were about to give Bloom a lecture in political science. "The Republican party was born one hundred and thirty years ago in times exactly like these. It grew out of a period of political stagnation in the 1840s and 1850s, not unlike the stagnation that struck our parties in the seventies and early eighties. One ineffective president after another brought the American people indecisive government in Lincoln's time, allowing public policy to drift, without a rudder, toward eventual civil war. Don't you see the parallel?"

Bloom was taken by the insight of Davis. He knew his history. More important, he knew how to manipulate it to make a point.

"Abraham Lincoln," Davis continued, "won election with a plurality, *not* a majority. He had only thirty-nine percent of the vote. And he won because the Republican party represented a fresh, strong, and decisive political philosophy."

"Then why couldn't your history work for Anderson in 1980?" Bloom asked.

"John Anderson failed because he didn't have us." Davis gestured with his hand to acknowledge a silent Hattie Lewis, the candidate, and Bloom. "He didn't have our instincts and your talents."

Bloom had to hand it to Davis. He had chutzpah even though he probably had never heard the word in his Texas drawing rooms and country clubs.

"Granted, we're all good at what we do, but I don't know if we're all *that* good."

Now Wendell joined the conversation again. "Jerome, my associate is quite right. We have—or *could* have, with you—what John Anderson did not have."

"I'm not so sure, with all due respect."

"Let's get back to history again, Mr. Bloom," said Davis, not raising his voice, but clearly showing his impatience. "Abraham Lincoln was elected as a minority candidate because he read the times. He capitalized on fragmented politics, when people were tired of the old parties. You, yourself, just outlined the very same scenario taking place today. You pointed to the Harris poll, to the alienation."

"But Lincoln had the issue of slavery and its divisive effect going for him," countered Bloom.

"And we," said Davis, "have the issue of survival working for us. The American people seriously question whether we will survive our economic crises, our moral breakdown—a world war, Mr. Bloom, a final, devastating nuclear war! Those concerns dwarf the issue of slavery."

Bloom looked toward Hattie at Davis's mention of slavery. She smiled ever so slightly, nodding at Bloom. He wondered why she sat silently, choosing not to challenge Davis.

Wendell broke the silence. "And speaking of the

threat of nuclear war, Jerome, I wanted to get your opinion of a new notion of mine."

Bloom waited, curious about what Wendell would have to offer on that vital issue.

"I'm going to promise, as my first order of presidential business, to create a new agency, which will deal with all the issues concerning peace and world conflict. It will be called the Agency for Peace and Conflict Resolution. Its director will have the autonomy and influence of cabinet directors.

"The Peace Corps," he continued, "will be moved into the new agency, as will the Peace Academy. The director will be involved with arms control negotiations and with the peaceful resolution of conflicts which threaten the peace, such as those in Central America and the Middle East. I envision an agency that will function on the level of the National Security Council, with a secretary of peace, if you will, who will be able to challenge the secretary of defense when necessary. What do you think?"

Bloom sat silently. He was taken totally by surprise. He found the idea fascinating, even bold. And he was confounded by this surprising side of Wendell.

"I think it could have a profound impact," Bloom finally said. "There's no more important issue. And your proposal would make a positive statement about the administration's view of the peace question."

Wendell nodded and smiled. He looked at Davis, who did not smile.

"And you see," said Davis, "we are offering more in the way of substantive alternatives than John Anderson did. Also, we have the advantage of better planning than he had in his campaign. His efforts were too hastily organized, at a point too late in time. He had to spend his efforts trying to get on the ballot in all states, one by one. Our candidate is already on the ballot in every one of the fifty states."

"I agree," said Bloom, "that the court decision was a major breakthrough. And I compliment you on your strategy. You went out and got six million signatures on Wendell petitions, enough from every state to convince the Supreme Court you were entitled to a place on all ballots. I still don't know how you got the names so quickly."

Wendell smiled and said, "As Harrison said, Jerome, we have history on our side. We read the times. And we acted upon them quickly."

"You see," Davis said, "we're not going to make the same mistakes John Anderson did. Instead of running on issues, he ran against candidates—two of them. His campaign was anti-Carter and anti-Reagan. Our campaign is *for* something. And we'll take advantage of timing, because we know that the voter climate is now ready for a new party. John Anderson in 1980 was like John C. Frémont in 1856. Neither candidate was capable of succeeding, of taking advantage of the times. But we *will* seize the opportunity, giving birth to a new party, with a strong moral cause to stand upon."

Bloom had to respect Davis for his understanding of history, but he didn't have to like him. In fact, he wasn't liking him at all. He was too zealous in his ambition for his friend Wendell. There was something about Davis that warned Bloom to be cautious.

"Today," Davis continued, leaning forward again

to stare deep into Bloom's eyes, "the people of America are leaving the left and the right. They are no longer asking which political party can best lead the country, but whether either of them can. The center is open, wide open, to someone who is ready to step into it and who understands how to give it credence."

"Well," said Davis, "I'm afraid I've lectured too much on the subject of political history." He looked at his watch. "Besides, I must attend a campaign finance meeting, so I'll excuse myself."

Davis left the room. Hattie finally spoke. "The man knows his politics," she said, obviously for Bloom's benefit.

Wendell smiled. "Harrison Davis," he said, "is the most astute political tactician I have ever encountered. His value in my campaign is immeasurable."

Wendell invited Hattie and Bloom to join him for an after-dinner drink to continue their discussion, with the promise of not keeping the weary Bloom from getting some much needed rest. The governor led his guests through the heavy oak doors of the dining room.

As he walked past the large paintings and the grand period furniture, Bloom wondered if any slaves had ever worked in the mansion. He fixed his eyes on Hattie, the descendant of slaves, and wondered what she was thinking.

Wendell took Hattie and Bloom into his garden room, which was a large solarium, lavishly filled with exotic tropical plants and furnished in antique wicker. There was a waterfall and a fish pond. A cage of finches added the finishing touch of sound to the environment created within the room. Bloom sat in a high-backed wicker chair, which had a regal look about it. Wendell sat facing him in a less imposing chair and Hattie was to the side on a garden bench, next to the pond. It seemed a strange place to hold a political discussion. Somehow, Bloom would have expected an oak-paneled, poorly lighted, and smoky study or conference room. This setting was far too comfortable and clean for what he knew they were going to discuss.

"Jerome," Wendell began, "I've been accused of a good number of things in my political lifetime. But the one thing they've never charged me with is beating around the bush."

Hattie laughed. "You're safe on that one, Stephen." This was the first time Bloom had heard Hattie call the man by his first name.

Wendell smiled and continued. "You may have heard that David Mattson, my good friend and media consultant, has decided not to continue in his previous capacity for the remaining nine weeks of the campaign."

"I heard you fired him." Why should Bloom beat around the bush either?

"It was a mutually agreed-upon move," Wendell said. "David has had some health problems that require rest and change of scenery. He, of course, will continue to be an important part of my effort, but only in an advisory capacity."

Bloom had heard the story before. A media consultant suddenly develops health problems. A "mutually agreed-upon" termination is announced. The consultant is a "good friend" and will continue in an "advisory capacity." And he is never seen or heard from again in the campaign, because he has been fired for what his candidate and campaign staff view as incompetence. A new man is brought in to turn things around. The way Bloom had been brought into the Braun-for-Senate campaign in California.

"And that brings us to the reason for our meeting," Wendell said. "How would you like to carry my presidential campaign to its successful completion in the two months that remain?" He made no effort to add any drama to his question. He asked it in as low-key a fashion as if he had asked Bloom whether he'd like another glass of brandy.

Bloom felt no particular twinge. He had fully expected the question to come sooner or later, although not *this* soon. Besides, he had felt all the shock, and all the twinges, earlier in the day, when he had been phoned by Davis, when he had been talked into flying to Dallas, and when he had found his friend and political heroine waiting for him in the Wendell home. Nonetheless, he made an effort to show some surprise. It was expected, he supposed.

"I'm afraid you've caught me unprepared to give you an intelligent response," he said. Which was far from true.

"That's not true and you know it, Jerome." Well, Bloom thought, at least the guy knows when I'm jerking him around.

"I immediately see two problems, Governor."

"And they are?"

"First, you haven't even reviewed my work—my sample reel of what I've been doing lately—to see if I'm the right fit for your campaign."

"Well, that's one problem we can forget about, right, Hattie?" Wendell asked the congresswoman.

Hattie leaned back and laughed. "Jerry, you've got it made. Your work is so notorious, you don't have to put on your dog and pony show anymore."

"That's right, Jerome," Wendell added. "I've seen all the commercials you've done for Hattie. They're brilliant. I've been shown your campaign for the governor of Arizona, and for Senator Steele in Montana. Now that was quite a job you did there, convincing a conservative electorate in Montana to elect to the Senate the former presidential campaign manager for John Halloran."

"Thank you. But I can't take credit for Senator Steele's success. All I did was show the man for what he really is, to correct the picture being painted of him by his opponent and by the press."

"Perhaps. But you *did* have to convince the voters that Steele wasn't a wild-eyed liberal, bent on disarming every hunter in Montana, nor committed to frivolous government spending."

"That was part of it, yes. Because he was being labeled a knee-jerk liberal, when, in fact, he's a Jeffersonian populist, with a conservative view of fiscal matters."

"But he was branded a radical by some simply because of his close association with Halloran's campaign, and his opposition to the Vietnam war."

"That's right."

"How unjust," Wendell continued, "that Senator Steele was handed a label by the press, simply because of his presence on—what did they call it— the Chicken Express?"

"Dove One," Bloom corrected, "is what *we* called it."

"Guilt by association, created by an insensitive press, can be so damaging to a man's career, can't it?"

Bloom realized how cleverly and easily Wendell had painted him into a corner, how he had set him up to a point where he couldn't deny the similarity between Mark Steele's political problems and Stephen Wendell's troubles. He was angered. With both Wendell and himself. He felt the perfect fool.

"I'm afraid the difference is in my view of the ideologies Senator Steele was tied to, and the ones you've been associated with," was all he could think to say in response.

"Jerome, surely you realize that no matter what I've been accused of—even if it's hacking my grandmother to death—I have been as unjustly treated as Senator Steele if the accusations are untrue."

"If they're untrue."

Both men now looked at each other, remaining silent. All that could be heard was the bubbling of the waterfall and the chirping of the caged finches. Hattie was smiling, shaking her head. She finally spoke.

"Jerry, the governor *does* have a point. Bum raps are bum raps. Wanting them to be true doesn't make them any less bum."

"Thank you, Hattie," Wendell said, sounding genuinely appreciative of her defense. "You said you saw two problems," he said to Bloom. "We've resolved the first one—my need to know more about your work, which is the best in the country, I believe. What's the second problem?"

"We've covered that one also," said Bloom.

"You mean my past associations, and your view of them?"

Bloom nodded. "Governor Wendell, it's not my place to sit in judgment of your past. But the fact remains, no matter how right you might think I would be for your campaign, I would be of little value to you if I represented your candidacy professionally when I couldn't feel committed on a personal level."

"You're saying you have to agree with everything I say and stand for before you can serve as a professional consultant?"

"No, I'm not saying I have to agree with everything. But I certainly can't give you what you need if I find that what you represent is in conflict with what I believe."

"That sounds fair enough. However, I trust you will give me an opportunity to offer a true picture of what I *do* represent, one that just might be different from what you have heard to date."

"Of course."

"Spoken like a real civil libertarian, Jerry," said Hattie, with her deep, strong laugh.

"Another thing, Jerome," Wendell continued, "is the question of fair and reasonable access."

"To what?"

Wendell smiled. "To you, and to your work. Don't you believe that every candidate is entitled to good media representation, regardless of his point of view, just as every defendant in court is entitled to a good defense?"

Bloom was stunned by the question. Just hours earlier, in a classroom in Phoenix, he had asked that same rhetorical question in defense of his own profession. Reason told Bloom that it was mere coincidence. The late hour, though, and the events of the day and the evening, gave him a feeling that it was more than coincidence. But how could Wendell have known what he had said to a radical young student several hours earlier and a thousand miles away?

Wendell reminded Bloom then that it had been a long day for all concerned, especially for Bloom. He suggested they continue their discussion the following afternoon as he accompanied Bloom and Hattie Lewis to the foyer of the mansion. The young driver, Hyman, was waiting, with Bloom's suitcase, at the front door.

"I trust you'll be comfortable at the Adamson, Jerome. It's our finest hotel."

Bloom was aching with fatigue. His eyes burned from the jet lag of the flight from Phoenix. "I'm sure it will be pleasant. In fact, anything with a bed and a shower would be nice at this point."

"By the way, I forgot to mention one thing," Wendell said, turning to Hattie. "Would you excuse us for a moment?" He stepped into the parlor, waiting for Bloom to follow.

"I have to make a phone call, anyway. So I'll say good night now, Jerry." She took Bloom's hand between her two and held it firmly. "You get yourself a good night's sleep, imagemaker."

"Will I see you tomorrow?" Bloom spoke softly,

hoping Wendell would not hear him from the adjoining room.

"You don't think I'd run out on you now, do you? I'll be here."

"I want to have a chat with you, lady. An important one." He appeared to be scolding a child as he spoke to Hattie.

"Yazzah, Massah Bloom," she mocked as Bloom shook his head and went into the parlor, where Wendell stood waiting. The former governor slid the pocket door closed when Bloom was in the room.

"I forgot to mention one item I'd like you to consider, Jerome, when you weigh our request to have you join us."

"All right."

"It's about money. The fee we wish to pay you for your services."

"Well, it's still a bit early to discuss that," said Bloom, irritated by the presumptuousness of the man.

"Well, I just wanted to make our position clear. We wish to pay you what you're worth. One million dollars."

Bloom truly could not speak.

Wendell smiled. "It's a good round number and, therefore, not easy to forget. Wouldn't you agree?"

Bloom stared at Wendell. Then he laughed uncomfortably. He was about to ask if this was a joke. But he knew the question was pointless.

Wendell opened the door again, calling out to Hyman. "Mr. Bloom is ready now, Alex." He turned back to Bloom. "Get some rest, Jerome. And if you need anything, just let Alex know. We'll phone you in the morning."

"Thank you" was all he said. Walking down the steps to the waiting car, he tried to picture a check, payable to Jerome Bloom, in the amount of $1 million and no cents. He also tried to imagine the look on a young bank teller's face as he presented her with the million-dollar check and requested fifty dollars back in cash. Would she ask for a driver's license?

7

As Bloom sat at a corner table in the Brittany Room of the Adamson Hotel, he reflected on the full morning of phone conversations he had had. First, he had called home to let Anne know he would be staying in Dallas for the day and, perhaps, another night. Anne had taken on a new air of indifference in their conversation. Gone was the sarcasm and anger of the previous day. That worried him. She was not ordinarily given to indifference about virtually anything, especially about Bloom's prolonged absences.

Next, Wendell had called to see if Bloom had reached any decision about handling his campaign. No, he had not. He still needed some time to think about his schedule and present commitments. At least that was the excuse he gave Wendell. He really needed time to try and make some sense out of the absurd options with which he found himself faced.

Hattie called right after Wendell. She wanted to meet for lunch in the hotel at noon.

Bloom looked around the overdecorated dining

room. Flags of various European nations hung limp and time-faded around the oak-paneled walls. Prints of French and English country scenes were hung alongside musty displays of heraldic art. The waiters were dressed formally. They were all pale, and conducted themselves in a cool, but polite manner that bespoke more eastern snobbishness than southern hospitality. The entire Brittany Room seemed out of place to Bloom for a hotel in Dallas, Texas. Why not an Alamo Room? he mused.

Bloom looked at his watch, then took another sip of the black coffee he had ordered. Twelve-fifteen— Hattie was late. And Bloom was uncomfortable with the waiting, with the dining room and its atmosphere. He looked toward the entrance and saw Hattie looking out over the tables. She spotted him as he waved at her and she smiled to the unsmiling maître d', indicating she had found her luncheon companion.

"Well, well, image man, you're looking right at home," Hattie said, beaming, as she reached Bloom, who had not bothered to stand. Remaining seated when a woman arrived at the table was something new to him; it was Hattie herself who had told him the old chivalrous gestures, like rising for a woman and opening doors, were anachronistic customs of a chauvinistic society. He had simply replied bullshit, it's just common courtesy.

"I'm hungry, and you're late," said Bloom, tapping his wristwatch. "You said noon for lunch."

"You know how we folks are, never on time," she replied, shrugging her shoulders and taking the seat the waiter held out for her.

The waiter did a slight bow, handing Hattie a

large, leather-covered menu. "Enjoy your lunch, madam," he said.

"Actually," Hattie said, cheerfully, "I would have been on time. But I got tied up on a long phone call with Jonah."

"I hope he was talking some sense into you." Bloom could imagine the look on the Reverend Jonah Kirk's face when Hattie told him of her support for Stephen Wendell. Kirk had been an aide to Martin Luther King and, after King's death, had quickly ascended to the top of what remained of the American civil rights movement.

"Actually," Hattie said, "Jonah might just come around to my point of view."

"He could no more support Wendell than I could work for Jesse Helms. Come on, Hattie, Jonah isn't going to do anything like that. Jesus, he's carrying around a big *K* on his chest to remind him who are, and are not his friends." Among other painful reminders of his marching days, Jonah Kirk had the scars of the letter *K* welted permanently on his chest. The ugly, large letter had been seared into his skin by a gang of hooded Klansmen outside Birmingham in 1964.

"That's the past, Jerry," Hattie chided him. "Besides, that was Alabama, not Texas."

"Try and tell Jonah that."

"I don't have to. He knows it. He laughs now and calls it the first monogrammed shirt he ever owned. And a laundry can never lose it."

"What's going on in this country?" Bloom suddenly became aware of fatigue overtaking him, as though he might fall asleep right there at the table, in midsentence. He couldn't understand the feeling. He was frustrated, he was anxious, blood kept rushing to his face. Yet he was suddenly sleepy. Hattie jolted him back to wakefulness.

"You okay?"

"No, I'm not okay."

"What's wrong? You looked like you were about to pass out, just staring off."

"I'm simply trying to figure out how in hell I got where I am right now. What am I doing in Dallas? What are *you* doing in Dallas? What is Jonah doing, encouraging you to be here?"

"Let me ask you something, Jerry. How would you feel about a woman vice-president?"

"Of what?"

"You know damn well of what!"

"And *you* know you don't have to ask how I feel about it. I felt great about it in eighty-four, with Ferraro, even though the voters didn't. You and I have been through that before."

"Yes, we have. But how would you feel about a *black* woman vice-president?"

Bloom stared at Hattie. His brow showed the creases of puzzlement. He started to smile, then stopped. A rush of air came out of his mouth. It was part of a laugh and part of a gasp. He held his hands up, which gave him the appearance of blessing his coffee cup.

"I'm waiting," Hattie said, softly.

Bloom finally spoke. "For what?"

"For your answer. What would you think of a black woman as vice-president?" She uttered the words more precisely this time.

"Are you trying to tell me that Stephen Wendell is going to put you on the ticket with him?"

"I'm not trying to tell you anything. I'm trying to find out your sage political assessment of such a notion."

"On a ticket with a former Democrat from Texas? Ask me to assess the mating of a salmon with a canary. I could probably make more sense out of that."

"Thanks, Jerry." The way she said it showed that his comment had hurt her. And Hattie Lewis was not one to show hurt. The years had conditioned her against it.

"Besides," said Bloom, with more compassion in his voice this time, "I don't see how we can even discuss the notion. Wendell *has* a running mate. He can't dump Henry Blandemann at this point."

"Maybe not, but he ought to. It just doesn't make sense to have an all-southern, all-white, all-male ticket—not if Wendell wants to broaden his candidacy and cut into both parties."

"You should have told him that a few months ago, before his so-called convention picked Blandemann. Besides, that's the way all of Wendell's supporters would want it. If something should happen to Wendell as president, they'd get another one just like him to step right in."

"No, that's *not* the way all his supporters want it. There are a whole lot of disenchanted Democrats— Ferraro Democrats—who are getting behind Wendell. And they're going to hold his feet to the fire."

"Fine. But all they're going to get is a former governor from a state that turned back the ERA."

"Talk about guilt by association. You ought to know about that. You got on a couple of FBI lists just for having a few beers with some SDS members once upon a time."

Bloom saw the faces of those old friends who had made so much sense to him, who had been so beautifully committed to the same things he believed in. He had never been able to bring himself to embrace their notions of revolution. But he had had no trouble at all sharing their goals. They had wanted peace and justice in the world, just as Bloom had wanted it. But to Bloom, getting it with violence recalled the line from *Hair*: "Fighting for peace is like fucking for chastity."

"I don't know, Hattie. I just don't know what the hell is going on. Maybe I *am* overreacting. Maybe I'm knee-jerking. But, Jesus, you know and I know what this Wendell thing is all about. It's an old idea—the third-party alternative, like Anderson, like the old Dixiecrats. But this time it's different. Because they've finally got a candidate who's smart as hell. And attractive. Plus, he's got money—big, big money. Plus a level of discontent in the country that exceeds anything we've seen before. And all that scares the living shit out of me."

"Have you decided, sir?" The question, coming from the waiter who stood behind Bloom's shoulder, startled him with its irony. He leaned toward Hattie and spoke softly. "The whole world wants to know what I'm deciding." Then he turned to the waiter, smiled, and said, "I'll have the club sandwich and some iced tea."

The waiter nodded and looked at Hattie. "Madam?"

"Chef's salad, please, with a little vinegar. And coffee."

When the waiter departed, Bloom stared at Hattie again.

"I guess I haven't answered your question about the vice-presidency," said Bloom.

"That's right, you haven't."

"Has it been offered?"

"Damn, it's true about you people."

"What?"

"Jews answer a question with another question."

"You think that's what I'm doing?"

"Don't you?" asked Hattie as she leaned back and laughed. Bloom caught the joke also, and joined Hattie with the first honest laugh he'd had in days.

"Okay, okay," Hattie said, her face quickly changing to its more serious, and more familiar, attitude. "No, Wendell hasn't offered or promised anything. But Jonah thinks he's considering it. Apparently, Wendell's been talking to Jonah, being very cagey, sniffing out the possibilities of black support for a ticket with someone like me on it."

"Well, I think both Jonah and Wendell are smoking something. Blandemann isn't about to be dumped. And even if he were, the people who started this whole Wendell push would go crazy with a black—a black woman—on the ticket. It just isn't going to happen."

"But if it did, don't you think it would give Wendell an enormous new opportunity?"

"I can't see it. Blacks voting for Stephen Wendell? Even with a Hattie Lewis on the ticket, there's no way."

"You've seen the polls, Jerry. The Democrats are only getting forty percent of the black vote—the vote that helped elect Jimmy Carter president with ninety percent! And the GOP is only getting twenty percent. That leaves forty percent of the black vote sitting there undecided, not willing to go for either major candidate. And the forty percent Gary Hart has now is soft as hell. Just think what a ticket with a black on it would do for the undecideds, and how it would erode the votes that are weak for the Democrats."

"You're a very convincing lady, Hattie. You've got a couple of nice victories to prove it. But you can't convince me that you actually believe Stephen Wendell would want you on a ticket with him, or that his army would accept you." He paused and looked down at the tablecloth, not wanting to see Hattie's eyes. ". . . *Or* that you would consider doing that to yourself and to the rest of us."

Hattie tapped an index finger firmly on the table and spoke more loudly than she normally would in a restaurant. "Let me tell *you* something, my dear but sometimes forgetful friend. The war isn't over yet. Not by a long shot. Black people are still getting the short end of the stick all over this land. Getting elected mayor here and there, a few management jobs in big corporations, sleeping in white hotels— that's all terrific. But it's not victory yet. When unemployment hits, it hits blacks first and hardest. And that's something Stephen Wendell understands. He's worried about our own huddled masses. That's us. When this country isn't generating enough jobs for its own people, we've got to make sure our underclass and unemployed get jobs *before* we let illegal aliens in. There's a direct competition between blacks and aliens for jobs. And blacks are tired of seeing all kinds of newcomers, whether they're from Vietnam or Mexico, come in and take the jobs that should go to them. Listen, Jerry. We got tossed a lot of bones during the civil rights struggle. Some of them look pretty to a lot of people who never had anything before. But we still don't have what we need: power. A piece of the action, a slice of the economic pie. Governor Wendell understands that—a lot better than most white politicians. His immigration position proves it."

Hattie stopped and stared into Bloom's eyes. Bloom stared back, expressionless. He could hear someone at a nearby table whispering. He thought he heard the name Hattie Lewis spoken.

Bloom shook his head. "I don't know what to say, Hattie, to you or to Wendell. I think I want to go home and see Anne and the kids. I want to think about things, and I need to be around them when I do that thinking."

"Maybe that's a good idea. How is Anne?"

Bloom recalled Anne's words on the phone the previous day: "Jesus—even Hattie!"

"Anne's fine. A little cranky about all my traveling. But fine," he lied. He felt an aching as he thought of how much deeper than crankiness Anne's feelings were running.

Bloom lay on the king-size bed of his lavishly appointed hotel room, staring at the television screen. He was watching a pantomime of an old "M*A*S*H" rerun; he had turned the set on, leaving the sound off. It was a little game he frequently played, creating his own dialogue to go with the action. He was waiting for a call from Wendell headquarters to confirm a late-afternoon meeting with the candidate and his running mate. This was as good a way as any to pass the time.

The phone beside the bed rang, just as Bloom was about to assign some dialogue to the nurse standing over an injured soldier.

"Hello?" inquired Bloom, expecting the ingratiating voice of Wendell, or Davis, his equally ingratiating friend.

"Jerry. Where the hell are you?" It was the confidently strong voice of Senator David Braun, Bloom's client from California.

"I'm taking a little vacation."

"Oh, that's just great. They're eating me alive out here, and you're taking a vacation. In Texas. If you're going to goof off, at least do it somewhere worth visiting."

"You're right. I should have gone to Newark."

"How're we doing on the new spots?" Braun asked.

"Didn't you get the scripts?"

"No. Did you send me some?"

"I put them on the transceiver this morning to your L.A. office. Becky took the transmission."

"Shit, I'm up in San Francisco."

"Sorry. I thought you were going to be down south today."

"Well, I did, too. But we had a polling update to look at, and our boy genius couldn't take the time to go down to L.A. with it."

Bloom felt his usual distaste for the young research specialist Braun referred to. Tim Denning, the hottest item in the political poll-taking business. At age twenty-eight, he had already worked for a dozen successful Senate candidates, and was now doing some special assignment work for the presidential campaign of Gary Hart. Denning was good. And very, very cocky. Bloom's favorite little trick was to mispronounce his name, calling him Dunning, and then apologize for his forgetfulness. The last time it had happened Denning had written a memo to Senator Braun, asking him if he would kindly inform Bloom that his name was not Tim Dunning.

"What's Dunning got for us?" Bloom asked.

Braun laughed. "Careful, I don't want another memo about his name. Anyway, what he's got isn't what I want. He says we just lost another five percent from our *strong* column."

"Where did it go? To undecided?"

"No, it's not that bad. It all went into the soft column."

"Well, your opponent's bound to get through to some of those folks. It's predictable."

"That's what Denning says. You two guys must be talking to each other."

"Not when I can help it," said Bloom. "But if that's the only slippage so far, I think we're still okay. The new spots ought to help. When can you look at them?"

"I'll have Sarah shoot them up on the wire right now. Tell me, do they have the old Bloom touch?"

The question troubled Bloom. "I hope you don't have any reason to think they wouldn't be up to par."

"Wow, you sound a little uptight. See what happens when you go to Dallas? You lose your sense of humor."

"Sorry. Just a little edgy today."

"Well," assured the senator, "we all get that way nine weeks out. I know the spots will be great, as usual."

Bloom wished he could share Braun's faith. He also hoped his deteriorating self-confidence wouldn't be noticed.

"Let me know what you think. I'll be here the rest of the day, then back to L.A. tonight or tomorrow."

"Your wife said she didn't know when you'd be back."

That, too, bothered Bloom. Anne knew damn well that he would have to return the next day.

"If you don't get back to me tonight, I'll call you when I get in tomorrow and we can schedule a meeting," Bloom said.

"Fine. By the way, you still haven't told me what you're doing in Dallas."

"Just checking out a political situation a friend of mine asked for some help with." It wasn't, after all, a lie. Hattie *had* asked him to take a look at the Wendell race.

"Just be careful you don't run into Stephen Wendell. Isn't that his hometown?"

The electric shock ran through Bloom's head again. "We had a terrific dinner together last night," he said with perfect matter-of-factness.

Braun laughed loudly. "I'll bet you did! Out at the bastard's ranch. Well, it's okay. You don't have to tell me who you're really seeing down there. It's probably just as well I don't know."

"Talk to you soon, David." Bloom could see the senator laughing, shaking his head, even sharing the joke with one of his staffers, about Bloom having dinner with Stephen Wendell.

114

"So long," Braun said as he clicked off the line. The dial tone came on, but Bloom continued to hold the phone to his ear. Then the tone was interrupted by a clicking sound, as though an extension phone were being hung up. But it couldn't be at David Braun's end; the connection from California had already been broken. It was there, in Dallas, in the hotel perhaps. Probably just a quirk in the switchboard. Bloom wondered. A wiretap? Come on, he warned himself, don't start playing this one like a Woodward-and-Bernstein episode. He hung up the phone and tried to picture someone down in the basement of the hotel listening on a headset, operating a tape recorder.

Bloom held Jeanette Wells's business card in his hand and considered returning home to California. But he also thought about seeing this intriguing woman again. He manufactured a set of rationalizations that could keep him in Dallas another night, including the late hour at which he would arrive in Los Angeles and, more importantly, the unresolved business with Stephen Wendell.

He decided to stay. But only, of course, if Jeanette Wells was still interested in having the "friendly" dinner she had proposed on the plane.

Bloom was pleased when she answered the phone in her hotel room.

"Hello, Jeanette. This is Jerry Bloom. We met on the plane last night."

She laughed. "Yes, Jerry, I do happen to remember you. How's your trip going?"

"Oh, it's going all right. In fact, it's been interesting."

"I don't imagine any of your trips are ever dull. Are we having dinner tonight?"

Bloom was pleased that she brought up the subject of dinner. That way he didn't have to work around to it himself. He was not, after all, overly confident with women.

"If you can still make it, yes, I'd like to do that."

"Well, I *would* still like to make it. There's no sense in both of us having dinner alone in Dallas."

"Have you chosen a restaurant?" Bloom asked. "I still don't know my way around the city. Except how to find the School Book Depository."

"I'm not surprised you went there," Jeanette replied. "Actually, I thought some all-American beef might be in order. Are you up for a steak?"

"Sure. Might as well try the local fare."

"I tell you, though," she laughed, "they probably import the steaks from Omaha or Denver. But I do happen to know a very pleasant steak house. Where are you staying?"

"The Adamson."

"Good. It's within walking distance of the restaurant. Why don't I meet you at the hotel."

"You sure you don't want me to call for you?"

"Why on earth would you want to do that? It's way out of your way."

Bloom felt very foolish. Without thinking, he acted as though he were young and single again, at a time when men "called for" their dates at their home, no matter how much out of the way they would have to go.

"Actually, I can't think of a reason why I'd want to do that. Shall we make it for eight?"

"Sounds fine. That will give me some time to finish up my work. What room are you in?"

Bloom had to look at the telephone. He was that preoccupied. "Seven-twenty-two."

"Fine. I'll buzz you when I arrive." She paused. "And then you can come down and call for me, if you'd like."

"Very funny. I'll wash the car, too."

"Looking forward to it. 'Bye," she said.

"I'm looking forward to it, too. See you then."

As he hung up the phone, Bloom realized how much, in fact, he was looking forward to dinner with Jeanette. It was enough to make him decide to shower and shave for the second time that day, and to do anything else he could to make himself presentable.

8 THE RESTAURANT JEANETTE CHOSE was more pleasant and inviting than he had expected. Instead of something loud and brassy, it was subdued, even inviting. The waiters wore black ties and long white aprons, giving the place an atmosphere more like New York and less like what Bloom would expect in Texas.

Bloom thought Jeanette looked lovely. Her eyes had a shine to them that he hadn't noticed on the airplane. Her mouth was just slightly seductive when she formed words; her hands occasionally touched his when she made a particular point, and she would lean forward to expose just enough of the top of her breasts to be provocative. But nothing that she did looked planned. She simply possessed a confident sexuality.

"Tell me about your family," she said as the waiter was pouring the after-dinner coffee.

Bloom had not mentioned Anne or the children during the entire meal. "I'm blessed with two wonderful children. A boy and a girl. Like most fathers these days, I don't see as much of them as I'd like to."

"I'm glad you didn't say as much as you *should*."

"Not that I don't have my share of guilt. It's in the genes. But being with my children is something I do strictly for my own pleasure, not out of some sense of duty. They're a genuine kick to be around. I can't tell you how much I learn from them."

"It sounds wonderful. I haven't had children. And until"—she stopped herself—"unless I have any of my own, I don't think I'll fully appreciate what they can bring to a person's life. Like teaching you something."

"Well, I can only wish for you that you have children some day. I promise, you'll love what they bring to your life."

"It's not that I haven't wanted them. Or planned on them. But," she paused again, and her eyes seemed to be welling up, "you know what happened to my plans and wants." She looked down, lest Bloom see the tears forming.

"Your husband was a good man, a very talented young man. And it was terribly unfair and unnecessary, the way he lost his life. But I hope you don't think his death foreclosed on all the plans you had made for your own life. Children—they can still happen for you. You're obviously young enough to plan for them again."

"I suppose I am. But the new things that have come into my life since Jeff was killed have changed my priorities."

"Your work?"

Jeanette nodded. "I don't know that I could find

room now for a marriage and for children, and work, too."

Bloom started to speak, but then he stopped. He laughed. "You know something? I was about to tell you a lie—that your work need not interfere with family, and family need not intrude on work. Neither has been true for me. But I don't love my kids any less. And I don't need my work any less. I just try and accommodate as much as I can."

"What about your wife?"

Somehow, Bloom felt it would be inappropriate to talk of Anne while having dinner with a beautiful woman. Even though it was billed as a "friendly" dinner.

"It's not the easiest thing to talk about. Because we don't happen to be gliding along as smoothly as we'd like to be right now."

"Is it your work?"

"I suppose it is. My wife is a strong and mature woman. She has enough of her own challenges and wants, which extend beyond family and home, to avoid the familiar housewife trap. Right now, I guess, it's what I seem to be doing in my work, rather than the work itself, that's become a problem." Bloom had the feeling he was talking in circles, not making much sense.

"You mean she doesn't like your politics?" asked Jeanette.

"No, she and I have pretty much the same politics. It's more a question of whether or not I'm being true to what I claim to stand for." Bloom reminded himself that he had not yet chosen to work for Stephen Wendell. He had only talked to the

120

man, as he had tried to reassure Anne. And his conscience.

"Sounds like a story of two ideologues. That can
make for an interesting marriage, what with all the
testing you might do of one another."

"Well, so far we've survived the tests." He wanted
to change the subject. "You know, you still haven't
told me what brought you to Dallas."

"Didn't I? I thought I told you I was here to work
with a client."

"But you didn't tell me anything about the client.
Is it politics?"

"I'm sorry. I know I was being evasive. But I felt I
had to protect client privilege, at least until we
agreed to formally work together. And now we have.
So I can tell you." She sat up straight in her chair,
took a breath, and spoke without a smile. "I'm going
to do the polling and research for Governor Stephen
Wendell's campaign for the presidency."

Bloom was stunned. For a moment, he could do
nothing but stare at Jeanette. Then all he could say
was "Holy shit."

"Is it really so surprising?" she asked.

Bloom watched a series of faces flash across his
consciousness—Wendell, Davis, Hattie Lewis,
Anne, Senator Braun. They seemed to be chasing
one another. Or him. "Maybe it's not so surprising.
Or, at least, it shouldn't be by now."

"Then why are you looking at me as though I had
just confessed a series of ax murders."

"It's just that I find it incredible—what I'm doing
here in Dallas myself."

"Is the idea of your doing the media for Wendell so preposterous?"

"You know about that?"

"Really, Jerry. Don't you think I know of the campaign's interest in you? Surely you realize I'd hear about it if I'm working on their polling. We're talking to the same people."

"And you don't have a problem with Wendell? With what he stands for?"

"I don't have a problem with what he's offering the country."

"And what's that?" Bloom asked, somewhat facetiously.

"An alternative. A logical alternative to a political system that has lost its relevance."

"You don't think he's an opportunist?"

"Of course I do. I wouldn't want him to be anything less, if he's interested in winning the presidency. It's a business that's all about opportunism. And the word can also convey flexibility, a lack of ideology."

"I guess it's a semantic problem. Opportunism isn't always a positive notion."

"That's true. And neither is it always a character flaw."

"My wife might disagree with you," said Bloom, recalling her reaction to his visit to Dallas.

"Are you going to work with the campaign?"

"I haven't given them an answer yet. I must say I'm impressed with the people who are joining the ranks. But I'm still reluctant to turn my back on a party that has given me a chance to do something that matters."

"Don't you think Stephen Wendell can give you that kind of chance?"

"Right now, no, I don't think so. He appeals to a constituency that, frankly, turns me off."

"Is that what we do?"

Well, Bloom thought, he now had managed to offend someone he was hoping to become close to. Which, he acknowledged, was fairly typical for him. "I'm sorry. But that's not what I meant. I'm talking about his coalition—the voters—the fringe groups he seems to attract."

"But he's also attracting a lot of people just like you."

"I know. And that's probably what frustrates me more than anything else."

"He's even managed to get a former John Halloran groupie like me."

It was another surprise for Bloom. Now Jeanette presented herself as a one-time supporter of the most liberal candidate the Democrats had run since Roosevelt—Halloran, the peace candidate, who had been so soundly defeated by an electorate that was not ready to move that far to the left.

"I guess I shouldn't be all that surprised. I knew your husband was involved in the Halloran campaign. In fact, I saw some of the film work he did for John."

"Actually, that's how Jeff and I got to know each other. I wasn't always a pollster. I flew for a living while I was taking my graduate work."

"Did you get to meet Halloran in your travels?"

"As a matter of fact, I got to know him reasonably

well. I was first flight attendant on his chartered campaign plane."

Bloom whistled softly. "You flew on Dove One?"

"The plane some people took to calling 'Chicken Express.'"

Bloom recalled the previous evening, when Davis had used the same expression, much to Bloom's distaste.

"I imagine it was quite an experience for you, traveling with the campaign. For me, it was the only losing campaign I've been involved in that felt like a victory. They don't happen like that anymore."

"He's the most unusual human being I've ever met. He could have been a magnificent president."

"America wasn't ready for a Halloran. Maybe we'll never be," said Bloom, feeling nostalgic as he recalled those earlier, more uncomplicated days.

"You know, I rediscovered poetry through John Halloran."

Bloom smiled. "I can understand."

She continued wistfully, "When we'd get airborne, all his aides would reach for printouts of polls, the latest political columns, all the usual garbage to read. But John Halloran would reach into that worn canvas bag he carried and get out a book of poetry. I was bringing him his dinner one night, on the way to Michigan for the primary. He saw me looking at his book. He asked me if I had read 'The Love Song of J. Alfred Prufrock.' I told him I had read it only once, in college. And then he said, 'Read it again sometime, and see if it doesn't remind you a little of what we're doing on the airplane . . . peering in at something we're not really a part of, but to which we're more a witness, making a visit. "Oh, do not ask, 'What is it?' Let us go and make our visit."'"

Bloom was moved, as he had been moved by the hopeless campaign of John Halloran. And by the humiliation of so enormous a defeat at the polls, for so good a man.

"This country doesn't want to be led by poets," he said. "We want lawyers. Or generals. Men of action, not men of thought."

"It's too bad," she said. "We ought to try a poet, just once."

"I agree. But until we do, we still have to make sure that we choose the best of all possible lawyers or generals—or farmers or whatever."

"I suppose so," she said.

"The governor isn't a poet. At least to my knowledge."

"No, he's not," she answered. "But he's an honest man, which is becoming as hard to find as a good poet."

"Perhaps he *is* honest. But why do I find it so hard to pin him down, to put him into a box where I can identify what he's all about?"

"I think," said Jeanette, carefully choosing her words, "and I hope you won't take offense at this, but I think maybe you're having trouble with your ideological road map."

"My what?"

"Don't you think that, given your years of loyal service to a set of principles, to one wing of one political party, maybe you have to see everything as taking only one of two roads? It either goes to the left, where you accept it, or off to the right, where you reject it."

"Wait a minute," said Bloom, sensing a tightening in his body. "I have a feeling you're giving me the left-wing, knee-jerk business."

"I'm not giving you *any* business. I'm just trying to remind you you're coming from a bias. An understandable bias. You believe in your view of the world, which comes from a definite political persuasion. And you believe in it with an intensity that helps make what you do so good. But it also tends to get in the way of objectivity, at least when it comes to politics."

Bloom did not want to respond too quickly. Otherwise, he might have gone on the attack. Which he clearly did not want to do. He waited, nodding—not in agreement, but in search of an appropriate response.

"It takes more than an ability to understand to make the system work. It takes a lot of believing in things, too." Bloom knew he was being defensive. So, apparently, did Jeanette.

"I agree. I'm only saying that a strong commitment can sometimes make it hard to accept an alternative."

"And you think Stephen Wendell is a real alternative?"

"Yes, I do. For me, and for an awful lot of other people who are getting every bit as impatient for change as you and I were in the seventies."

"That depresses me," said Bloom.

"That people want change?"

"No," he said, shaking his head, "that you're a product of the seventies. I'm a sixties radical.

Which makes me, according to your logic, not only irrelevant, but old."

Jeanette took advantage of Bloom's wisecracking. She leaned back and laughed. "It's not like I wasn't there. I was probably in a preschoolers' march against war while you were burning your draft card."

Bloom turned serious again just as quickly. "Tell me about Jeff. I only know what I read about him and his work."

Jeanette's shoulders drooped, and she looked down at her folded hands. Finally, she looked up at Bloom. "What can I say? Except that he loved his work with an unyielding passion. Just as, I imagine, you do."

Bloom nodded.

"And he loved me."

Bloom was moved by Jeanette's reverence for the word, *loved*.

"Which explains," she continued, "why his work was as good as it was. And why our marriage was as strong as it was."

"Commitment," said Bloom.

"That's right. But it also gave him a naiveté. A fatal naiveté. He made the mistake of feeling safe among the oppressed, who would harm no one. He believed it right to the end, when a bullet from one of the oppressed killed him."

Bloom couldn't stop himself from reaching out and placing his hand on hers. "I know I can't make you hurt any less, but I wish I could."

"Thank you," she said, softly. "The nice thing is, I believe you."

They said very little more to one another in the

restaurant. Bloom paid the bill and suggested they take a walk in the pleasant Indian-summer air. Jeanette agreed, and they walked together past some of Dallas's more elegant shops, stopping here and there to admire a window display or to marvel at some show of opulence. Before they had walked far, Jeanette slipped her hand under Bloom's arm. The contact was pleasing to him. And promising.

When they stopped for a red light at a deserted intersection, Jeanette looked at Bloom, smiling. "I'm enjoying being with you," she said.

Bloom felt a rush. He could only laugh nervously. "You know, this is like a *date*."

"Of course it is. We had dinner together. We talked a lot. Now we're taking a walk. All of which makes for a date. A nice one, I might add."

"I'd hate to tell you how long it's been since I've been on one."

"I have a feeling it's been since you proposed to your wife."

"Just about," said Bloom, wondering if a few harmless luncheon flirtations or an occasional fantasy over cocktails with attractive business associates qualified as *dates*.

Jeanette took her hand away from his arm and held it out to him. "Thank you for a lovely evening."

"What do you mean?"

She motioned behind him to a marquee. "This is my hotel," she said with a subdued giggle.

He quickly turned to see the hotel's name on a shining brass plaque. He smiled and shrugged, as if to say he had better be on his way.

"But I certainly hope you won't leave me standing

out here on the street. You will come in to say good night, won't you?"

"Sure." It was all he could say. He knew his desire to stay with Jeanette was sufficiently obvious.

When the elevator doors shut out the hotel's lobby, Jeanette turned to Bloom, this time with a warm, inviting smile on her glistening lips. "I hope you won't find it inappropriate for me to do this on our first date," she half whispered. She leaned up to him, placed her hands lightly on his arms, and kissed him. He responded, very gently, as though wanting not to break some illusion. He felt both a warmth and a lust, yet he did not so much as move his arms to embrace her. They remained motionless until the sound of a soft bell signaled the stopping of the elevator's ascent at the eighteenth floor. Bloom could still taste the confectionlike flavor of her lipstick as the doors slid open.

He felt an anticipation that, for the moment, eased some of his concerns with the way in which things had been closing in around him for the past two days. Jeanette said nothing, but smiled both knowingly and warmly as she led Bloom to her door. She opened it and went inside, making it clear that she expected him to follow.

There was very little to say. Nor did Jeanette seem compelled to speak. She turned on a lamp, put her coat over a chair, and came back to Bloom, who was looking out the window at the sprawling lights of the city. Still saying nothing, she stepped closer to him and waited. He very naturally put his arms around her, and they kissed again.

Bloom became completely overwhelmed by the

comforting warmth and surging desire Jeanette brought to his body. What followed did so quite naturally, without conversation, without questioning, without caveat. Jeanette began to undress, and Bloom helped her. Then, he, too, began to remove his clothes. And without ceremony, but with the excitement of discovering and exploring each other for the first time, the two of them led one another to the bed, where their passion continued to build. During the entire time in which they moved together toward a climax, Bloom spoke only once: "You make me feel wonderful." Nothing else.

And all that Jeanette said, before they had begun to move passionately, and then almost violently, was "I want you to feel that way."

Only after they had climaxed, together—and Bloom was certain it was spontaneous and genuine—did they begin to speak, as they lay close together, embracing as though not wanting to let go of so enjoyable a union.

"I fully expect I should be feeling some deep guilt now," said Bloom. "But the pleasure of the moment seems to be forestalling it. Either that or I've stopped being a typical Jewish male all of a sudden."

"You don't have a corner on the guilt market," laughed Jeanette. "Didn't anyone ever tell you about Irish Catholics?"

"Sure. You folks run a close second to us."

"Our guilt didn't stop with anguishing over what we had done, either. We then had to feel guilty about not telling it all to the priest."

They continued to joke about such issues, as Bloom felt himself sliding into a very comfortable, euphoric state. There seemed to be neither reason nor need to move away from Jeanette's body or out of the bed. They talked of some things that had nothing at all to do with their lovemaking. And then they talked of things that had a good deal to do with it. They complimented each other on their bodies. They assured one another how much they enjoyed being together. And soon a very pleasant, comforting fatigue overtook Bloom. He found himself on the verge of falling asleep in midsentence, with Jeanette in his arms, the length of her body lightly pressed against his. He settled softly into euphoric slumber for what seemed to be hours. But when he awoke, and glanced at the clock radio beside the bed, he saw it was one in the morning. He had slept only half an hour. Jeanette was now sleeping, breathing peacefully, her head tucked down against his chest. He reached down and gently kissed her on the forehead, and her eyes opened. She looked at him, smiled, and closed her eyes again. "I'm sure it can't be morning yet."

"No. But I'm not much in the mood to sleep," he said.

Jeanette put both hands on his face. "I'd like you to be with me again."

Her touch aroused him even further, and he gently caressed her. Again, there seemed to be no need to speak. Jeanette responded warmly and enthusiastically to Bloom. They made love again. Bloom enjoyed the feel of her body, as well as its fragrance and its taste.

Finally spent again, they both let sleep come. And it was not until light poured in through the sheer window curtains that Bloom opened his eyes. He lay still, enjoying watching Jeanette, still sleeping, but with her back to him, and enjoying the feeling of peace that had come over him. It was six-thirty. Bloom had been gone from his hotel for twelve hours. He wondered reflexively if anyone had tried to reach him. But he didn't really care. Phone calls would wait, including any from his various candidate clients. And especially from Stephen Wendell. It was, altogether, a sense of confidence that existed for him. All could not be too bad, he thought. He had spent an incredibly satisfying night. And the fact that he had been seduced, for whatever reason, did not detract from his notion of self-worth. He almost, but not quite, accepted the notion that he had simply been desired.

Bloom lay still, lest he awaken Jeanette, and took an inventory, to help him deal with the enormous decision with which he was faced. He held in his hands an opportunity to step up to the pinnacle of his career, to make more money than he ever had thought possible, to take on the challenge of a lifetime in a campaign for the presidency, the most important position in the entire world. He could be a part of it. Although victory still seemed unlikely, it was clear that the American electorate was as close to being ready for an alternative candidacy as it would ever be. Stephen Wendell, as enigmatic as he was to Bloom, had won to his cause so many of Bloom's ideological universe: Hattie Lewis. This beautiful woman, Jeanette, to whom he had made love so passionately—she, too, had found sufficient reason to commit herself to this remarkable crusade.

What would his colleagues say? How would the

candidates for whom he worked react to such a move? Would they condemn him or ridicule him? Would they cite his ambition? His greed? Or would they grant him the opportunity to pursue his career needs while he explored the first genuine new idea to present itself in the country's electoral process in decades?

Ahead would be challenge. The chance to create. To make a difference. There would be time away from Anne, while there would be time with Jeanette. Would it be an opportunity to give a tired marriage a needed rest? Or would it merely be an opportunity for self-indulgence, Bloom wondered, looking at the peaceful Jeanette lying next to him. He was reminded of his dear friend and former business partner, Chuck Hanselman, who had more than once warned him "Always keep your business decisions between your ears, never between your legs." How much effect could a few glorious hours with Jeanette Wells possibly have on so major a decision? Come on, Bloom thought, how much? The returning warmth, down deep inside him, told him he was, indeed, being influenced perhaps more libidinously than Chuck Hanselman or he, himself, would want him to be.

What makes a worthwhile politician? Bloom asked himself as he continued to search for the decision he had to make soon. Certainly not only a pure heart, or Jimmy Carter would be better remembered. Wendell was an effective governor; Bloom could not deny that. He had run his state effectively and efficiently. His "High-Tech Texas" campaign was a model for economic development. He called himself a "jobs Democrat," and his efforts had won bipartisan acclaim. He had promised "100,000 new jobs for Texas" during his first campaign, and he had delivered. His eight years as governor were years of real prosperity for Texas.

Bloom had been bothered, though, by Wendell's calling out of the National Guard during a chemical workers' strike. But even that was morally and politically complicated. The Guard was not called until after the strikers had resorted to violence. "When the baseball bats come out, so does the National Guard," Wendell had explained when he announced his decision to act. Bloom had a hard time arguing with the reasoning. Still, he was bothered by the fact that Wendell had gone to the scene to set up a command post close to the plant gate—and easily accessible to the media. Where does conviction end and self-promotion begin?

Bloom mentally added up the plus side of the yellow ledger sheet he saw in his mind, the column in which he saw the $1 million, the responsibility that came with the money, the prestige, the power, the strength and independence with which Hattie Lewis had marched into a new camp, a camp which offered bold ideas, like the proposed peace agency. And there was the chance to work with, to be with Jeanette.

Across the page was the minus column. In it was the break with the Democratic party, that institution that had offered him an ideological home and that had helped provide him with a good living. He had made lasting friendships there with his clients, with his fellow quixotic ideologues. Further alienation of his wife—that glared up at him, too. But the minus column was too short in comparison to the plus side. As he neared his decision, he wished that column were longer. At least, he thought he wished it.

Jeanette's soft voice interrupted his accounting process.

"You look like you've got something on your mind, sailor."

Harrison Davis stared intently at Jeanette across the desk in his law office. The midmorning sun streamed in through venetian blinds, creating a striped light pattern across Jeanette's face.

"Is he with us?" he asked.

"Yes, I think so." She showed no emotion, but she seemed reflective.

"How do you find him?"

"He's quite intense."

"That could help make him quite a good media consultant for our project, don't you think?"

"I would imagine. It certainly makes him interesting to know," she said.

"Perhaps it does. Which would make your assignment an especially pleasant one, correct?"

Jeanette shrugged and stared into the sunlight.

9

ARAM SARAF SAT IMPATIENTLY AT ONE
end of the large mahogany conference
table. He looked indifferently at the
various diplomas and citations framed on the walls.
Most of them either had the name of Stephen Wendell or Harrison Davis on them. The smell of
Saraf's expensive, but strong cologne seemed an in-
trusion in the otherwise staid, leathery atmosphere
of the room. Saraf didn't bother to rise when the
door opened and Davis came through it.

"Mr. Saraf?" Davis reached his hand down to
Saraf, who took it, almost reluctantly, and smiled,
still not bothering to stand.

"I am pleased to meet you, Mr. Davis."

Davis sat down at the table.

"Well, Mr. Saraf, things are falling into place for
us."

Saraf smiled. "Miss Wells spent the entire night
with our Jewish friend."

"You mean Mr. Bloom?" Davis was very calm, but
deliberate, in his chastisement of Saraf.

Saraf shrugged. "I realize that you are much

more sensitive about these things in this country than we are at home. However, when I see a Jew, that is all he is—a Jew—who represents my country's enemy."

"I understand, Mr. Saraf. But we do have to be careful about these things. Anyway, Miss Wells thinks Mr. Bloom will decide to accept our offer."

"Bloom is now on his way back to Los Angeles, but it seems he would prefer to be here in Dallas with the beautiful young woman with whom he had his chance meeting." Saraf seemed to be leering as he spoke.

Davis changed the subject. "I understand you have another contribution for our effort."

"Of course. As promised, my associates are pleased to contribute three million dollars to Citizens for an Independent Congress." As he spoke, he slowly pushed a rich-looking, leather attaché case across the table toward Davis.

"Excellent. It will be of great help." Davis grasped the case by its sides and moved it in front of him. He stared at it for a moment, and then opened the two gold latches. He raised the lid sufficiently to glance at what lay inside the case. His face did not give away any emotion at all as he saw the stacks of large bills, all new, bound by paper bands.

"Excellent," he said again, closing the lid on the case and smiling at Saraf.

"My associates are concerned about something, Mr. Davis."

"And what is that?"

"They want to be certain that their contributions will serve the purposes they intend to see served. Some of them have asked why they are contributing to campaigns for congressmen and senators, when, all along, their interest has been in the presidency and Mr. Wendell."

Davis's face flushed ever so slightly, but his expression remained unchanged. "I thought we had made it sufficiently clear to your generous associates that one of the keys to our success is victory for the House and Senate candidates who can be counted on for support of our positions. Perhaps some of your people overlook the reality of our system, which has carefully provided that the power of the presidency does not become absolute."

"Perhaps some of our people need to become better acquainted with your government's structure."

"That could be," Davis agreed.

"What would you suggest, Mr. Davis? A correspondence course?" Saraf seemed eager to engage Davis in a verbal duel.

"I merely suggest that your associates keep in mind the various legal limitations and constraints under which we are required to function."

"I will try to get the message to my people. But I hope you will be patient with us. After all, we are little more than nomads living in desert tents and wearing absurd garments on our heads, as your Hollywood would have all the world believe."

"I can assure you, neither Governor Wendell nor I have much influence on the motion picture community or the media in this country."

"Perhaps not. But this Bloom and his like have a great deal of influence. However," he said, his eyes narrowing, "we shall soon see some changes there, as well as in the political system in this country."

"We wish you well in your efforts," said Davis, his voice lower than it had been.

"We are confident we will succeed. Arab interests are coming very close to controlling positions in two major film corporations and in a television network. It's very interesting, how the American people view our nations with such contempt while they fight with one another to buy our oil, helping us to get the influence they fear so much."

"Yes, self-interest can sometimes explain behavior that would otherwise be totally without explanation." Davis was still remaining aloof, if not patronizing.

"I think we will see how that self-interest works in November, Mr. Davis, don't you agree?"

Davis stared silently at Saraf. He then spoke more quietly. "In November we expect to see self-interest put aside for a nobler purpose, Mr. Saraf."

Saraf grinned broadly. "Of course. It would be, as you say, more of an act by the American people to give themselves the gift of new moral leadership, as your campaign literature has said." Saraf seemed uninterested in concealing his cynicism.

Davis looked at his watch, his face still somewhat flushed. "The governor is expecting me to join him. Do we have any further business to discuss?"

"There is still the question of Senator Blandemann," said Saraf. "It is clear that the ticket cannot win with him on it."

"You seem to be picking up on the nuances of our system rather well," said Davis.

"Your polling experts have discovered that two

men from the southern United States cannot be victorious. Correct?"

"Yes, it's true. And, as you know, we fully intend to make an appropriate change in that regard."

"How did the senator become the vice-presidential nominee in the first place? Surely the governor must have known he would be a liability."

"That," said Davis, "is one of the impediments we carry with us in this effort. The senator is an old friend of the governor's. He shares his views on the immigration issue. And he, like the governor, has been a friend of labor over the years."

"And Stephen Wendell would never abandon his friend, even if it meant losing the election?" asked Saraf.

"Our candidate is a man of abiding principle. He feels very strongly about commitments to people, as well as to causes. No, he would not walk away from his friend without good cause. And yes, that would be the case, even if he knew it meant losing the election."

"How commendable. He would make a very fine president," said Saraf quite sarcastically. "Or a priest, perhaps. But Hattie Lewis must be on the ticket with him. My associates will accept nothing less. Nor will the American voters."

"I don't think we disagree," said Davis. "By the way," he continued, seeming not to want to look at Saraf, choosing instead to look out the window, "how *are* things progressing in Florida?"

Saraf smiled. "I am told the demand for medication is increasing every day, and the supply"—he opened his hands wide—"well, it is being kept up with the demand. Our medical specialists are doing everything they can for the senator's comfort. He is in a great deal of pain these days."

"I see," said Davis. "Well, then, that should ease your concern about our ability to continue with our plans for the congresswoman."

"It would, if the governor were not so idealistic and naive about loyalties."

"I can assure you, Governor Wendell will come to grips with the problem of continuing to carry a running mate with a serious drug problem. Then the question will go beyond loyalty and friendship. It will pain him, but he will do what he must do."

"And my associates will continue to do their part."

"With sufficient discretion and safeguards, I trust."

"Please, Mr. Davis. You are not dealing with amateurs or simple idealists. We rely upon highly skilled professionals in such matters. Just as we do in taking care of our financial arrangements. By the way, I want to assure you that our current contribution to the campaign is quite clean."

Davis raised an inquisitive eyebrow.

"The three million dollars," Saraf explained. "It has been thoroughly laundered, to use your political idiom. The CIC financial report will show it as the result of a massive collection effort, in which thousands of people contributed small sums of hard-earned money to this noble cause." Davis nodded approvingly. "But I assume I can assure my people that Mr. Wendell acknowledges—discreetly, of course—the generosity of today's donor?" Davis lowered his eyelids and nodded again ever so slightly. "And that he can look forward to meeting

141

with Mr. Wendell soon about matters of mutual interest?"

"That's correct, Mr. Saraf."

"Good, Mr. Davis. I'm sure he will appreciate knowing this. By the way, before I forget, there will be another contribution coming in within a few days. Perhaps a million dollars—which would cover your Jerome Bloom's fee."

"Also from today's donor?"

"No, this will not be from His Eminence. It will also appear as individual contributions."

Davis was curious. "Interesting. Can you tell me who has been so kind?"

Saraf smiled broadly. "Of course. It's very ironic, considering Mr. Bloom's involvement."

"In what way?"

"The million dollars is in actuality a gift from the group known as Fair Treatment for South Africa." Davis could not mask his incredulous reaction. "That's right, Mr. Davis. They are quite supportive of the governor's campaign."

Davis looked concerned. "I'm not sure about this. That group has been accused repeatedly of racist leanings. It's dangerous."

"You can relax, Mr. Davis. The funds are as thoroughly clean as are those that you have in that briefcase. There will be no connection with the Fair Treatment group. It will show as small contributions."

"I see," said Davis, looking down at the leather case.

"I find it very interesting how people of modest means in this country will scorn a beggar who seeks only a few coins in the name of human compassion, only to give their last ten dollars in the name of racial superiority."

"That doesn't bother you—a non-Caucasian?"

"How could it? Remember, these so-called racists are impotent—except when it comes to raising money. Besides, we cannot be looked upon too unfavorably by them, since so few of us have chosen to emigrate here."

Davis rose from his seat. "I really must go now, Mr. Saraf. Please extend our continued gratitude to your associates."

Davis started to offer his hand to Saraf, but quickly stopped himself. Saraf remained seated.

"I will convey your message, Mr. Davis."

Davis opened the door to the hallway and held it, waiting for Saraf, who finally rose. The young Arab walked past Davis into the reception area, leaving behind his unmistakable scent of strong cologne. He paused, turning back to the expressionless Davis.

"*Salaam*, Mr. Davis." His bow was mocking. "Or, should I more appropriately say *shalom*?" He did not wait to see Davis's reaction. He turned and walked through the law firm's massive oak door.

When Bloom stepped through the automatic doors at Los Angeles International Airport, he walked into the familiar warm dampness, the visual chaos of passengers being discharged into the sprawling city, the sounds of recorded warnings.

"Unattended vehicles will be ticketed and towed away." The threatening voice was totally indifferent. Tired and perspiring chauffeurs in gray or black uniforms craned beside parked Mercedes-Benzes or

Rolls-Royces, searching the endless stream of harried travelers for the familiar faces of their wealthy employers. Bloom put his two bags down on the sidewalk and searched the three-deep row of cars for his sensible family car, a 1984 Volvo station wagon. He had felt just a little saddened that none of his family had been waiting at the gate when he stepped off the plane. But he and Anne had agreed that such ceremony was unnecessary when the airport was crowded, which was the case virtually all the time these days. As he stood in the warm California sunshine, tinged with the gray-brown of automotive exhaust, he noticed a familiar face coming through a crowded exit. One of the waiting chauffeurs ran up to the man, an aging film actor whose name eluded Bloom. He tried to picture the pudgy, balding man in his younger days. His memory was helped by the chauffeur, who grabbed the man's suitcase and said, "Hello, Mr. Richman. Have a good trip?" Good God, Bloom thought, is that really John Richman? Look at him—pale, looking like a coronary poised to happen, overweight, and very, very unhappy. Must be seventy, at least. He thought back to one of his favorite motion pictures, *Beyond Hope*, in which Richman had played the leading role, the part of a hopeless alcoholic, a performance that had won him an Oscar. Bloom wondered what he himself would look like in not too many years, when there would be little demand, if any, for his services, as was the case these days with the now obscure Richman.

A honking car horn got Bloom's attention away from the aging actor. He turned to see his red sports car, the impractical two-seater, instead of the family car, with Anne at the wheel. Her arm was held out the window to get his attention. She was not smiling, just waving at Bloom. Still more of a feeling of sadness came upon Bloom as he wondered why the children hadn't come with Anne to meet him. They usually seemed to enjoy going to the airport to greet their father, particularly if they took the slower route home, through Marina del Rey, with a chance to look at the enormous flotillas of luxury boats, then on to the interestingly shabby streets of Venice.

Bloom worked his way through the crowds and stacks of luggage to the curb, and then threaded between some nearly touching parked cars to his own. Anne got out to move to the passenger seat, allowing Bloom to drive home. She merely brushed his cheek with her lips on the way around the car, saying nothing more than "Hi. Good trip?"

He stared at her. "Yeah. Terrific, thank you."

As Bloom started into the steady stream of traffic headed for the freeways, he spoke again, after a lengthy silence. "Where are the kids?"

"Danny has soccer practice. It's Thursday, remember?" Her voice showed no more emotion than it would have if Bloom had been gone for just a few hours, instead of three days.

"And Beth?"

"She disappeared when it was time to leave for the airport. I couldn't wait for her."

Bloom made no comment about Beth's apparent disinterest in going to meet him. He silently reflected on what she might have chosen to do instead of making the trip with her mother. Go to the drugstore to look at magazines? Sit on the front porch down the street with one of her friends? Or some other diversion that would be of more interest to her than greeting her father? Get off this self-pity trip, he warned himself.

Bloom found himself looking, out of the corner of his eye, at Anne comparatively as he continued his silence. She looked fresh and clean; she must have bathed just before leaving to meet him. Jeanette had looked fresh and clean, also. The age differential between Anne and Jeanette—some ten years— wasn't all that apparent. Anne had an unusual ability to appear much younger than she actually was. And she didn't need to work at it. She smelled particularly good to Bloom. He was reminded of the fragrance of Jeanette again. He worried that the comparisons would continue.

Anne now chose to break the silence. "What went on in Dallas?"

Bloom couldn't help but toy with the irony of his wife's question. "Not much exciting."

It was time to take a walk along the beach. Whenever things weren't going well for Anne and Jerry Bloom, they seemed to deal best with issues on a long walk, which usually began at the Venice public beach and ended on the Santa Monica pier. They would take off their shoes and walk in the sand at the water's edge. Today they needed one of those walks, one of those discussions.

"How have we been able to keep this marriage together for twenty-one years?" Anne asked. She seemed to be asking the question of the Pacific Ocean.

Bloom seemed to be answering the sand. "Some luck, I guess. And three separations."

Anne smiled. "How quickly they forget. It's four. Remember?"

"Sure, if you count those four months in New York."

"Why shouldn't we count them? You were living there. In your own apartment."

"I came home on most weekends."

"Okay. You say three separations, I say four. You say to-may-to . . . I say to-mah-to. Let's call the whole thing off?"

Bloom stopped. Anne went a few steps farther before stopping and turning. "You know something?" asked Bloom.

"What?"

"You're getting flip in your old age. Why don't you cut the comedy? This is serious stuff we're talking about."

"Believe me, sweetheart, I know how serious it is. In fact, I was up all night thinking how serious everything has become in our lives. And I came up with only one conclusion."

"What's that?" asked Bloom, as they began walking again.

"If we're going to separate again, this one's for good. No more reconciliations. No more attempts at picking up all the little pieces again."

"You're giving me an ultimatum."

"Call it that if you want. I see it more as survival. I don't think I can endure another trip through the revolving door. Nor can the children. If we have to remove ourselves from one another's lives one more time, I think we will have sufficiently demonstrated we can't make it through life together."

"I just have a real problem with ultimatums. You're threatening me. That's not what we came here for."

"That's right. We came here to discuss what's going on in your world."

Bloom looked out at the sea. A tanker was lumbering southward, belching out a column of black smoke. Closer in to shore, a large sailboat was running parallel to the beach, with wind-filled spinnaker. And still closer, a flock of gulls was diving into the breakers for food. Lives were simpler on the freighter, aboard the sailboat. It all seemed so removed from presidential politics. From crumbling marriages.

"I'm going to do it," he finally said.

"What, pray tell, are you going to do?"

"The campaign. I'm going to take it."

This time it was Anne who stopped walking. She put her hands on her hips and looked at Bloom. "You're serious?"

"Of course I'm serious."

"You're going to turn your back on everything you stand for and on everyone you believe in?"

"Goddamm it, I'm not turning my back. I'm taking the opportunity of a lifetime. I've got a chance to take a career step that I may never have again. And I'm doing it with some of those people you say I'm turning my back on. Or have you forgotten how much Hattie is a part of my career—of our lives?"

"I don't know what they did to get Hattie on their team. Maybe I don't want to know. But I'm sure she has her reasons for doing what she's done. I also suspect they're reasons you couldn't possibly have."

"And why not?"

"First of all, you're not black. Or a woman."

"But I *am* trying to make a living."

"A million dollars isn't making a living. It's a killing."

"They're willing to pay it. And they must think I'm worth it. Although you'd obviously disagree with them."

"I'm not saying you're not worth it. Christ, for all I know, you may be worth ten million dollars. I don't discount your talent. You're the best at what you do. I know it. Stephen Wendell obviously knows it. But David Braun also knows it. What are you going to do about his campaign?"

"I'll turn it over to Chuck Hanselman. He's good. And David likes him."

"You're talking about David's Senate seat. Not his car. You don't just *turn it over* to someone. He needs you."

"Look, what do you want me to do? Maybe you're forgetting what it is I do. I help people who think they ought to be elected by the people. It's part of the process by which we govern ourselves. David Braun is a client. He doesn't hire me because he likes me. He hires me because he believes I can help get him elected. When someone better comes along, and David's political future is on the line, don't you think he'll hire him?"

"Or her."

"Very funny. Yes, or her. The point is, I'm in a business. Granted, I'm in it because I want to make a difference while I make a living. That's why I do political commercials instead of soap commercials. And when choices present themselves, like the choice to move up to the top of the mountain, do you want me to say 'No thanks, I'd rather not make the climb'? Besides, I think David Braun would be the first to tell me to go for it."

"Why don't you ask him how he feels about the idea before you make your decision?" Anne wouldn't let up on her husband.

"Because I've made my decision."

"And you only *assume* David would advise you to abandon him."

"You know something? You're not interested in discussing this. You're writing a fucking editorial."

"I don't like that kind of language. Never did."

"I'm sorry. My manners must have gone out the window with my integrity."

"This is one of those arguments no one's going to win. We're both too angry," said Anne.

"Do you really think I've lost my integrity?"

"No. If you had, you wouldn't be as angry and frustrated as you are right now. But if you were to ask me if I think you're letting people down, I'm sorry, but I feel you are."

"Well, it's a decision I felt I had to make. And now I'll have to live with it."

"Will *I*?" Anne stopped again to look at Bloom.

"I suppose that depends on whether you want to live with *me* any longer." They both looked at each other, as though they were wondering who would strike the next blow.

"I'm sorry I'm on the attack. I'm angry with you. But not nearly as angry as I am with Stephen Wendell. Let the man run for president. Let him win, if that's what the people of this country want. But why can't he do it without my husband? Why can't he find himself another genius of the media? Yes, I want to continue living with you, if our marriage is something you still believe in, if it's something you still view as important enough to keep your commitment to it, and to me. But I get this feeling you're having an affair."

Bloom was struck by a shock wave that raced from head to foot.

"Well, in a manner of speaking," Anne continued, "it's an affair I think you're having with politics. It excites you. It offers you something more attractive than I can—power, wealth, maybe a place next to the throne. That's tough stuff to compete with."

Bloom could find little relief in discovering Anne was merely speaking metaphorically. He still felt the shame of having violated his marriage vows, of having broken the trust.

They continued their walk along the beach, both remaining silent for some time, looking down at the shells and debris on the sand or out to sea, as the sailboat quickly moved out of sight and the tanker continued to lumber across the horizon. A younger couple, their jeans soaked up to the knees and their arms around one another, passed by and smiled at them. Both Bloom and Anne seemed equally uncomfortable with the contrast they presented to the happy couple. Bloom wished he wanted to be walking with his arm around his wife. But in truth, he wanted to be somewhere else. With someone else.

When they were at the end of the Santa Monica

pier, staring out over the railing, Anne delivered another ultimatum.

"I'm going to work against you in this campaign. I hope you realize that."

"Hey, it's still a free country. I just hope you don't work against Wendell solely because I'm working *for* him."

"No, it's simply because I think he'd be very bad for the country. I think he should be stopped."

"And I think he should be president. Which makes for some interesting weeks ahead for the two of us."

"I'm serious," said Anne. And Bloom couldn't help but wonder just how far she might go to work against Stephen Wendell and, therefore, against her own husband.

As for the state of their marriage, nothing was decided that afternoon. At least the status quo was preserved, if not their relationship.

Some three thousand miles away from the beach where Jerome and Anne Bloom had taken their walk, less than a mile offshore from Palm Beach, Florida, a gleaming, white sportfishing boat cruised slowly in the warm gulf-stream current. The boat, *Florida's Pride*, was rigged for surface trolling for sailfish. It was Senator Henry Blandemann's proudest possession. And fishing aboard it was his favorite leisure activity. Today, however, the boat was not carrying the usual group of happy sportsmen. A pale, deeply concerned, and obviously depressed Blandemann sat slumped in his fishing chair, oblivious to everything around him, except the conversation he was having with Harrison Davis.

"Senator," said Davis, who looked as imposing in his fishing clothes as he did in his impeccable three-piece suits, "I'm sorry, but the problem has become unmanageable for us."

Blandemann stared off to the open sea, perhaps wondering if any sailfish might take the mullet bait being offered them some hundred yards beyond the wake of the boat. He finally spoke, in a low, troubled voice. "I don't know what I can do at this point. I have a problem that I'm trying to lick. But I just haven't been able to yet. My entire career is at stake."

"As is Stephen's," said Davis, still stone-faced.

"I know. That part is even worse than what I'm doing to myself. But Jesus, do you know what it's like to be hooked on those damn drugs? You start out taking them for the pain, when it gets so bad in your spine that you have to stuff the bedclothes in your mouth, just to keep from screaming. Someone comes along and gives you a shot. It knocks you out. You sleep six hours; for the first time in three months, you sleep. You almost feel like a human being the next morning. But then the pain comes back, and the doctors say no more shots. They could be addictive. But they don't take the pain away from you. Only the drugs. So you try anything. Liquor. I hate the stuff. But it helps cut the pain. And then, out of the blue, someone comes along with another needle. You don't ask questions. You thank God that it's going into your arm to take away the pain again. To let you sleep for a few hours. And, after the needle, someone gives you some pills. Before you know it, your body no longer belongs to you. It's owned by the goddamn pills, and the needles and the booze. It does what those things allow it to do—nothing more, nothing less. But I'm telling you, Harrison, I'm going to beat it. I'm going to dry out completely. No more liquor. No more drugs. I know I can do it."

"I'm sure you can, Henry. But not while you're running for vice-president of the United States. You know how unfairly the press will treat this. My God, look what they did to Thomas Eagleton."

"They goddamn near killed him," said Blandemann, tears welling up in his reddened eyes. "They're not going to kill me."

"We want to help you in these difficult times," said Davis, as sincerely as a used-car salesman. Blandemann looked as though he understood just how much Davis wanted to help.

"What do you want me to do?" asked Blandemann. "What does Stephen want me to do?"

"We must choose what is best for our mission, and for our country."

Blandemann thought a while before speaking. "You want me to get out, to step down, right?"

Davis shrugged and looked away from Blandemann.

"Why isn't Stephen here to ask me?" Blandemann continued. "He's been my friend for years. He should be here today."

"He's also been *my* friend for years, Henry. And I know how much this entire matter pains him. He would sooner abandon his own career goals than abandon a friend like you, I can assure you. But he now realizes it's not his personal career that's on the line. It's millions of people who believe in him. Little people, who have given their grocery money to this cause. How can he turn away from them?"

Blandemann put his head down in his hands. He was silent, looking at the deck of the boat.

"Are you all right, Senator?" came a booming voice from the flying bridge. It was the boat's skipper.

"He'll be fine," Davis shouted back to the man, who nodded and returned his attention to the waters through which the boat was cruising.

Blandemann continued to remain silent, just staring down at the maroon decking. Davis looked toward the shore, and then checked the time on his gleaming, gold wristwatch. And the boat's name, lettered in bronze on the transom, seemed incongruous. FLORIDA'S PRIDE. Its owner, however, seemed like a man who had lost, perhaps irretrievably, whatever pride he might have once possessed.

Aram Saraf was on the phone, speaking long-distance from his hotel room in Dallas to an associate in Key West.

"I hope you can increase the senator's dosage a little," he said.

"No problem," said the voice, with a southern accent, on the other end of the line. "We can keep him nice and comfortable."

"And you are certain you can continue to do it discreetly?"

"Hey, man, you're not dealing with minor leaguers down here. We know what we're doing. But our fees are going to have to go up, naturally."

"Naturally," replied Saraf. "Just let us know what is required."

"Oh, we'll be sure to do that, all right. By the way, our patient told me he's not going to be needing my help anymore. Says he's going to dry out and kick it completely."

"Perhaps he will," said Saraf. "He's very strong, I am told."

"Like I said, you're not dealing with minor leaguers. No, he's not about to give up heaven for the kind of hell he'd be buying. Trust me."

"We have no choice," said Saraf.

"As a matter of fact, you don't," said the voice, laughing.

The next morning, Henry Blandemann put in a call to his friend and running mate. His hand was steadier than it had been for some time. Perhaps the fact that, only ten minutes earlier, he had received an injection of morphine made for steadier nerves. What followed was the most difficult conversation he had ever had in his life.

10

THE PRETTY YOUNG CHILD, A girl of about five, stooped to pick a flower from a lush summer hillside. A daisy. She began to pick off the white petals, one by one. As she did, a man's voice counted with her. Backward. Nine. Eight. Seven . . . She continued picking the petals, all her attention concentrated on the act. Three. Two. One. Then the little girl was gone in a blinding, searing flash of white. Followed by an ominous, omnipotent mushroom cloud.

Stephen Wendell, sitting in his hotel room in Washington's Hyatt Regency, leaned forward and turned off the video recorder, and the image on the television screen faded to nothing as the words VOTE FOR LYNDON JOHNSON appeared on a black field. Harrison Davis had a faint smile on his lips. He said nothing as he looked across the room to an expressionless Bloom, slumped in the brocade sofa.

"That, Jerome," said Wendell, "is what I want in my television commercials."

Bloom continued to stare at the blank, gray television screen, as if expecting to see more of what Wendell wanted. "You want a child vaporized by a nuclear explosion?"

"Why don't you save your gallows humor for your off-year writing endeavors?" snapped Davis.

"It's all right, Harrison," was Wendell's condescending reassurance to Davis that the remark should be ignored. "Jerome is a man of abiding moral conviction. Although it is interesting that this particular commercial was created in the interest of one of the great moral issues, nuclear disarmament. It was also the most brilliant piece of work in modern campaigning."

"It was the cheapest shot ever fired in politics."

"Really?" prodded Wendell. "As long as we're using superlatives, I've always thought it was the most effective piece of persuasion ever developed for a presidential campaign. It cut right to the heart of people's innermost fears about Barry Goldwater. While Barry was saying 'In your heart you know I'm right,' Johnson was saying 'In your heart you harbor a nightmare of total and final nuclear devastation if Goldwater should be elected president.'"

"The commercial also helped seal Johnson's victory," said Davis, "even though it was aired only once."

"The people who made that commercial," countered Bloom, "knew from the start it would play only once. They bought the biggest prime-time audience available on the network. Then, when everyone cried foul, the Johnson people pulled it off the air. And with all the hell that was raised by the media, the commercial got even more exposure on every major network newscast. Very few voters escaped seeing the spot. Smart planning—dirty politics. Put the two together, and you've got a bomb capable of swaying millions of votes. Of changing history."

"Changing history. Precisely," said Wendell, with a definite tinge of triumph in his voice. "That is what this campaign is about. We are going to change the course of American politics. And you are going to help us. It's a good way to secure a place in the chronicles of our times, Jerome."

This man is clever enough to keep you wondering where the bullshit ends and political acumen begins, Bloom thought, staring at his shoes, wondering how many new Bally's he could buy for $1 million. At a hundred and eighty a pair, let's see, one-eighty into two hundred, once, carry the twenty—fuck it, too many zeroes. Chronicles. Bullshit or acumen?

"What am I to make of your silence, Jerome?"

"I'm just thinking what a thin line we walk in this business."

"Oh, yes, that line between propriety and recklessness. We walk it daily when we're pursuing a goal as awesome as the presidency."

"And Lyndon Johnson stepped over it. No, he *jumped* over it, with that commercial. Now the president of the United States—not some TV censor—is crying foul at us, in defense of his party's candidate. He thinks we've crossed the line and violated fair campaign practices."

"He's grasping," Davis chimed in. "He knows we're going to hurt his candidate with the immigration spot. And the only way he can think to stop us is to frighten us off with his charges of ethics violations."

"I know he's planning to use the famous Johnson bomb commercial to make his point. I also understand," Wendell continued, in his cool, matter-of-fact style, "that he intends to show the commercial to the entire White House press corps, along with your storyboard for the immigration spot."

Bloom was startled enough to sit up straight. Wendell's words had been like a splash of cold water, just as he was feeling his familiar, protective drowsiness approaching. Jesus Christ, Bloom thought, now the president's people had gotten a copy of his storyboard. What the hell is going on, another Watergate? The whole issue was becoming more absurd by the moment. The chief executive of the United States was using dirty tricks to prove the use of dirty tricks. How did he get the 24" × 30" display of eight television frames with the script for the commercial typed in white panels below each frame? Who had gotten into Bloom's locked office files?

Wendell spoke as though he had read the question in Bloom's mind. "The Republicans probably got a copy of your board somewhere other than from your office. He wouldn't risk something as foolish as a break-in. Didn't you have your film people go over the storyboard for purposes of production planning?"

"I trust my people," snapped Bloom defensively. "They'd never violate a confidence like that. It would finish them in the business."

"I know it's a poor cliché, Jerome, but doesn't everyone have his price?"

Bloom felt a shock wave of anger jolt his body. He wanted very much to call Wendell a smug, arrogant son-of-a-bitch. But he settled for the thought. Live with it. Roll with it. The man is your client. He's paying you well, even if he's turning around and accusing you of being a Judas on his behalf, with his own pieces of silver. But if his film production people didn't give the storyboard to the Republicans, who did?

Anne Bloom had not yet learned how to look comfortable sitting alone in a restaurant. She had spent too many years of her life being with someone in public. In most cases it was her husband. Occasionally, it was with a friend for lunch. Twenty-one years of married life, with the occupation of "homemaker" putting perimeters on her contact with people who have lunch with other people, now made her self-conscious as she sat waiting for the man she was to have lunch with at Cyrano. Not the Sunset Boulevard Cyrano, but the one in Marina del Rey. Which was a good choice. For Anne had no friends whom she would run into anywhere in the Marina, which was frequented for the most part by tourists, conventioneers, "fast-lane" singles, and Republicans—all groups with which she had no contact.

Anne looked several years younger than her age. Her Los Angeles tennis tan gave her a healthy glow. It also called attention to her youthful, firm figure, as did her white linen shirtwaist dress. Her long auburn hair fell down to her shoulders and framed her calm, pretty face. The men who passed her table, some smiling, some just making it clear they found her attractive, did not see a nervous or uncomfortable Anne Bloom. She seemed, instead, a confident, desirable woman. But then, Anne had always been able to mask her feelings and state of mind. It was an acquired skill, a prerequisite for life with the unpredictable, sometimes mercurial moods of her husband, the media mover.

"Mrs. Bloom?" It was half question, half greeting, the voice of a man she had not seen approaching her table. She smiled cautiously, a little nervously, and nodded. "Mark Cassidy," he said, identifying himself as he pulled out the other chair at the table to join Anne. His appearance was predictable to her. No surprises, from the conservative, three-piece gray suit to the blue oxford shirt, the striped tie, the neat haircut, and the uninteresting eyes. Probably made love to his equally predictable wife in the dark.

"It was easy finding you," he began, avoiding her eyes, smiling at his place setting, "I just looked around for the most attractive woman in the restaurant."

She smiled mockingly. "What do you do when you meet a man you don't know for lunch?"

He finally looked at Anne. He shrugged helplessly and spoke with a nervous chuckle. "Guess I ask the captain to show me to the right table."

"I see." She was expressionless.

"Well, Mrs. Bloom, I bring you greetings from the president."

It was one of the funniest things Anne had heard in a long time. What greetings? A box of candy? A Hallmark card—from the president?

"Thank you. I suppose I should be taken by that.

How many people today can say they've been greeted by the president?"

Cassidy tried to relax, but was not successful. He engaged in dull small talk, about the weather, the restaurant, about things that wouldn't lead to awkward situations. He seemed to sense the alienation. He was, after all, director of media communications for the Committee to Elect Jack Kemp. And he was having lunch with the wife, albeit the recently separated wife, of Jerry Bloom, a member of the enemy camp, a liberal Democrat working for an independent candidate who was coming dangerously close to the presidency.

Anne had to get her disclaimer out. She wanted this man to know what she was—and was not—up to. "Look, Mr. Cassidy, let's make one thing perfectly clear." She stopped to laugh at what she had just done, using Richard Nixon's famous words.

"It's okay," Cassidy said, also laughing. "I thought Mr. Nixon was a clown, myself."

"Richard Nixon did more harm to this country than any clown could do." Cassidy said nothing. "But that's beside the point. I gave you my husband's storyboards for one reason. That reason is to try and keep Stephen Wendell from getting into the White House. I would rather have cooperated with the Hart people, because I would rather see Gary Hart president than Stephen Wendell." She paused. "Or Jack Kemp."

Cassidy flushed. He obviously didn't like hearing about Anne's preference for Hart. "I realize your political preference, Mrs. Bloom. And I understand why you were willing to give us the material. But why didn't the Hart people want to use it?"

"To quote Gary's campaign director, 'Dirty tricks aren't part of our strategy, even to expose someone else's dirty tricks.' Don't forget," Anne continued, "Gary Hart was George McGovern's campaign manager."

"We don't view exposing violations of fair campaign practices as dirty tricks. In fact, the president is doing a service to the elective process by confronting the Wendell people with his charges."

"How is he going to expose the Wendell strategy?"

Cassidy looked at his watch. "At nine tomorrow morning he's meeting with Wendell, Harrison Davis," he paused, "and your husband. He plans to challenge the immigration commercial. If Wendell is willing to either keep it off the air or modify it substantially, the Kemp Committee will drop its charges."

"And if Wendell refuses?"

"The president will go to the American people. With Congressman Kemp, at a press conference. He'll also ask the networks to keep your husband's commercial off the air."

"*Wendell's* commercial," she corrected.

"Whatever. The point is, Mrs. Bloom, your husband is likely to be the center of quite a storm."

"He already is, and has been, ever since he agreed to work for Stephen Wendell."

"And you don't want to try and talk him out of what he's doing? I don't understand."

"If that were a possibility, I never would have stooped to taking confidential material and passing it along to your committee." She made the word *your* sound undesirable.

164

"You make it seem as though we're involved in some sort of crime," Cassidy said, clearly showing his defensiveness. "You merely furnished us with evidence of what we already know. It was available to you and you saw fit to pass it on to us."

Anne turned her gaze away from Cassidy. She took in the rest of the crowded restaurant. Her eyes didn't stop at the swarthy young man two tables away, a man with large, tinted, horn-rimmed glasses. He was aiming a small camera at the windows and the view of the marina outside them. Or at least that was what Aram Saraf appeared to be doing. When Anne fixed her gaze on the large, rounded condominium building across Admiralty Way, Saraf was fixing his Nikon on her. He clicked the shutter, just as Anne turned back to look at Cassidy, laughing.

"You do realize the irony of sitting here, looking out at that building?"

"Which building?" Cassidy asked.

"That big white one," she said, discreetly pointing a finger under her chin. "Know who lives there?" Cassidy merely shook his head in anticipation. "Segretti. The Watergate Segretti."

"Yes, I know who he is."

"And here we are, in view of his balcony, pilfering campaign material. I wonder if we're being watched," she mused, still not seeing Saraf snap his shutter, just as Anne leaned forward in a gesture of mock confidentiality.

Bloom was alone in his Washington hotel room, two floors below Wendell's Hyatt Regency suite. He was tying the lace on one of his running shoes, looking out the window at the dome of the Capitol building two blocks away. He was dressed in shorts and T-shirt, preparing for a five-mile run with his new client, Stephen Wendell. Just when the atmosphere in Wendell's suite had come close to the explosion point, the candidate had abruptly changed the subject and invited Bloom to run with him. It took Bloom by surprise. He simply had not expected the smooth former governor of Texas to be a runner. He just didn't seem the type who would sweat. But Wendell was a man full of surprises for Bloom.

The Capitol was beginning to take on a slight reddish-orange cast, as the late afternoon sun began to tint the nation's capital with the warm hues of sunset. The country and the world had survived for another day the debates of the legislative, the decisions of the executive, and the deliberations of the judiciary. Now the hundreds of thousands of men and women who daily populated the marble and granite buildings that housed the lumbering machinery of American government were bound for home or the cocktail lounges. Some, like Bloom and Wendell, were bound for the streets and running paths.

Waiting for the phone call from Wendell to summon him for the running expedition, Bloom focused on the large piece of art board that had become the source of so much controversy. In fact, it was possibly about to become the subject of a nationally televised press conference to be convened by the president. The black cardboard, propped against the wall on the hotel-room desk, contained eight panels in the shape of a television screen. In each was an illustration; below each illustration was a white panel in which dialogue and action descriptions had been typed. It was a step-by-step blueprint of a thirty-second commercial. Not just any commercial. This was the one Kemp's people had seen and complained about. They had been given a photostatic copy of the original storyboard. Bloom was still angered and puzzled by the question of how the candidate's staff got a copy. Who would violate the confidence with which Bloom and his associates were committed to work on the Wendell campaign? Who would sell out to the other side? Once again Bloom reviewed his commercial, just as he had dozens of times before, prior to presenting it to the campaign committee and, again, while planning its filming with his production crew. Had he gone too far? Had he committed a foul, and violated fair campaign practices and principles, as the Kemp people were charging? There was that thin line again. Only it was now becoming thinner. More imperceptible. It's funny, Bloom thought, how a million dollars can blur your vision of the line that separates right from wrong, moral from immoral.

In the right-hand corner of the storyboard, a typed identifying label read: WENDELL FOR PRESIDENT, 30-SECOND TV/ANIMATION. TITLE: "IMMIGRATION/LIBERTY." The commercial would be an innovation in political advertising, in that it would be the first use of animation, at least to Bloom's knowledge, in a major political campaign. The rule had always been to use only live-action techniques, with real people and places. Bloom had always found it ironic that candidates and campaign managers would spend enormous sums to make their filmed messages look like they cost very little. The

167

stated goal was always to make it look inexpensive, rough around the edges, real-life. Animation, Bloom had been told, would look too slick, too much like fantasy. Never mind the fact that candidates would spend hours with wardrobe specialists, makeup artists, and speech coaches to make themselves look real and spontaneous. Forget that political filmmakers would use special lenses to make a candidate look taller or thinner. Reality was what everyone was after, no matter how hard it was to fabricate it.

Bloom had prevailed with Wendell and Davis. When he explained that the only other alternative was to destroy the nation's most cherished national monument on camera, the candidate and his campaign director relented, agreeing to the use of animation.

Bloom went over the commercial one more time, going through each panel of illustration and typed copy. He really did not need the board any longer; he had every detail of the commercial indelibly etched on his consciousness. But still he studied it, searching for some help in deciding whether he had gone too far.

The commercial opened with a close-up of the head and upheld arm of the Statue of Liberty, proudly standing guard over New York's harbor. In the background, the viewer would hear music, a full orchestration of "America the Beautiful." So far, everything was patriotic and upbeat. What could be more positive than a tastefully animated rendering of that great American symbol of freedom, together with music to make even the most cynical feel a twinge of warm respect for his country?

But as the camera pulled back, a fleet of small boats was seen arriving at the base of the statue. Next, groups of brown-skinned men, who were, in fact, illegal refugees from Caribbean nations, began swarming around the statue, as if they were capturing it. Their angry conversations, mostly in Spanish, were a frightening contrast to the patriotic music in the background. Close-ups of determined, even menacing faces were intercut. The aliens climbed on the statue. And now there were hundreds of dark men, swarming all over the statue, seeming to violate a woman who had previously been chaste. Cracks appeared in the arm of the statue and, then, in its head. The sounds of a building collapsing drowned out the music and the cries of the men, as the statue crumbled in upon itself and fell into the waters of the harbor. An off-camera announcer said solemnly, "Stephen Wendell has fought to protect our cherished way of life against the crushing tide of illegal immigration . . . a tide that steals jobs from our people and creates crime in our streets. We must continue the fight, in the name of liberty." The screen went black, and Wendell's name faded on, together with the words LET FREEDOM RING AGAIN, followed by the striking of a large bell, the ringing sound lingering to the end of the commercial.

Bloom could still hear the bell's echo as he stared at the last panel of the storyboard, half admiring what he felt was probably his best work, half condemning himself for creating it. His thoughts were jarred by the shrill ring of the telephone next to his bed. He was in no rush to answer it, for he knew who would be on the other end of the line.

"Are you ready to run a relaxing five miles?" asked Stephen Wendell, who didn't wait for an answer, but went on to instruct Bloom to meet him in the lobby in five minutes.

The early evening air, heavy with humidity, was made slightly refreshing by a light breeze as they made their way along crowded sidewalks toward the Capitol. A few people did double takes as they were passed by the two runners, not because it was unusual to see runners out on the sidewalks of Washington, but, obviously, because it was unusual to see a man who looked so much like presidential candidate Stephen Wendell running without a cadre of Secret Service agents for security. What most people didn't notice was the van that kept pace with Wendell and Bloom; nor could they possibly have seen through the blackened windows inside, where four men, dressed in warm-up suits and carrying .45 automatics in shoulder holsters, watched every move the candidate made. Wendell had received a great deal of press attention about what appeared to be a total absence of security when he went for his daily runs. Reporters were merely told that Wendell preferred to free himself of tight security measures, just as he desired to free the nation of its restricting obsession with crime. It was another of the publicity gimmicks Wendell kept in his bag of tricks, most of which seemed to be working.

"Have you ever seen a more awe-inspiring sight?" Wendell asked Bloom, as they waited for a green light just across the street from the Capitol grounds.

Bloom shrugged. "The Statue of Liberty is also very impressive," he said, pointing to the green light and feeling some satisfaction as he watched Wendell first shoot a reprimanding glance toward him, followed by a quick, politicianlike change to a nodding smile.

"Touché, Jerome. You've not lost your touch."

"I can't afford to now." It felt good to Bloom to be outside, to be stretching out his leg muscles, to be taking deep breaths of air that was, in spite of the presence of automobile exhaust, far more fresh and invigorating than the atmosphere of hotel suites.

The sun was dropping quickly now and the orange sky darkening as Wendell and Bloom turned toward the Washington Monument. Headlights were coming on in the streams of traffic. Bloom was perspiring heavily already. He saw that Wendell's shirt was still dry. *The son-of-a-bitch doesn't even sweat, he's so damn cool. What else doesn't he do like normal people?*

"Is the pace comfortable for you?" Wendell asked.

Bloom nodded. "Fine." Actually, it was just a little quick for him. Which is why he said no more. The runner's rule of thumb says a pace is too fast if a comfortable conversation cannot be held.

"Good," replied Wendell, smiling. "I was afraid I might be holding you back." His conversation wasn't the least bit labored.

As they headed back out to the sidewalk leading past the Smithsonian buildings, they passed the bumper-to-bumper string of pickup campers and small motor homes that always seemed to be parked near the Capitol. Parked among the recreational vehicles were similar-looking trucks belonging to souvenir vendors. The area always looked like the assembly point for a farmers' protest.

"Why isn't the secret service with us?" Bloom finally asked, trying to conceal his labored breathing.

"Why in the world would we need security out here?"

"You just never know. There are a lot of nuts running around these days. Some of them would just love to take a shot at a presidential candidate."

"If we can't be safe within sight of the nation's Capitol, there's no place left for men to walk free, unencumbered by fear." Bloom had heard those same words before, in newspaper coverage of Wendell's speeches on immigration. Now he was hearing the words from the source. And they were spoken with conviction. There was a time when Bloom hadn't accepted the logic that illegal immigration was a major contributing factor to urban crime. He thought back to his conversation with Jeanette about her late husband, about his death on the streets of Los Angeles. Bloom's traditional, liberal views, which had never been particularly flexible, were being challenged by Wendell, by Jeanette, by changing times.

As they approached the old, red buildings of the Smithsonian Institution, now shrouded in the cloak of twilight, Bloom's gaze fell upon the figures of three men, struggling with each other. He saw one of them go down on the sidewalk and heard a shout. His adrenaline began racing. Bloom couldn't deal with adults fighting. What was worth coming to blows over?

"Looks like someone's trying to prove a point the hard way," he said to Wendell.

Wendell squinted in the dim light. "That's not a fight. Come on." And he broke into a sprint.

Bloom followed Wendell reluctantly. He shouted after him, "Wait a minute. Maybe they're armed." He realized how absurd, how totally unheroic he must have sounded. He struggled to keep up for the last fifty yards or so, realizing, as he and Wendell drew closer, that they had come upon a mugging, one of those famous Washington street attacks that take place within plain view of the nation's Capitol. He quickly glanced back over his shoulder, as if to make sure it were true. The Capitol was there all right.

When they reached the three men, they saw that the one lying on the ground was neatly dressed in a dark suit. He was covering his head with his arms while one of the men standing over him kicked him in the ribs. Everything happened so quickly. He heard the man shouting, "I don't have any more . . . I don't!" Another voice, coming from the second attacker, shot out a staccato stream of Spanish. Bloom didn't understand what was being said, but whatever it was had a mixture of fear and anger. Bloom couldn't tell how long he and Wendell stood watching the scene. The talking assailant, a small wiry man, saw the two runners and raised his hand, pointing at them, while he shouted to his accomplice. Bloom could make out one word: *"Vamos!"* The man doing the kicking stopped and turned to face Bloom and Wendell. He started to walk toward them and Bloom felt a taste of something sour rising in his throat. He also felt a tingling in his hands and feet, a sensation that, he had once read, was caused by blood rushing from the extremities, a part of the fight-or-flight phenomenon.

The man, who was angrily looking at Bloom, started to take a few steps away. Bloom felt a flash of relief. Maybe they were going to run off. But Wendell had another notion. He shouted to Bloom, "Come on. Let's get them!"

Oh, no, Bloom thought, get them! It was then that he saw the knife in the hand of the man who had been doing the kicking. Bloom could picture the gleaming blade finding its way into his abdomen. Before he could warn Wendell to stand still, the candidate, looking quite unheroic in his running shorts and T-shirt, was throwing himself on the attacker. Bloom bolted after the other man, shouting a warning over his shoulder to Wendell.

"The bastard's got a knife!" He caught up with the fleeing man in an instant and lurched toward him, arms open wide. He felt himself falling on top of the man. As they were going down to the pavement he heard Wendell muttering through clenched teeth.

"He doesn't have a knife now!" The sharp sound of metal hitting concrete rang out reassuringly.

Bloom heard another stream of Spanish invective as the mugger tried to break his hold. Bloom muttered back at him, "Hold still, dammit, or I'll break your fucking arm!" As if to show he could do just that, Bloom grabbed the man's arm and doubled it back on itself into a hammerlock, turning him over on his stomach at the same time.

Now Bloom found himself sitting on top of his captive, forcing the arm up higher until the man shouted out in pain, "*No más, no más!*"

Bloom, his chest heaving more than it ever had on any run, looked over to see Wendell standing, holding the other attacker from behind in a half nelson. The man was gurgling, gasping for air.

Bloom shouted toward two young men he had not noticed before. They simply stood, watching the action. "Call a cop. Do something!" One of the men nodded, as though he had been awakened from a trance, and jogged out to the curb, waving his arm at passing cars. A screech of brakes was of some comfort.

Running footsteps gave Bloom even more comfort. He looked over his shoulder to see two uniformed officers who had arrived in a patrol car. There was a hand on Bloom's shoulder, a firm hand, pulling him.

"It's okay, sir, we'll take it from here." The voice was cool and confident. Bloom looked at the officer. He was a member of the District of Columbia police force. The cavalry had come to the rescue. *After* the attack. But, nonetheless, they had come.

Wendell pushed the man he had wrestled the knife from and wiped his hands on his running shorts, as if trying to remove dirt.

Bloom sat down on a step leading to the Smithsonian's main entrance. He looked at his knees. He saw a deep gash in one of them, feeding a stream of blood running down his leg and into his shoe. He reached to touch the blood and saw still more on the back of his hand. Another gash. He had felt no pain during his struggle to subdue the mugger. He wondered if his head had been split open, too. He felt his forehead and found nothing. His right cheek began to burn. When his fingers touched the spot, he felt the first pain. The sidewalk, or maybe a shoe, had raised what felt like a very large welt under his eye.

"We'd better get you looked at, Jerome." Wendell was standing over him, eyeing the hot spot on his cheek.

Bloom raised his hands and shook his head. He spoke, barely above a whisper. "It's okay. Nothing wrong." Nothing except a couple of gashes and a possible fractured cheekbone. Plus the realization that he had come perilously close to becoming another of Washington's alarming murder statistics.

Bloom looked at the patrol car, still at the curb, with its doors wide open. He pointed to it. "Where did they come from?"

Wendell shrugged. "I imagine they were on patrol and spotted us."

Wendell turned and walked over to one of the officers, who was talking to the victim to whose rescue Wendell and Bloom had come. He seemed to be unhurt.

A small crowd had gathered. Some tourists. A few government office workers on their way home. And now three more District of Columbia police were questioning Wendell. Bloom stayed on the step, waiting for his turn to answer questions about what had happened. It couldn't have been more than three minutes later when he saw a brightly painted truck pull up. Emblazoned on the side were the words NEWS SCENE SEVEN.

Aching muscles had begun to tell their tale of the encounter five hours earlier as Bloom lay stretched out on his hotel-room bed. The television set was tuned to channel 7. He still hadn't had dinner. He had felt no appetite. Wendell had left him in the lobby, after finishing two television interviews, plus one with a reporter from *The Washington Post*. He had been summoned by the president for a briefing on an undisclosed matter. Some international crisis was undoubtedly brewing, and Wendell was to be informed of it. He was, after all, a major candidate for the presidency, and therefore entitled to such briefings.

Bloom felt an electric twinge run through his body when he heard the reporter introduce the story. Over the newscaster's shoulder was a photograph of Wendell, in his running clothes, in front of the Smithsonian. "Presidential candidate Stephen Wendell had a close call with street crime in the nation's capital earlier this evening. However, the former governor of Texas was not a victim. He was out running with his media consultant when he came upon two men committing robbery in front of the Smithsonian Institution."

Running with his media consultant. I've got a name. Bloom reminded himself his role was always in the background. But he still felt cheated of an identity.

"Ironically," the newscaster continued, "the alleged muggers, who were taken into police custody, are reported to be illegal aliens from Cuba. Wendell's most controversial campaign issue is the nation's immigration policies. He has been pointing continually to the crime problems created by the flow of refugees to this country."

Now Wendell was on camera, with a microphone thrust in front of his face. Bloom could see a figure sitting on a step in the background. At least he would be seen. But before he could see if he was recognizable, the camera moved from him and in closer on Wendell's face.

"I find it incredible that such brazen contempt for the law exists here in the shadow of our nation's Capitol. Why must the American people walk the streets of our cities in fear of such senseless attacks? When we allow other countries to empty their prisons onto our shores, we invite the kind of crime we have just witnessed."

Bloom drew in a long breath and slowly let it out in a sigh of frustration with Wendell's rhetoric. This was a candidate who never missed a trick. Events of the day were going better for him than they would have if everything had been scripted. And that troubled Bloom. He wouldn't have created a script this good. If he had, it would have been too implausible.

The phone rang. He was in no hurry to answer. It rang two more times. He finally picked it up.

"Hello?"

"Are you all right, Jerome?" Wendell sounded happy.

"Just sore all over."

"I have good news. I'm still at the White House. The president wanted to brief me on a new crisis developing in Guatemala." Wendell lowered his voice in confidentiality. "But he also wanted to talk about the commercial. He seems to have lost his enthusiasm for holding a press conference to attack my immigration position."

"He must have watched the evening news," Bloom said, not hiding his cynicism.

"I suspect you're right. In any event, he seems

much more open to discussion. I don't see how he can continue to press the issue of unfair tactics when the whole nation has just seen so vivid a demonstration of what we've been talking about."

"We couldn't have staged a better press event if we tried." Bloom conjured up a scene in his mind of a smoke-filled room, where Stephen Wendell was giving Cuban men instructions on how to stage a mugging.

"It's been quite an eventful day, Jerome. Tomorrow promises to be equally so."

"I'm sure it will be, Governor."

They agreed to meet for breakfast at six-thirty. Bloom hung up the phone and stared at the television screen. The newscaster was still reporting the mugging story. Bloom was troubled again when the picture of the victim of the attack came on screen. The face still looked familiar to him. The newsman told him why.

"The victim of the mugging attack is a graduate student from Arizona State University, visiting Washington to apply for admission to Georgetown Law School."

Suddenly the young man's face came into focus in Bloom's memory. It had been an angrier face, far more hostile. He was the one who had taunted Bloom in the graduate seminar on politics and media.

Bloom felt a sense of panic. What was he being caught up in? Only an utter fool could possibly accept coincidence as an explanation of what was happening in this campaign to elect Governor Stephen Wendell president of the United States. Bloom groaned and felt a surge of nausea overtaking him.

11

THE HUGE WHITE STATUE OF ABRAHAM Lincoln looked much too relaxed for what was about to happen to American politics. Stephen Wendell had chosen the Lincoln Memorial in Washington for the site from which to make a major announcement to the nation. He had chosen it for obvious reasons. Too obvious, Bloom had thought. Entirely too corny, this notion of standing in front of the Republican who gave America its first encounter with its own conscience on the issue of freedom and equality for blacks. Colored people, they had been called then. Negroes.

Bloom surveyed the gathering crowd. It looked to him as though between four and five hundred people had assembled at the bottom of the steps of the Memorial. Most of them looked liked the curious, the kind of people who just happen to show up at anything that resembles an event in Washington. Some were dressed for business, the business of keeping the offices working and the payrolls brimming in the various agencies of government. Others were the ever-present tourists, cameras around their necks and guidebooks in their hands. Bloom also noticed a number of college students, probably from Georgetown and George Washington.

The previous evening the Wendell organization had announced it would hold a major press conference at the Lincoln Memorial at noon. The timing assured a good lunch-hour crowd. More important, it gave the television networks time to cover the story and then analyze it for the early evening news. The nation's newspapers would come out second best, since the most important ones were morning editions, and the news, therefore, would be on the stale side for them. But Wendell's press people knew that maximum impact and opportunity existed in the nearly 200 million television sets in America's homes. They also knew the networks, as well as the representatives of scores of local stations around the country, loved the kind of visual opportunity the setting of the Lincoln Memorial provided. As Bloom had once reminded a naive press aide to a Senate candidate, "Television reporters aren't reporting events—they're making them. They're far more interested in being creative than in being informative. Give them a boring story, but set it down in front of an attractive background and let them think they've discovered some brilliant irony in it all, and they'll make you the lead story on the six-o'clock news. Plus they'll come back the next time you call them with another boring story."

Well, Bloom thought, it must still work. Because dozens of television camera crews were setting up their equipment in front of the bottom step of the Memorial.

In a black, four-door sedan, parked at the edge of the surrounding lawn, sat Stephen Wendell, his running mate, Henry Blandemann, Harrison Davis, and Hattie Lewis. All four were looking at sheets of white paper, as though in a final rehearsal.

Bloom felt a surge of excitement when he saw Jeanette walking toward him, dressed in a brown tailored suit and carrying a leather attaché case. She looked both very businesslike and very alluring. She smiled broadly as she approached.

"Nice day for a press conference, don't you think?"

"Great day for photo opportunities," he answered. "Nice to see you again. I've missed you."

"Thanks. I've been thinking about you. But these are the weeks of a campaign when you forfeit your private life. From now until November first, every hour belongs to the crusade, except for the ones we manage to steal for ourselves now and then."

"That's funny. I used to find myself saying that a lot."

"To your wife, I imagine."

Bloom nodded. "Can I see you tonight?"

"I'd like that. It might be a good chance to go over the latest numbers with you," she said, smiling coyly.

Bloom hadn't paid much attention to the five buses that had pulled into the Memorial parking lot. It was, after all, one of the more popular stops on the Washington tourist circuit. But then he noticed that all the passengers getting off the buses were black. Most of them seemed young. And they did not proceed to the Memorial. Instead, they gathered behind the already assembled onlookers.

"What's going on?" he asked Jeanette.

"Beats me. I would imagine they're here to witness the press conference."

"Obviously," said Bloom, not without facetiousness in his voice. "But don't you think the publicity people have gone a bit far with contrivance?"

"I take it, then, that this isn't one of your media strategies."

"Hardly. This one belongs to publicity. The opportunity people."

"Would you have recommended against any of this?" asked Jeanette.

"Probably. And that's why they generally don't seek my counsel on press relations. I would have suggested something far more mundane for today's announcement, with far less exploitativeness. And the campaign would have ended up with far less coverage."

The busloads of blacks were now in place. As if that were the cue to begin, the doors of the sedan opened, and its passengers began walking toward the steps of the Memorial. Wendell and Hattie walked side by side, followed by Davis and Blandemann. Some applause began from the gathered crowd, and it became louder and fuller as everyone seemed to get the signal. By the time the small group reached the microphones, virtually everyone, except, of course, the press, was applauding.

Wendell moved up to the podium that had been placed on the fifth step, and Hattie, Davis, and Blandemann stood behind him. Wendell waved at the crowd, which encouraged them to applaud even more enthusiastically. He continued to smile and to wave, playing to the television cameras below him.

At the precise moment when it seemed as though the press had had enough applause and waving, Wendell held up his arms to silence the crowd. The applause tapered off and, when it had nearly stopped, Wendell spoke.

"My friends and fellow Americans," he boomed, his voice reverberating heroically off the marble walls behind him, "I want to thank you for coming here today to share with me what I believe will be the making of history." He was interrupted, to his obvious satisfaction, by the resumption of applause. And he waited patiently for it to die down before speaking again.

"I must begin my announcement today with news that I know will sadden you as it does me. My good friend and running mate, Henry Blandemann, has come to a very difficult decision. Before he tells you of that decision, let me first say that there is no more courageous, no more loyal public servant than Senator Henry Blandemann. He has been an inspiration to me all the years I have known him and worked with him. And now, I ask him to tell you of the decision he shared with me yesterday morning."

Blandemann looked pale and tired. He managed to smile, however, and to wave at the crowd in acknowledgment of the applause he received. His reception was far less enthusiastic than Wendell's had been, which would surprise no one. Very few voters, in fact, had been able to identify Blandemann as the vice-presidential nominee on the Wendell ticket, according to Jeanette's most recent poll.

"My friends, my colleagues, Governor Wendell," he began, in a subdued voice. "Those of us who have accepted the public trust, by becoming elected representatives of the people, must also accept only the highest standards of personal conduct. I have always gladly acknowledged those standards and tried my best to lead my public and private life in a manner that would withstand the closest scrutiny. For that reason, I have chosen to share with you a problem that has made it impossible for me to continue as a nominee for vice-president of the United States."

The crowd didn't register any particular surprise. A few people whispered to one another, but everyone, for the most part, remained silent and attentive, waiting to hear the rest of Blandemann's statement.

"Tomorrow morning," he continued, "I will enter a private sanatorium, where I will begin an intensive therapy program to deal with a problem of drug and alcohol addiction. In recent months, the lower back injury that I suffered during the Korean War became so incredibly painful that I found myself becoming increasingly dependent upon both alcohol and pain-killing drugs for the temporary relief they gave me. The rest of my story is a tragically familiar one. I soon became addicted, totally dependent, on whatever substances could allow me just a few hours of relief, of precious sleep.

"Until my doctors are convinced I have overcome my dependence, I shall be on medical leave from the United States Senate, and, of course, I am today resigning as candidate for vice-president.

"I discussed my decision yesterday with Governor Wendell. He at first asked me to stay on as his running mate, if I felt I could deal with the stress and demands of the campaign without endangering my health. I appreciate the governor's loyalty, but I cannot accept his offer to remain on the ticket. The mission upon which we have embarked is far too important to the future of this nation to allow my present condition to interfere with its success in any way.

"This campaign, however, has my pledge to continue to support it and work for it in any way humanly possible. I shall miss being on the campaign trail with my old friend. But," he said, turning to Wendell, "I will be with you in every city, at every stop, along every route you travel from now until election day. I wish you good luck and Godspeed on this magnificent journey."

And now the crowd came alive again, roaring its approval of the senator's decision to step aside, but to continue supporting Wendell. Wendell embraced Blandemann, whispered something to him, and then stepped forward to the microphones again.

"Thank you, Senator Blandemann. Our thoughts and our prayers go with you, for a speedy recovery and for your return to public service. We shall never forget the achievements you have made in the past, and we look forward to more of them in the future," said Wendell, now turning back to the crowd.

"Senator Blandemann was the first to say we must carry on our mission with all the energy and all the zeal at our disposal. We are standing on the leading edge of history in our effort to win the presidency, and we *will* win it—not for a political party, or for any special interests, but we will win it for the people of the United States of America."

The crowd roared its approval. What had been

billed as a press conference was quickly becoming a rally for Stephen Wendell.

Bloom, his arms folded, turned to Jeanette and smiled. "The man's hot today."

"By tonight's newscast, he'll be scorching, I promise. And as corny as it sounds, it's giving me goose bumps."

"Along with this news that so saddens us today, I am here to bring you an announcement that should bring joy to the hearts of every American who believes that the door of true and equal opportunity for all should be opened wide enough for the American dream to come through and flourish in the way in which it was designed to flourish.

"Four years ago, the Democratic party took a historic step forward when it nominated Geraldine Ferraro for vice-president. There were some who said the country was not ready for such a step. There were others who said we were ready, but the party that tried to make history didn't understand history enough to succeed. I prefer to believe the latter, that the Democratic party had the right idea, but the wrong ideological platform from which to launch it. The party of Jefferson, Roosevelt, Truman, and Kennedy became the party of the NEA, the AFL-CIO, and the UAW—not of their memberships, but of their management.

"The party of Abraham Lincoln, on the other hand," he said, lifting the level of his voice and pointing to the statue behind him, "the party that built a republic by and for the people—that party walked away from the people—and from the enormous problems facing them—and gave the nation the opportunity to mark time rather than to make history.

"Well, my fellow Americans," he continued, sounding more and more like Lyndon Johnson, "those of us who were ready to write some important new pages of American history are still here. But the difference is, we have gathered together under an entirely new political banner, one that recalls the humanity of Abraham Lincoln, one that looks to the courage of Franklin Roosevelt, and proclaims to the nation and to the world that it is time for a redeclaration of independence!"

This time the crowd bettered its previous outburst of enthusiasm and approval. Wendell's words moved them to begin chanting his name: "Wendell!! Wendell!! Wendell!!" Arms were stretched high and hands were clenched into fists. Bloom looked around and felt himself being carried along in the emotion of the moment.

"You did it," Jeanette said into his ear. "He bought your new theme. More important, the crowd has bought it. Look at them. They know we're going to the top of the mountain."

Bloom felt pride seeing and hearing the crowd respond to the theme line he had created for the campaign: The Re-Declaration of Independence. He also felt awed by the inestimable importance of what was taking place, and the part he was playing in it.

"The American dream is not dead, my friends," Wendell continued. "It has merely been put aside by some forces that find it unimportant. But it has never been more important than it is today, at a time when we are challenged by the incredibly rapid winds of change that are sweeping across our nation and around our planet."

He paused for dramatic effect. Then, lowering his voice, he continued, "Standing with me today, making me proud to never have stopped believing in the American dream, filling me with renewed hope that emancipation has become more than a word inscribed on this great memorial in tribute to one of our greatest Americans, joining me in the rekindling of our most important dreams, is the next vice-president of the United States, Congresswoman Hattie Lewis."

And the crowd of hundreds sounded like thousands, cheering, now shouting two names: "Wendell—Lewis! Wendell—Lewis! Wendell—Lewis!"

Hattie stepped forward, on signal from Wendell, and smiled broadly, waving to the crowd. Wendell held out both his hands to her, which she took. Then, he pulled Hattie toward him, though she hesitated for an instant, and embraced her. Television cameras rolled, still cameras clicked and whirred, and Bloom felt deeply moved by the scene before him. A man of the south now stood beneath the approving statue of Abraham Lincoln, embracing a black American woman and asking the American people to let the two of them ascend to perhaps the most important and powerful offices on earth—to walk together through the front door of the White House.

And now it was Hattie Lewis's turn to speak. When she stepped to the microphones, the gathered crowd seemed to understand the cue to quiet down for her. She looked out over the audience and past them, up to the spire of the Washington Monument, past it to the dome of the Capitol, as if surveying a domain, as though she believed that she could one day rule from it.

"Governor Wendell," she began, her voice containing a melodic quality, as though she were about to begin singing a hymn, "my dear friends and fellow citizens of this great nation. Thank you for both the honor and the challenge you have given me today. I am deeply saddened by the circumstances that have taken Senator Blandemann from this campaign, and Senator," she said, turning to Blandemann, "I, too, pray for your recovery. . . ."

In his cluttered office at his network's headquarters in New York, Grant Chase shook his head as he watched Hattie Lewis's image on his television monitor. Helen Dumont, the reporter who had covered Wendell's union endorsement story, sat on the corner of Chase's desk, smiling.

"You know, it just occurred to me," said Chase. "Wendell's like Jerry Brown, in some respects. He paddles a little on the left, then a little on the right. He started out a liberal, but he saw some new reality and became a jobs Democrat. He saw the implications of illegal immigration, and now he's challenging the old notions of America's open arms and doors."

"Do you hold that against him?" asked Dumont.

"I guess I've just never met a Texan or a politician that I liked."

"Not a bad line. Going to use it on tonight's commentary?"

"I may possess balls, Helen, but not quite that large."

On the monitor, Hattie Lewis continued speaking. "And now, I join this magnificent mission, this redeclaration of independence that has been created by Governor Wendell."

"Shit," said Chase. "Now *she's* using that goddamn line. I wonder what hack came up with it."

"And our redeclaration," Lewis continued, "will be carried across the land in the remaining two months of this campaign. It will be carried not by any special interests, by any corporations, by any power structure. It will be borne, proudly and strongly, by individual Americans who want to shape their own destinies as we move into the future together. The banner will be carried by white hands and black and brown hands, by young and old hands, by laborers and bankers, teachers and students. Out of the disunity that has been spawned by our political parties, we will create a new unity. And I will be there, alongside Stephen Wendell, as the banner and story are taken to the people of America.

"It will not be an easy task. But no historic change has ever been achieved without hardship and adversity," she said, her voice stronger and even more melodic. She pointed back to the statue of Lincoln. "Emancipation did not come without pain and hardship. But he overcame—just as we shall overcome!"

Chase nodded at the screen. "Smart lady. Bring back the Reverend King now."

As though she had heard Grant Chase, Lewis

said, "Yes, my dear and good friends, my brothers and sisters throughout this nation, the Reverend King told us not long ago that, one day, we shall overcome. As we take this mission to the American people, we fear not the resistance, the skepticism, the intolerance that will be rallied against us. No, we do not. Because, deep in our hearts, we know we shall march forward together to a new and rare opportunity, to heal a divided people, to restore the unique American dream, to rebuild American confidence, to rediscover our pride and purpose. We shall write history between now and November. I ask every American to join with us in that magnificent process. Let your best dreams and hopes guide your decision when you cast your vote for the next president of the United States of America. If you do, you will choose, as I have chosen, Stephen Wendell.

"Join hands with us now, lift up that banner with us, march throughout America with us, and help us overcome whatever challenge may stand before us. Thank you, and may the Lord bless you!"

A cheer burst forth from the crowd. And faintly heard, behind the cheer were voices, singing, "Deep in my heart, I do believe . . ." And then more voices joined. "We shall overcome some day." The singing grew louder and stronger, until Wendell and Lewis joined raised hands, and they, too, began singing, together and, for many Americans, ironically, the hymn of the American civil rights movement.

The floor director signaled Grant Chase to stand by. In the large, high-ceilinged studio, everything remained darkened except the one corner in which Chase's set stood. Overhead lights, covered by opaque, white fabric, cast a soft, forgiving glow on his head and face, covering, together with makeup, many of the lines and creases of too many days in the sun of the Caribbean and the Maine coast.

The familiar signal to begin came from the young man standing next to the television camera, along with the red light that winked on, telling Chase he was now being seen by several million Americans.

"And now, let's go to Grant Chase, standing by in our New York studios. Grant, what has happened today in Stephen Wendell's campaign?" The question, coming through a small studio speaker, was asked by Clay Bennett, one of the network's Washington reporters.

"I would say that Governor Wendell took a rather sizable step forward today, with the announcement that his running mate will now be Congresswoman Lewis. He's written some history, on more than one front. Not only has he chosen the first black woman in history to be a vice-presidential candidate, but he has also become the first independent candidate to seriously threaten both major-party candidates. His is a genuine coalition. He has selected a liberal Democrat to share his independent, conservative ticket. He is a pro-lifer, running with a pro-choice advocate. It all makes for one of modern politics' most interesting set of paradoxes."

"You're saying, then, that Wendell's chances have substantially improved?" was Bennett's next question.

"They would have to be. You cannot form the kind of coalition Wendell has without benefiting from it. I would venture a guess that his campaign will gain several points in the next few days. And, interestingly enough, the gains should come equally from the Democrats and the Republicans. Many black Democrats will find a new home, now that Hattie Lewis is in it; women Republicans will find a new reason to step away from the party that walked away from them in 1984. Not to mention more and more blue-collar Americans who can now begin to believe Wendell's claim that he is trying to safeguard their jobs with his seemingly radical immigration position.

"Yes, I would call it a very good day for Stephen Wendell. In fact, it might become a spectacular day for him. You can rest assured the machinery for measuring today's success is already running full speed, as the polling specialists are directing the thousands of phone calls required to present an accurate assessment of voter preferences. It's my guess that Wendell's research people are already rubbing their hands, while his opponents' people are wringing theirs."

Bloom was writing a radio script that needed to be produced the next day—a script that was directed toward urban blacks—when he heard the knock that had to be Jeanette's. He went to the door and opened it, excited at seeing her again, although it had been less than twenty-four hours since they watched the Lewis announcement together. They kissed briefly, and Jeanette walked past Bloom, smiling broadly.

"Six points since yesterday. Six points in twenty-four hours!" she exclaimed. "Can you believe it?"

"I guess I can. You already have the numbers?"

Jeanette patted the side of her attaché case. "Of course. What do you think I did all last night?"

"I don't know. I was wondering."

Jeanette looked at him, showing puzzlement. She shrugged. "Well, I was up until four going over the spreads as they came in." She sat down on the bed and flipped open the lid of her case. "We did well across the board," she said, pulling out a thick stack of computer printouts.

Bloom sat down next to her, looking more at her face than at the stack of papers. Jeanette ignored his misdirected attention and continued. "We pulled up a full twelve points with black men, and fourteen with black women. Look at this," she said, pointing to a column headed with C M/F + 30. "We gained two points with Caucasian undecideds over thirty. And the party breakouts are fascinating. Here, Republican men, down one point, *but* Republican women, up five points for Wendell."

"You're excited as hell about the way things are going, aren't you?" asked Bloom.

"Of course I am. Do you realize what this all means?" she asked, putting her hand down on the spread sheets.

"It means what was a crazy damn dream a couple of weeks ago is becoming the possible."

"That's right. And we're part of it. I can't believe how calmly you're taking it all. You're doing absolutely brilliant work—your commercials, the themes you're developing. But you're acting like I just showed you the latest football scores, instead of a turning point in American history."

"Maybe I don't pay the proper respect to polling.

But it's probably only because I don't understand it enough. I still have trouble believing people will tell strangers the truth about how they're thinking and voting over the telephone."

"We're getting better at accuracy all the time. The techniques we're using now are getting the error margin down to one half of one percent when we sample seven hundred respondents."

"What are you doing different? People will still tell you only what they want you to hear," said Bloom. "Someone may tell your interviewer he likes the idea of a black woman vice-president, and that he'll vote for her. He thus proves to some stranger that he's really a tolerant man. But then maybe he turns around on election day and says, in the privacy of that little booth, 'I ain't about to vote for a guy who's going to have a nigger waiting for him to get killed so she can take over.' I think people in your business call it the 'halo effect'—voters telling you what they want you to think about them, instead of what they're really all about. I know it happens with television ratings. 'I only watch news and public TV.' But they really spend forty hours a week watching sitcoms and football."

"But we have much more sophisticated techniques now," said Jeanette. "We've developed a feedback system that actually tells us if we're being given false data by a respondent."

"I don't get it. Feedback?"

"We do it with our computers. When we get you on the phone, your conversation back to us is fed into a data processor that takes audio input. We first set up a quick profile of you with our early questions. What do you do for a living? What's your education? Where do you live? Where do your children go to school? You'd be amazed how our computer can draw a picture of your personality in just seconds. Then we ask the kind of questions that set up cross-references against known data. If the computer says your answer doesn't ring true, it kicks in a few more test questions. If you still answer inconsistently, we know it, and your interview is discarded."

Bloom whistled. "Jesus, you're giving people lie-detector tests without them knowing it."

"It's only the beginning of where technology is taking us in politics."

"You mean there's more? What's better than one half of one percent margin of error—other than no percent? Then what?"

"Don't get nervous, but we're getting into your area next."

Bloom was becoming increasingly uncomfortable. He had been concerned for some time about the role that data gathering was playing in campaigning. On several occasions he had felt it necessary to remind polling consultants that their role was to provide information, not to persuade voters. He had always maintained that campaign commercials written by pollsters would do nothing to voters except put them to sleep. It was part of a creative petulance Bloom was known for and, generally, forgiven.

"What are you and your computers going to do for us—or *to* us—next?" asked Bloom, playfully holding Jeanette by the shoulders.

"Look at this," she said, picking up a computer-typed letter from her stack of papers.

Bloom glanced at the typed page, which had a salutation of *Dear Mr. Doe:* It was a brief letter. Its opening paragraph got right to the point. *Has either political party done anything to help you stay out of debt? What have either the Republicans or Democrats done to help you make it from paycheck to paycheck?*

The rest of the letter was predictable. It urged the reader to invest ten dollars to help get himself, and his fellow Americans, back to financial solvency. More important, the letter said, was the recipient's vote in November for Stephen Wendell, the candidate who offered a solution to the public debt that had become the private burden of millions of Americans.

"What's different?" asked Bloom. "It's the same debt story Wendell's been telling all along, except maybe that it's pitched more directly to people who think they're in financial trouble."

"That's precisely the difference. This letter will go out to fourteen million people who had personal financial trouble in the last year—people who had their credit cards canceled for nonpayment, car repossessions, mortgage defaults. Those are the people who Reagan's economic blunders hurt most—and who the Democrats' promises can help the least!"

"Wait a minute. You mean you're getting lists of people in trouble, and you're going to mail to them? Come on. First of all, there's no legal way to get that kind of data."

"Oh, no? Are you familiar with credit-reporting bureaus? Every bank and credit operation in the country belongs to them, and has the right of access to their information."

"Sure, banks and stores have access. But not political campaigns."

Jeanette smiled. "The campaign fund-raising operation set up a time-payment plan for individual donors, remember? That put them in the credit business. And it got them membership in every major reporting bureau."

Bloom was angered by what he was hearing, but also impressed by the shrewdness of it all. "Jesus Christ, talk about the end of privacy! That's terrible. If I get delinquent on my car payment, a politician can find out about it and use the information to his advantage. Talk about cheap exploitation."

"I know. It's awful," said Jeanette, feigning guilt. "It's sort of like appealing to people who love their country with a television commercial that tells them immigrants are going to tear down the Statue of Liberty."

Bloom glared at Jeanette. "Touché," he said, grabbing her and pulling her down on top of him on the bed. They both broke into laughter. "Guess none of us in this business is a virgin anymore," he said. And he kissed her, hard and long. Her body responded to his embrace.

"I can't," Jeanette whispered into his ear. "I've got to meet with Davis in half an hour."

"That gives us twenty-five minutes," said Bloom, beginning to unbutton her blouse. "His office is a five-minute walk."

"You're incorrigible in your lust," she whispered,

pulling him closer to her. "But then, so am I. You're beginning to do that to me."

They did not remove any more clothing than was necessary to allow them to make hasty and intense love, taking full advantage of the short time they had.

The formality of Davis's office had always made Jeanette uncomfortable. Today, however, she had reason to be especially uncomfortable as she sat in the wing-back chair facing Davis, who sat erect behind his massive mahogany desk.

"You're late," he said.

"Only five minutes," Jeanette replied.

"Where were you?"

"I stopped by to show Bloom some of the new numbers." She disliked referring to Bloom by his last name. She did it as some kind of reassurance to Davis that it was strictly a business relationship she was pursuing with Bloom. Nothing more involving than that. But her mind's focus was still on him, on what, just minutes earlier, had taken place.

"Perhaps you should have been just a few moments later, my dear. That way, you could have finished buttoning your blouse."

Jeanette's hand went reflexively up to her blouse, which had one button still open, revealing the top of her lace brassiere. She dropped her hand down again, though, defiantly.

"I trust Bloom liked what he saw." He paused and smiled. "The new numbers."

"Look," said Jeanette. "I'm paid to do a job for you."

"For the organization," Davis corrected. "And you're paid extremely well."

"And I think I'm earning my fee." She now reached up and took care of the open button.

"I simply want to remind you that we have an enormous task ahead of us, and that nothing can come before it."

"I'm well aware of that," said Jeanette. "Have you seen today's tracking figures?"

"Yes, I saw a copy of the printout only an hour ago. The movement we anticipated as a result of the Hattie Lewis announcement is up to our expectations. Your polling people are operating efficiently. As for our friend Bloom, he's an eminently useful component of this operation. An emotional man, but you, fortunately, are not a very emotional woman. You can help get his total loyalty and his best effort for us. However, if you become emotionally involved, you might not be able to perform to full capacity. That was my point."

"It's amazing," said Jeanette, fidgeting in her chair, "how you are able to totally dismiss people as nothing more than useful objects, as you've done with Jerry Bloom."

"As I said, my dear, you are not an emotional person. I suspect you have the ability to be as objective as I can."

Jeanette's eyes welled with tears, and Davis noticed it immediately.

"Perhaps I'm wrong about your unemotional nature. Your tears are a new phenomenon for me."

"I'm sorry. I had forgotten how perfectly free of emotion you prefer me to be. But, dammit," and her voice began to break, "I'm human—sure I can control my emotions. But I'm not devoid of them."

"I haven't yet told you my plans for tonight."

"Sorry. Just what *are* your plans? I'm sure they must involve me."

"We shall have dinner at eight. I want to discuss some additional analysis we will require starting tomorrow."

Jeanette stared at Davis, who neither smiled nor showed any anger. He looked as though he were posing for a portrait to hang in his library—nothing but business.

"I'll be here at eight," said Jeanette, her voice barely audible to Davis. She picked up her attaché case and walked to the door, opened it, and left the room.

Back in her hotel room, Jeanette paced nervously with an energy level that would not let her sit. She went to the telephone, picked it up, and began to dial the number of Bloom's hotel. Before she finished dialing, she hung up. She wanted to speak with someone other than Harrison Davis. She missed Bloom's company. And she felt the recurring, painful loneliness when she thought of her late husband, Jeff. She went to her attaché case, opened it, and took out a handsome brochure. The title on the cover read THE JEFFREY WELLS MEMORIAL FILM INSTITUTE. She opened the cover and looked at the picture of Stephen Wendell. Beneath it was a letter to the reader:

It has been an honor to serve as chairman of the Jeffrey Wells Memorial Film Institute. The Institute's programs will encourage new, young film documentarians to record through their art and craft the events of our times, as Jeffrey Wells did so brilliantly in his brief lifetime. His enormous talents will serve as an inspiration to other young filmmakers, who have the courage to search for truth and meaning with their cameras. Mr. Wells's film on the immigration crisis facing this country, which was in progress at the time of his death, will soon be completed and distributed through the auspices of this institute. It is our continuing hope that the work of the Institute will serve as a living tribute to Jeffrey Wells, and to the work he stood for.

Sincerely, Governor Stephen Wendell.

Ever since the fatal shooting of Jeff Wells, Jeanette had been consumed by the unfinished work he had begun, and by her need for some form of either justice or revenge for his death. In Stephen Wendell, the man responsible for the creation of the film institute, Jeanette had found both a fitting tribute to her husband's work and some small sense of justice, through Wendell's continuing campaign to substantially change the country's immigration policies. Jeanette somehow had held millions of illegal aliens responsible for the death of her husband in the Los Angeles riots. Her obsessive outrage at her husband's death had caused an inconsistent ideological change in her. Once the committed liberal, the champion of most liberal and minority causes, she was now an ardent nativist. And the Stephen Wendell candidacy offered her the chance to see her views furthered. But now she felt another change beginning to take place, and she was not comfortable with herself. It was the return of something visceral, a signal of a rekindling. And it occurred when she thought of Jerry Bloom. This was precisely the kind of feeling she had vowed would never return, and she told herself to be careful. As Davis had reminded her, there was work to be done. And she wasn't being paid to become emotionally involved with anything or anyone.

Jeanette went to the bathroom and turned on the water in the tub, making it as hot as she could stand it. A scalding bath, she had found, generally helped when she feared she might once again have to deal with feelings.

12

NO ONE HAD MORE TO DO WITH the shaping of Stephen Wendell's life than his friend and associate of thirty-five years, Harrison Davis. They had met at the University of Texas College of Law, when Wendell was a first-year student and Davis a senior. Wendell was trying to earn his own way through law school. His parents, who had suffered through a lifetime of barely successful farming, had no money with which to educate their son. Wendell had managed to scramble through undergraduate school with a combination of scholarship aid and a series of odd jobs, from waiting tables in fraternity houses to scrubbing floors in the student union.

It was September 1953, when Stephen Wendell received his first taste of political activism. He had worked all summer on an enormous ranch in west Texas. He was an all-around hand, helping with the cattle roundup and branding, as well as working on the harvesting of orange groves. Most of his fellow laborers were migrant workers from Mexico. At first he had assumed they had been brought to the ranch through legal means. However, when he finally won the trust of some of the men, he learned they were all illegal aliens. The ranch owner had been paying them less than half of what he had promised when he had first recruited them. When they realized how much they were being cheated, a handful of the laborers met late one night in their Quonset hut and talked about taking action. They invited Wendell to their meeting and discussed their problems with him. Several of the men were opposed to taking any action; they felt they would be turned over to immigration authorities and deported, with no pay at all. They had also heard rumors that other aliens who had protested their treatment and conditions had been beaten by the foreman. In one case, a Mexican national had been shot and killed.

Wendell addressed the men in Spanish. "You have the right and the power to get justice. Clarence Peterson owns this ranch, and all the cattle and all the orange groves on it. But he does not own you. Yes, you are in this country illegally. But you were recruited in Mexico by Peterson's people. Therefore, he is obligated to pay you what he promised you. He also must be held accountable for your poor living conditions and for not providing decent food for you. Our country has not tolerated abuse of its own working people. We must remind the government that mistreatment of alien workers will not be tolerated either.

"There are two hundred and fifty Mexican nationals working on the Peterson ranch. There are at least another two thousand working on other ranches within fifty miles of here. I have heard that conditions on other ranches are as bad as they are here. There are cattle to be rounded up and branded, and there are orange and grapefruit trees to be harvested. You must realize that if you refuse to work anymore, this ranch, and other ranches and farms nearby, will lose valuable crops, and cattle will not get to market.

"You must gather together. You must organize, so that you can deal with Peterson through strength. None of you has the voice to be heard alone and to cause things to change. But all of you, together, have one voice that can be heard, and that can cause things to change."

A small, thin man in his fifties, looking tired and hungry, his eyes reddened, with a scruffy beard framing his face, stood up and spoke in a low voice to Wendell. "Mr. Wendell, you have been a friend to us. It has taken us time, but we have come to trust you. We know you want to help us. But you cannot ask us to form a union to go on strike like the Americans in your cities do. We are Mexicans—spicks, panchos. Your police, your courts, they would laugh at us—or spit on us—if we were to try to act like American workers, and to form your unions. We are at the mercy of Mr. Peterson. We must ask him to understand that we are hungry, and that we need the money we were promised. If he does not wish to honor his promise, we have no choice, except to finish our work and go home when it is done."

A younger Mexican worker, leaning against a bunk bed, yelled, "No! Peterson does not care to listen to our complaints. He only cares to use us, and to steal from us. Mr. Wendell is right. If we do not band together, with one voice of strength, there is no hope. Let us get all the other Mexicanos in Texas to join with us, and we will strike, and there will be no orange harvests or cattle roundups this fall. Will you help us, Mr. Wendell?"

Wendell looked around the room at the men. They were all awaiting his answer. He saw their hunger, their anger, their fear. He nodded slowly. "Yes, I will do whatever I can."

"Be careful, my friend," said the older, bearded man. "The American authorities will not be happy with you if you try to help us. The only thing worse than being a Mexican here is being an American who wants to help Mexicans."

"Perhaps it's true in some cases," said Wendell. "But I still have faith that there are people here in Texas who understand your troubles, and will help you. Remember, this is a country that was built and made great by people from other parts of the world. And it is also a country that has learned to recognize its wrongs and its injustices, and has eventually taken steps to correct those wrongs."

That night, in a Quonset hut on a sprawling Texas ranch, Stephen Wendell promised to help Mexicans seek redress. Nothing was decided in the way of taking action. But the men promised to talk to their fellow workers, and to form an organization and appoint a spokesman to present their grievances to Peterson and other ranchers.

When fall classes began at the law school, Wendell left the ranch and returned to Austin. Before he left, he reminded the men he had befriended of his pledge to help them. He didn't think, however, that he would hear from them again. He understood how difficult it would be for them to band together and risk their safety in a hostile, foreign land.

Wendell was taken by surprise one evening in late September when he was told he had a visitor waiting to see him outside his dormitory. The visitor turned out to be the older Mexican man, who had been fearful of organizing on the ranch. He was now clean-shaven, and his shoulders were not nearly as sloped forward as they had been that night in the Quonset hut.

"Mr. Wendell," said the man, "we are ready."

"You're ready to band together?" asked Wendell.

"No, my friend, we have already banded together. We are now ready to act. We are going on strike in the morning. Fifteen hundred of us will refuse to work tomorrow. We will gather outside the main gate of the Peterson ranch."

Wendell felt a tingle run throughout his body in anticipation of what would happen the next morning. His pulse quickened, and he felt a surge of pride in having worked with these men and having encouraged them to take action in the interest of justice.

"Do you want my help?"

"Yes, we need to know that it is not just us making this protest, asking for justice. We need to know there are Americans who feel as we do, who are willing to help us. And I think your authorities here need to know that."

Wendell thought for a moment. He remembered the promise he had made in the summer. He had seen the fear and desperation on the faces of the men that night when they talked about unity, about righting wrongs. And here, at age twenty-two, without money, but with the means with which to be heard, Stephen Wendell decided to step forward and be counted for something more important than his studies and his career. And, in the back of his mind, he could not help but think that standing up and speaking out might, in fact, be helpful to him at some time in the future.

The next day at eight o'clock on a warm, bright Texas morning, Stephen Wendell took the first step on the road that led to his prominence in politics and to his eventual belief that virtually anyone can go to the top of the political mountain, a belief that one day would lead him to the brash conclusion that he could be president of the United States.

Wendell had no car. He left his dormitory at 4 A.M. to begin hitchhiking the seventy-five miles to the front entrance of the Peterson ranch. Only because he stood in the middle of the state highway did he get a pickup truck to stop for him. He offered the driver, an old and weathered farmer, the last $4.84 he had in his pockets to take him where he needed to go. The farmer mumbled something about damned crazy college kids, told Wendell to keep his money, and agreed to give him a ride. Wendell arrived nearly two hours before the scheduled protest time. This gave him the chance to mingle with the men as they pulled up in trucks or arrived on foot. He must have shaken the hands of six or seven hundred people by the time eight o'clock arrived. Many of them called him by name and thanked him for what he was doing.

A few minutes before eight o'clock, a yellow school bus pulled up in front of the gate to the

Peterson ranch, and some thirty uniformed Texas rangers climbed out. Following directly behind the bus were two television news cars filled with reporters and photographers from Austin television stations. Wendell was not very surprised at the sight of the rangers. He was, however, surprised to see the television news crews arrive. He assumed they had been told by someone in the rangers that trouble was anticipated at the ranch gate. The officers formed a single file in front of the gate and stood at parade rest. They did not attempt to make contact with the gathering demonstrators. The members of the two television news crews quickly set up their equipment and stood by.

At eight o'clock, the old man who had twice spoken to Wendell stepped forward. He raised his arms, asking the crowd to be silent. To Wendell's surprise, the man who only a month earlier had been fearful of even discussing any form of protest, was now emerging as a leader. He called out to the crowd, in Spanish, "My friends, my brothers. Please, be quiet. Please pay attention."

The crowd didn't seem to hear him. They were talking to one another, looking concerned about the rangers. Someone in the group walked forward and handed the man a portable bullhorn and gestured at him to use it. The man looked at it inquisitively, and held it to his lips.

"Please, my friends and brothers. Can you hear me now?"

The gathered protestors now became quiet. The man introduced himself. "My name is Rudolfo Martinez. I have been asked by many of you to be a spokesman on our behalf. I feel that I am maybe too old to lead a group like this. I have worked on the ranches and in the orchards for many years, alongside some of you, and alongside your fathers. Today, it is time to ask for justice and fairness from the people who come to our country and bring us north here to work. Until our demands are met for fair treatment and for the pay we are owed, we will do no more work on these ranches."

The crowd applauded and murmured approvingly. The uniformed officers still remained silent. Wendell felt something very important was happening today. And he knew he had made the right choice in becoming part of it.

Martinez continued talking to the crowd, giving them instructions on how to conduct themselves during the strike, offering words of encouragement. Wendell was startled to hear his name mentioned.

"And Stephen Wendell, who has also worked with us in the fields, who is a North American, but one who understands the wrongs we must make right, is alongside us today. He will help add to our voices, the voices of our friends in the United States who wish to see justice for all of us. I now give you Stephen Wendell, our friend."

Wendell went to Martinez, who was smiling and who held out the bullhorn to him. Before taking it he looked back at the line of rangers. He saw one of them smiling and whispering to the man next to him. He heard several of the Mexican nationals in the crowd shout his name, then some applause as he took the bullhorn and faced the group.

By now, the television cameras were rolling, and they were filming Wendell as he began to speak, in Spanish. "You have done a wise thing to join together today. You have also done a courageous thing. I urge you to carry out this protest peacefully, and to break no laws. I know you are lawful men. I also know most of you are fearful that because of what you are doing today, you will be sent back home to Mexico with no pay at all. The officers behind me are members of the Texas rangers. I am sure they have been called here by Mr. Peterson and the other ranchers, who found out what you were planning to do today. I want you to know that these officers have one purpose here today. That is to frighten you enough to make you go back to work and drop your demands. My friends, this is America, a free and fair country. Do not be frightened by the presence of these officers. If you do not break the law, you have nothing to fear. Yes, it is possible you may be deported. But I know enough about our law to tell you that since you were brought here by the ranchers, you have a right to remain here as temporary workers until you are paid. And I will help you claim that right.

"Let the word go out to all the ranchers and farmers who each year bring you across our borders that a new day has come for migrant laborers. You will be paid a fair wage and you will be given decent living and working conditions, or you will not work, nor will any of your brothers from Mexico come up and replace you. These ranchers need you. You now must withhold that work until your demands are met. There are legal channels through which you can become temporary, working residents of this country. There are also channels through which you can eventually become citizens. I am pledged to help you find those channels. But first you must pull together and say to the ranchers who abuse you 'No more work! No more work!'"

The crowd picked up Wendell's rallying cry and began to chant. Wendell felt a tapping on his shoulder. He turned to see a face he had seen only in newspapers, the face of the owner of the huge Peterson ranch. "Wendell, my name's Peterson. You've gone and stirred up an awful lot of trouble that we don't need here. I hope you're prepared to answer for it."

Wendell stared at him and said, "You have heard what we are prepared to do, Mr. Peterson. We intend to operate completely within the law and to pursue the rights to which these men are entitled."

"Well, sonny, you can begin by getting your smart ass off my ranch property."

"I would be most pleased to do that, sir, if I were standing on your property. However, I am on a public, county road. I have no intention of entering your ranch. I do, however, have every intention of seeing work stopped on your ranch until you negotiate in good faith with these men."

Peterson backed away from the hand-held microphone that had been placed by a reporter between himself and Wendell. Wendell saw the microphone, but did not back away. He said, "No more work, Mr. Peterson, no more work."

That evening, shortly after the six o'clock local news, while sitting in his dormitory room, Wendell was visited by Harrison Davis, who had come by to introduce himself and to congratulate him. When Wendell answered the knock at his door, Harrison Davis entered through it, standing tall and erect, and smiling graciously.

"This has been one hell of a day for you, Wendell. Welcome to your first step onto the political ladder."

"Would you mind telling me who the hell you are, and what the hell you're talking about?"

"Gladly. I'm Harrison Davis. A senior. As far as what the hell I'm talking about, I'm talking about what you did out at the front gate of the Peterson ranch today, with those migrant workers. You've been on two local newscasts, and I've just heard that one of the networks is going to pick up the story. You're just barely into law school and you've carved yourself a nice little political niche around here. I like to think I can spot a winner, and you look like one to me: That's what I'm talking about."

"Wait a minute. What I did out there had to do with a whole lot of people who were getting nothing but mistreatment here in Texas. I don't know a damned thing about politics, and I'm not so sure I want to. These people need help, and they're not going to be able to cut through the bureaucracy on their own. In fact, they're not going to be taken very seriously. After all, they're just a bunch of wet-backs, right?"

"I admire your sense of commitment," said Davis. "It's that kind of commitment that gives people a start in the political arena. And I happen to think you have the stuff of which a good political career could be shaped. After all, don't forget this is that great country in which anyone—even a struggling law student who can't meet his tuition payments— can one day reach out for and obtain the very highest of political dreams. This is the country where any little boy and, someday, any little girl, can grow up and become president, remember?"

"Wait a damn minute," snapped Wendell. "What is this business about being behind in tuition payments? Where in hell did you get that information?"

"It's very simple," replied Davis. "I was impressed with you, and I made it my business to find out what I could. A friend of mine, who happens to work in the records office, told me, among other things, that you were behind in your tuition payments."

"Well, maybe it's true. But it's none of your business, or anyone else's. It's between me and the University."

"I appreciate your sense of pride," said Davis. "And I wouldn't want to see someone with the stuff you're made of denied the chance to finish law school and go on with his plans."

Wendell tried to figure out what this brash, presumptuous student was all about. Was he some rich man's son hoping to salve his conscience by helping out less privileged students? Or did he have other motives? Why did he want to be Wendell's friend all of a sudden? Surely it couldn't be just that he wanted to associate with someone who had a brief stint in the public limelight. He wondered if he had a homosexual on his hands. In those days such a notion was removed from reality, and if it ever came close to reality, it was viewed with repulsion. However, Wendell's concerns on that score were quickly put to rest. Shortly after they met, Davis invited Wendell to go to the Texas–Aggies football game. He said that he had run across an extra ticket and wanted Wendell to join him and "a couple of friends from Dallas" for the game and perhaps a few beers afterward. The "couple of friends" turned out to be two absolutely beautiful and, obviously, very wealthy women in their early thirties. That afternoon and most of the following night became the most memorable sexual experience in Wendell's young life. At halftime the two women decided the game was boring, and insisted that Wendell and Davis join them for some "more interesting fun." What ensued was a marathon party in a spacious suite of rooms at Austin's finest hotel. Champagne and Scotch flowed freely, the women's clothes came off quickly, and Wendell's question about Davis's manliness was answered with dispatch.

At four o'clock the next morning, an exhausted Wendell stumbled up the steps to his dormitory room with the help of Davis, who was managing the effects of the night's activity and alcohol far better than Wendell was.

"Why did you set all this up?" asked the weaving Wendell, as he tried to open the door to his room.

"Law school is an ordeal for those who take it seriously. Every now and then some strenuous diversion provides a welcome recharging. Tomorrow morning, when you've sobered up, you'll not need to worry about walking around with an unappreciated erection, at least for a while. You'll be able to concentrate more on your studies. When it's time to clear things out again, let me know, and I'll see if I can be of help."

"Sounds fair enough to me. I hope you can do as good a job recruiting next time."

Wendell fell into bed, and was quickly overtaken by a delicious sense of utter exhaustion. A thirty-five-year friendship was thus begun. Davis repeated his offer to help with Wendell's finances, and the offer was eventually accepted. Wendell had to choose between borrowing from Davis and dropping out of law school. Davis assured him that things would be kept on a businesslike basis, and that he would expect full repayment of the loan.

Wendell worked forty hours a week while carrying a full load of classwork. By doing so, he was able to repay Davis by midsummer of the following year. After Davis graduated and went to work in one of Austin's more prestigious law firms, the two men continued to stay in touch with one another, and their friendship flourished. Davis continued to encourage Wendell's efforts on behalf of migrant workers. Wendell became active in other civil liberties affairs, and became a prominent figure in what were the very early days of the movement, long before Birmingham and Tuscaloosa.

Wendell soon realized that Davis was right, that he had taken the first step onto the political ladder when he stood in front of the gate at the Peterson ranch with the protesting migrant workers. He had a strong sense of commitment to causes. In addition to the migrant workers, he felt a kinship with the small farmer in the southwest. He had watched his family struggle year after year to scratch out a living on a small farm. His parents remained ever loyal to the Democratic party of Franklin Roosevelt, and Wendell, although he felt let down by the party, joined its ranks as a delegate to the 1956 state convention. Davis introduced Wendell to the Young Democrats of Texas, and Wendell soon became an officer of the group. One year after he graduated from law school he became president.

After he finished his clerking, Wendell was invited to form a law partnership with Davis. It was flattering, yet not unpredictable. They opened a small office in Austin, and Davis pursued small-business clients, while Wendell specialized in immigration law. Wendell would one day realize the irony of his early work on behalf of aliens. His political career began with his efforts to open wider the gates of entry into the United States for immigrants, and it reached its culmination when he launched his campaign for the presidency, with a commitment to close America's borders to the tide of immigration that was posing so great a threat to, in his view, the country's economic and social well-being. But, as he once reminded his friend Davis, "Politics can forgive a man for being wrong, but it can never forgive him for being irrelevant." Wendell firmly believed he was as right thirty-five years earlier when he encouraged easier immigration, as he was today when he pledged himself to make immigration virtually impossible.

Davis was always at Wendell's side, as the young idealist pursued a political career in his home state. In 1960 he ran for the state legislature in a traditionally Republican district. He was unopposed in his party's primary, and won an upset victory in the general election, beating his firmly entrenched incumbent opponent by four percentage points. He was subsequently reelected three times, before moving to Dallas, where he ran for the state Senate and won that office. He and his law partner, Davis, opened new offices in Dallas. After two terms in the Texas Senate, Wendell was ready to step up to his long-planned goal: the governorship. He ran in a highly contested primary race for the Democratic nomination. He won, by a very small margin, and went on to win the governorship in a landslide, in a state in which the Democratic primary was the real deciding race for statewide office. One day Wendell would bolt from the majority party, over his high-tech posture and his new immigration policies, and register as an independent.

At his inaugural reception, Wendell was greeted by a man who looked familiar to him, but whom he could not quite place.

"Congratulations," drawled the man. "It's been a long road from my front gate to the state Capitol, Governor Wendell."

Wendell then recognized Clarence Peterson, the powerful and wealthy rancher against whom he had led the migrant workers in their protest of his treatment. Peterson had aged well, and still looked rugged and fit, in spite of his seventy-some years.

"Thank you, Mr. Peterson. I'm not sure that things began for me that day. But I've always hoped that all of us, who wish to treat our working people fairly, can make important strides forward by negotiating in good faith, as you did back then."

"I have a feeling, Governor," said Peterson, "that this is not the end of the political road for you. Yes, sir, something tells me this country is going to hear more from you one of these days. Who knows where you might go next?"

"Thank you, sir. However, I want to assure you that I'm quite content serving in this office, and I can imagine no more important goal for me."

"Well, we'll see about that, Governor. We'll see," Peterson said, smiling and nodding as he turned to walk away.

13

WITH JUST FIVE WEEKS LEFT until election day, Davis had to be very careful about his activities. Now that Wendell's candidacy was receiving full attention from the nation's press, it was becoming more and more difficult for him to meet with certain of his colleagues, most of whom were known neither by the public, nor by Wendell. That explained his trip to Denver. He had told Wendell that he needed to work with the Colorado organization and would spend no more than one day there.

At Stapleton Airport, Davis got into a cab and asked to be taken to the Fairmont Hotel, where he had reserved a room for one night. When he checked into his room, he immediately called a local telephone number and said to the party at the other end, "Good morning. I've arrived at my hotel. I shall be downstairs at the main entrance in twenty minutes."

He then dialed another number, and after hearing a voice with a Middle-Eastern accent answer, he said, "We will meet you in front of your hotel in thirty minutes. We will be in a gray Cadillac. Please wait out front for our arrival." And he hung up the phone.

The large gray Cadillac, with Colorado rental license plates, pulled up in front of the Fairmont entrance precisely twenty minutes after Davis's phone call. He went to the waiting car, opened the passenger door, got in, and shut the door. He said to the man driving, Clarence Peterson, "Thank you for agreeing to come here to meet with us. I don't feel comfortable meeting in Texas right now."

"No problem," said Peterson. "I think it makes sense. And it sure as hell keeps us out of range of those bastards in the press."

Davis gave Peterson directions to their next stop. They soon pulled up in front of a small residence hotel, the Evans House, just two blocks away from the Colorado State Capitol. Waiting in front was Aram Saraf, dressed impeccably in suit and tie, and wearing dark glasses. As soon as the car pulled to a stop, Saraf opened the rear door and got in. He said only, "Good morning, gentlemen," as Peterson drove away again.

"Well," said Peterson, "it looks like we've got us a meeting. I'm going to drive out toward the mountains. They look pretty this time of year, don't you think?"

Neither of the two men answered him.

Peterson tried to begin a conversation again. "Well, now, it seems to me Governor Wendell has made this thing a real horse race. I would say that right about now he's got both of the other candidates scared shitless, since he was the one who was smart enough to sew up every black in the whole damn country who was waiting to march behind their precious Hattie Lewis."

"I would hope," said Davis, "that we could exercise caution in speaking about the congresswoman. You know what can happen when the slightest offhand remark is made public."

"Dammit," said Peterson, "the reason I picked a car for a meeting is there is no way in hell anybody is going to listen to us here."

"It seems to me it's a rental car," said Davis, looking out the window.

Peterson said nothing, but shook his head, obviously not sharing Davis's caution.

Saraf finally spoke. "I think we should begin our discussion, which is about money, correct?"

"That's right," Peterson said, "we're here to talk about the next two million that's got to go into the direct-mail effort. The one that's going out from Citizens for Financial Responsibility."

"My associates would like to know more about your people," said Saraf. "We only know that they are very wealthy and very powerful men, like you, who are in the American oil business."

"That's right, they are. And that's about all the information about them that we're prepared to give your people."

Davis spoke up. "Why is it important to know names?"

Saraf replied, "Our people are cautious. You cannot blame them for wanting to understand who it is they're dealing with. They were only told that we all have a common goal, to help create new American policies through a new president, policies that will benefit your oil interests here in America, and the international goals of our countries."

"Right," said Peterson briskly, "we think we can see a policy come out of Washington that's going to get the price of our oil a hell of a lot higher than it's been since the liberal Jews and Commies got control of this country and put the clamps on us. And we're finally going to put a stop to all the immigration that's tearing down a country that some people put a hell of a lot of sweat into. You, on the other hand, are going to get a little more help in squashing that enemy of yours, Israel."

"There are, of course, no guarantees in this business," said Davis. "You are investing in futures, helping to rewrite a chapter in American history, by uniting behind a man who can truly make a difference. It is hoped that that difference will accrue to both your benefits. But, again, I must remind you there can be no specific promises."

"That's okay," replied Peterson. "You put all the disclaimers out there you want. But I know, and Mr. Saraf, here, knows, we're going to be a couple of damned important stockholders in Governor Wendell's administration if he becomes President Wendell."

"And what of the question of the names of your associates?" asked Saraf.

"Sorry. I'm afraid you're going to have to have faith in us, like we have faith in your folks."

"I will discuss the matter with my brothers, in the hope they will agree to proceed on that basis," said Saraf.

"Good," said Peterson. "I'll deposit our two million in the Financial Responsibility account this afternoon. It'll show as a collection of smaller contributions from smaller groups around the country—in cash, of course."

"And our matching contribution," said Saraf, "will go to the printing company as payment for printing and mailing services for my country's industrial development agency. We will, of course, have invoices and shipping receipts for appropriate verification."

"Very good, gentlemen," said Davis.

Peterson continued driving west on Interstate 70, until he arrived at the base of the foothills near Golden. He turned south toward U.S. Highway Number 6, which would take them back to Denver via another route. There was very little further conversation. What there was was limited to working out details of the next deposits of money from Peterson's colleagues and from the Arab factions represented by Saraf. Peterson went first to Saraf's hotel, where he again pulled up in front and dropped him off. Saraf said nothing when he left the car. He glanced back over his shoulder, as though checking to make sure no one was observing him, and went into the hotel. Peterson then drove on to the Fairmont Hotel and pulled into the entranceway. He held out his hand to Davis. Davis looked at it for a moment, and then offered his own.

"It's been real nice seeing you again," said Peterson.

"Yes," said Davis. "Your generous help is most appreciated. It's imperative, of course, that Governor Wendell does not know anything of the part you have agreed to play, or of Mr. Saraf's involvement. I'm sure you understand why. I cannot stress enough the importance of confidentiality."

"Remember, I'm not new to this game. I know how it's played. I treat it like most of my other investments," said Peterson.

"Good. It's clear we understand each other."

Davis opened the door and left the car. He did not glance back as it pulled away. The cheerful doorman said, "Beautiful day here in Denver, isn't it, sir?"

"Yes, indeed," said Davis. "A very fine day, thank you." And he went through the revolving door into the lobby.

Peterson did not drive back to the airport to return to Austin. Instead, after dropping Davis off at his hotel, he drove out of the city on Interstate 25, south toward Colorado Springs. Approximately thirty miles outside of Denver he turned off the highway and took a county road eastward, into an area known as the Black Forest. It seemed almost like an oasis in the dry, brown rolling hills. Dense groves of pine trees covered the hills and valleys as Peterson continued in a southeasterly direction until he came to another county road; this time it was dirt and gravel, not blacktop. The road wound around several hills and dropped down into a basin of tall grass. Peterson stopped at an iron cattle gate, which blocked a private road. A neatly lettered sign on the gate said PRIVATE PROPERTY. ATTACK DOGS PATROL 24 HOURS. TRESPASSERS WILL BE PROSECUTED.

Peterson parked his car and walked to a small wooden box bolted to a fence post beside the gate. He opened it and took a black telephone from its cradle. He dropped the phone and jumped backward as a huge German shepherd jumped from behind some brush and flew against the chainlink fence, teeth bared, snarling and growling, trying to break through the barrier and get to Peterson.

"You fuckin', goddamn mongrel, if I had a gun I'd shoot your ugly head off," shouted Peterson, embarrassed at his own reaction, picking up the telephone again. He heard a voice at the other end.

"Identify yourself." It sounded like a military command.

"It's Clarence W. Peterson, to see Thomas Kern."

"The colonel is expecting you. Security will be at the gate in two minutes. Please wait in your car until someone arrives."

"I wasn't exactly planning to sit on the gate with these goddamn dogs you got loose out here," said Peterson, turning to walk back to his Cadillac.

He didn't bother to time the arrival of the security guard, but something told him it was exactly two minutes later when a man dressed in green military fatigues pulled up to the gate in an open Jeep. He got out, leaving the motor running, said something to the dog, and reached to pat it on the head. He ignored Peterson until he unlocked the gate and swung it open. Then he motioned to him to drive through. Peterson started the car's motor and pulled up behind the waiting Jeep. The man came to the car, showing no expression at all. When Peterson lowered the window on his side, the man leaned closer and checked the empty backseat.

"If you'll follow me, Mr. Peterson, I'll take you up to the ranch house."

Peterson looked at the large holster on the man's hip. It held a .357 Magnum. "You expecting an invasion or something?" he asked.

"Security is very important these days," was all

the expressionless man said. He reminded Peterson of someone. He was in his early thirties, with an angular face, deep-set blue eyes, hollow cheeks, and a neatly trimmed beard that followed his jaw-line. The fatigues, the baseball cap, the aviator's sunglasses—it all added up to a picture Peterson thought he had seen recently.

After following the young man for approximately two miles, Peterson arrived at a large stone-and-frame ranch-style house, unimpressive in its design, but large enough to be respectable, even by Texas standards. With its brown-stained walls and porch and its green roof, the house almost had a military appearance. An oversize American flag, fly-ing from a tall, white flagpole, added to the re-semblance.

A tall, well-built man with closely cropped white hair, wearing silver, rimless eyeglasses, stepped onto the front porch from inside the house as the two vehicles approached. He, too, had a military air about him. His clothes were monochromatic; he wore a khaki bush jacket over an officer's shirt of the same color. His trousers were olive drab. His face didn't show much color either. His eyes were dull gray; the forehead that pushed back his hair-line was pale and his eyebrows were gray. The man was Thomas Kern, a retired army colonel who had, after twenty years of meritorious service, "struck it rich" in the oil fields of Texas and Oklahoma. He had begun as a wildcatter, with three shallow wells, and now was worth in excess of a billion dollars, according to gossip columnists and trade-press re-porters. But with all his wealth and all the power it brought him, he still cherished the rank with which he had retired from the army, and preferred to be called Colonel Kern, rather than Mr. Kern, Tom, or sir. Just Colonel. And Clarence Peterson knew it.

"Colonel, you're looking fit as ever," said Peterson, extending his hand to his host, who took a few steps forward, still unsmiling, to greet him.

"Clarence, it's good to see you again. It's been a while, hasn't it?"

"Too long, Colonel, much too long. We've got us some catching up to do."

Kern held the door to the ranch house open for his visitor, while the intense young security guard climbed back in his Jeep and drove off, back toward the front gate. Inside the house, everything seemed to be made either of thick cowhide or heavy pine, or a combination of the two. The wooden floor was too highly varnished. The few pictures that hung on the knotty pine walls were photographs, for the most part, of groups of soldiers and military memorabilia.

Over the mantel, where most men would hang a trophy head or large painting, was an oversize photo of Ronald Reagan, with a scrawled greeting: *To Colonel Hank Kern, a good soldier and a loyal friend. Ronald Reagan.* The room was, altogether, as inviting as a military barracks.

Kern offered Peterson a large leather chair, told him to make himself comfortable, and asked if he would have something to drink. Peterson looked at his watch before requesting a glass of bourbon, straight up. Kern obliged by walking to a pine cabinet, opening its doors, and pouring two glasses of Jim Beam. He sat down in a brown leather chair next to his guest, still unsmiling, appearing quite concerned about something.

"Clarence," said Kern, "I need to be brought up to date on these Arabs we're dealing with."

"I just met with our main contact, this fellow Saraf. He's holding up his end of the bargain. The money's coming in right on schedule, and it's clean as a whistle."

"But you said they were giving you some trouble."

"Well, as a matter of fact, they are. It's about us. They're asking for the names of everyone involved. Which is a switch. In the beginning, they didn't seem to give a damn who they were working with, just so long as we were helping them get a piece of the action."

"And that troubles me, Clarence. From the start, we've agreed that we can't risk public exposure. All it would take would be one persistent reporter to put our operation on the ten o'clock news, once he got a few names. We can't chance it, Clarence, we just can't."

"I know. And I told Saraf his people simply had to continue the way they started, operating in good faith, just the way we are, without a bunch of names that wouldn't mean a whole hell of a lot to them anyway."

"Well, I'll tell you something, it took two years and a small fortune to get our wire into Pennsylvania Avenue, and I'm not about to risk it now. Speaking of which, I found out today the president is still planning to cry foul over the immigration commercial. Just like everything else he's done for eight years, he's sat on the thing so damn long, we all figured he forgot about it. But he's planning a press conference for the day after tomorrow."

"From what I hear about the mood of the voters, I don't think he can hurt us at all. In fact, our friend the lame duck might just give us a nice boost. Now that we've got us a black woman on the ticket, Wendell isn't about to get in trouble with the liberals on that issue. They're beginning to think he's just a high-tech realist now, instead of a right-wing hard ass. If the president pours it on, they'll figure Wendell's being victimized by all us powerful conservatives. Shit, Colonel, we're smelling real good."

"Maybe we are," said Kern, staring into his glass of bourbon, "but we're not giving out any names to those people. Especially now, with our new associates in the picture."

Peterson shot a nervous glance around the room, making sure no one else was within earshot. "You mean the people who want to"—he paused, having trouble even whispering the words—"to take out Hattie Lewis? They're really serious?"

Kern nodded slowly. "It shouldn't surprise you. You've known all along that the people who are putting the real money into this effort would never tolerate a black vice-president—a female black vice-president, sitting over Wendell's shoulder, waiting for a heart attack or, more likely, a bullet to make her president."

"It's crazy," said Peterson. "The thing that can put us over the top now is Lewis on the ticket. She's bringing blacks and liberals—even some Jews— over in droves. But now we're saying she's got to go."

"Only when she has served out her usefulness. She can have her moment of glory. She can make history and be elected vice-president. But she cannot take office. She's pro-Israel, for one thing. We promised Saraf's people a whole new tough policy on Israel in this country. For the first time, the Arabs will be able to confront the Israelis without fear of military intervention from the United States. And when the OPEC ministers decide to turn off the oil flow, getting our prices all the way up to sixty bucks a barrel, we need Stephen Wendell in the White House, not a black Marxist."

Peterson smiled. "You see it going to sixty?"

Kern nodded again. "With the kind of help we'll get from those sheikhs, you can count on it."

"Good God, we're going to make us some change."

"Billions, before we're through," said Kern, "while we keep the country from falling into the hands of the Communists. They don't have to launch a single missile. They've got control of unions, the civil rights bleeders, practically the whole damn Democratic party. This is the real war, Clarence. If those people win it—people like Hattie Lewis and her friend Jesse Jackson—the oil business will be history. They'd nationalize it, like everything else. You and I wouldn't be selling crude, Clarence. We'd be lucky to have a job in the fields. With a Mexican for a supervisor."

"Who's going to do this thing—this Hattie Lewis plan?"

"A fanatic terrorist, of course. You know how brazen those people have become." Kern smiled for the first time. It was not a pleasant or happy smile.

"There's no stopping them once they get it into their head to carry out a suicide mission against their enemy. And they now believe that Lewis will be a mortal enemy if she is ever elected vice-president. They will see her elimination as the only way to protect Stephen Wendell, their new 'friend' in Washington, and, more important, to protect their plans for Israel. They can easily find a skilled lunatic willing to give all for a ticket to paradise." He splayed his fingers. "Poof. . . ."

"Jesus," said Peterson, "this isn't just a presidential campaign anymore."

"It never was, Clarence."

"Somebody's putting a contract out on a U.S. congresswoman. Who in hell is doing that?"

"You just spent some time with him, in Denver."

"Come on, that damn Saraf? He wouldn't take that chance."

Kern shook his head. "You're right."

Suddenly, Peterson turned much paler. He began to perspire.

"Davis?" he finally asked. "You're telling me Harrison Davis is fingering his own vice-presidential candidate?" He looked as though he had stumbled into a whole new world that was too incredible to be real.

"He 'fingered' no one. He merely counseled people who didn't fully understand the consequences of a Wendell–Lewis victory."

"Does Wendell have any idea of what's going on?"

"Of course not. How can you even ask? He doesn't know I exist. He thinks you're just an old adversary who got rich and wants to see him lose. And he knows nothing of our partnerships in the

Middle East. In fact, he's convinced that his new policies on Israel would actually help the Jews, by ridding themselves of the radicals in power. Stephen Wendell wants more than victory. He wants to be a president who will make a difference, who can have a positive dramatic effect on this country's course. And that's what makes him so useful. He'd be dangerous to us if he were in this for profit of any kind. His commitment to his ideologies will blind him to any of our goals."

Peterson simply stared out the window, troubled and deep in thought. He had done quite a few questionable things in his lifetime, most of them for profit, but none with the intent of breaking laws. He was now privy to—could it not be said a participant in?—a plan that had already broken several federal election laws, and which could eventually result in violation of man's most inviolate law. This business he had become a party to could end in murder.

"You look like you could stand some fresh air," Kern finally said. "Come on, I'll show you around."

Peterson agreed, saying nothing more than "Okay." And he followed his host outside. The young security guard had returned in the open Jeep. Kern motioned to it and got into the front seat, after Peterson sat alone on the rear bench seat. Kern nodded, and the driver pulled away. They drove off in a direction opposite from the main gate, up a steep, tree-covered hill. At the crest of the hill, Peterson could see down into a wide, flat valley, looking like the bottom of a bowl, with hills rising up on all sides. The bottom was three to four hundred yards across. Peterson was stunned by what he saw there. At least twenty strange-looking aircraft were lined up, wing-tip to wing-tip, in two rows. They were very small, with open cockpits and wingspans of no more than ten feet. The fabric covering their wings was painted in green and brown camouflage patterns. The collection of craft looked like an absurd, tiny air force. Several men were working around the little planes, gesturing, as though giving instructions to one another.

"Are those ultralights?" Peterson finally asked.

Kern smiled his strange smile again. "Not just ultralights. But the state of the art. There isn't a piece of metal in them. Everything's made out of fiberglass or plastic."

"Which makes them radarproof?"

"Exactly. And something else. Listen." Kern cocked his head, as though straining to hear something.

"To what?" Peterson was puzzled.

"That's the point. You can't hear their engines running, can you?"

"There's an engine running?"

"Four—wait, five of them are running," he said, pointing. "They've got a new muffling system that makes them as quiet as that Cadillac you drove down here in. They can fly low enough to be undetected, either by their sound or by radar."

"What are you planning, Colonel, some kind of invasion?"

Kern ignored the remark, in his usual, humorless fashion. "A pilot of one of those craft can go just about anywhere, especially at night, and stage a surprise mission at will."

"What kind of mission?"

"That's why I brought you over here. You're about to see a demonstration," said Kern, checking his wristwatch. "There," he said, pointing behind Peterson. The now incredulous Peterson turned to look back over his shoulder. He squinted into the bright sunlight and saw a small object, which at first appeared to be a crow, flying toward the two of them. As it came closer, Peterson could see it was one of the tiny aircraft, climbing up the hillside, no more than twenty feet off the ground. Then he could see a man stretched out in what appeared to be a harness, keeping him prone on the underside of the craft. The little airplane passed directly over them, and then took a sweeping turn around the ring of hills surrounding the basin. It came back and the pilot steered it down, still noiselessly, toward the center of the flat, grassy field. Just as its wheels were about to touch down on the surface, an explosive crack sounded and a large puff of reddish smoke engulfed the craft.

"Jesus, he crashed the thing," shouted Peterson.

Now Kern smiled again, shaking his head. "No, it landed just fine. And the pilot is all right. See? He's climbing out."

Peterson could see the smoke clearing away and, to his amazement, the small craft was sitting on its three wheels, quite properly. The pilot was coughing and trying to drive back the smoke with his flailing hands, but was, otherwise, all right.

"That was merely a simulated explosion, to test an altimeter-triggered fuse device."

"That was supposed to be a bomb?"

"That's right. It's armed before takeoff. A very precise altimeter, accurate to one foot, is programmed with the altitude of the target, which is, of course, always lower than the point of takeoff. When the pilot reaches his target, he needs to do nothing, as long as he has properly navigated himself there. The moment he hits the altitude of the building, the car, or the driveway, let's say, the explosive charge is automatically detonated."

"And the pilot gets blown away, along with his plane and his target," said an even more amazed Peterson.

"Pretty ingenious, don't you think, Clarence?"

"I guess it is, Colonel. It's like something out of World War Two. The kamikazes. But where are you going to recruit pilots for these one-way trips?"

"I'm sure you're aware of how easy it has been for Moslem causes to enlist operatives for their attacks on embassies and the like. Don't forget how easily they killed so many of our boys in Beirut. All it requires is enough conviction in a cause, especially if it's a religious one. Then you'll have volunteers lining up to serve."

"Not in this country, you won't."

"You're probably right. We lost the will to die for a noble purpose a long time ago. 'Better red than dead' was a self-fulfilling prophecy. No, when a mission must be carried out against the enemy, such as, let's say, hitting a limousine on the freeway, it wouldn't be hard to find a young pilot who wants to fly into his Almighty's arms, serving his cause and dealing a blow to his enemies."

"I see your point, Colonel," said Peterson, his hands beginning to tremble as he tried to picture a tiny aircraft plowing into the side of a black vice-presidential limousine, engulfing everything in flames, rather than in reddish practice smoke.

Twenty minutes later, Peterson was back in his rented Cadillac, driving much too fast along the winding, county roads, as though he were trying to escape from a pursuer just over the horizon.

14

WITH ONLY THREE WEEKS RE-
maining until election day, no
one could have possibly ex-
pected the National Association of Teachers to completely break with precedent for the second time in
the presidential campaign. Following a closed-door
meeting of the executive committee of the board of
directors, which lasted from six o'clock on Sunday
evening until 4 A.M. Tuesday, a telegram went out
to each of the fifty state association presidents. It
contained the following message:

> Our association decided in June to withhold en-
> dorsement of either the Republican or Demo-
> cratic presidential candidates for president, in
> an historic departure from our traditional prac-
> tice. We did so because our membership was
> convinced that neither candidate was suffi-
> ciently supportive of our goals and, more im-
> portantly, of the continued quality educational
> opportunities for America's children.
>
> However, we have been closely watching the

candidacy of Governor Stephen Wendell. As an independent candidate, he has offered some positive alternatives to the two major parties. During the late summer and early fall, we considered an endorsement of Mr. Wendell, but our board still had sufficient questions concerning his educational policies. Since that time, he has clarified his positions regarding education, including the reestablishment of the Department of Education, and he has provided insight into the threat to our public school systems that is posed by excessive and unregulated immigration.

Ten days ago, Governor Wendell once again demonstrated a commitment to the goals we hold in common, by appointing as his vice-presidential running mate Congresswoman Hattie Lewis, who has been a friend of public education since the day she first took office.

Early this morning, your national board voted unanimously to immediately endorse the candidacy of Stephen Wendell and Hattie Lewis. We urge you to ratify this executive action by telephone or wire, no later than six o'clock this evening, eastern standard time, so that we may maximize what opportunities for support are available to us in these remaining days of the campaign.

> Yours for better education for America,
> Dorothy Silver
> President, National Association of
>   Teachers

By five-fifteen, forty-nine state associations had

phoned or wired their ratification of the endorsement resolution. Only one state, Texas, had not been heard from. Since the pending endorsement had been known about and discussed for nearly a week, the ratifications amounted to little more than foregone conclusions, designed to satisfy the NAT's constitution. The president of the Texas Association of Teachers, a young science teacher at a Houston high school, Robert Hanson, told his board that Stephen Wendell's policies were clearly racist. The board members challenged him, pointing to the nomination of Hattie Lewis as hardly the action of a racist. Hanson held fast, and managed to convince three other board members to join him in refusing to endorse Wendell. At five forty-five, Hanson received a telephone call from Harrison Davis. At five-fifty-five, Hanson phoned Dorothy Silver and apologized for the delay. He was pleased to report the Texas association's support of the Wendell–Lewis ticket. He did not reveal to Silver the nature of his discussion with Davis, nor did he reveal it to anyone else.

In his private Washington office, Davis picked up the ringing telephone. It was Dorothy Silver, happily announcing the confirmed and unanimous support of the National Association of Teachers. She did not know what caused the young man in Texas to reverse his position, but she was pleased with his last-minute change. Davis didn't seem surprised, and he thanked Silver graciously. He hung up the telephone and turned to the personal computer beside his desk. He looked at the screen on which was printed the following data:

Hanson, Robert. Pres. Texas Assn. of Teachers. Science teacher, Hamilton H.S., Houston. Age: 36. Never married. Had homosexual relationship with former college roommate, John Steinman. No charges ever brought by students, but some Hamilton staff and parents suspect he made advances.

Davis smiled and hit the STORE key, and entered his personal code. The data instantly disappeared from the screen for electronic safekeeping.

Bloom fidgeted with a felt-tipped pen with one hand and held a yellow legal pad in the other, waiting for the president's press conference to begin. His hotel room at the Washington Regency was littered with storyboards for television commercials, and other various-size pieces of paper, some with typewritten copy and others with layout drawings on them.

"Ladies and gentlemen," said the voice coming from the television set, "the president of the United States."

The presidential seal was replaced with a close-up image of the president, who looked tired and somewhat troubled, in spite of his broad, familiar grin.

"My fellow Americans. I have requested this time to talk to you about a matter of utmost importance to the elective system by which we govern ourselves in this free nation of ours.

"As you know, this presidential campaign, in which, I am happy to report," he said, breaking into a slight chuckle, "I can sit on the sidelines and watch—or maybe do a little armchair quarterbacking—this campaign," he continued, no longer smiling, "has become a very unusual one. We have seen, for the first time, a third-party candidate receive enough support to be in close contention with both major party candidates. Now, a case can be made in favor of, and in opposition to, the concept of a three-party system. As a loyal Republican, it should come as no surprise that I continue to favor our traditional system of two major parties, although there have certainly been times when I would have welcomed a good alternative to both sides of the congressional aisle.

"However, what concerns me is not the notion of an independent candidate for president. Our constitution clearly provides for valid candidacies from more than the two major parties. What *does* concern me, very deeply, I might add, is the way in which the third-party candidate has been conducting his campaign."

Bloom wondered if the president would mention Wendell by name at all. He assumed some strategic advice had been given against it. He, himself, had given similar advice in the past: One mention on a national press conference, in prime time, can add five points in name recognition for a trailing candidate.

"The candidate," said the president, "has resorted to tactics that I find not only distasteful, but divisive. He has chosen, as his principal issue, immigration. I applaud his choice of that issue. It is, in fact, an issue I myself feel strongly about. My position on immigration reform is clear. We need to protect our working citizens from the consequences of unrestricted immigration of illegal aliens. But it is the excessive tactics the candidate is using with which I take issue.

"I'd like to show you a vivid example of the kind of campaign tactic I'm referring to." The president reached down and pulled up a large piece of black cardboard with eight frames of illustrations on it. Bloom felt a twinge surge through his body when he saw the camera move in to a close-up of a copy of his storyboard. Millions of Americans were seeing the blueprint for a television commercial he had created. It was a kind of notoriety that came with mixed emotions. He could not resist the feeling of pride in the implied importance of his work; he was angered at the premature exposure of it, before the finished commercial would begin airing the next morning.

"Tomorrow morning," the president continued, "a television commercial based on this visual outline will begin appearing on every television network. Let me read what it says."

It all seemed so absolutely unreal to Bloom. Now the president of the United States was going to read aloud from a script he, Bloom, had written. Frame by frame.

"Now some people might find that commercial clever. I find it not only offensive, but inflammatory as well. I have, therefore, filed a formal complaint with both the Federal Election Commission and the Fair Campaign Practices Committee. I have also asked the attorney general to seek, in Federal District Court, an injunction barring the broadcast of this particular commercial, because of its inflammatory nature.

"Most important of all," he said, in his most intense, sincere delivery, "I am asking you, out of your sense of fairness and decency, to reject this message, this misdirected attempt at political persuasion. When you see the effort for what it is—a new depth to which political campaigning has fallen—I am confident you will reject it. I am also confident you will think very carefully before you turn away from two fine men, one Republican, the other Democrat, who are running for the presidency."

Not too bad for an old lame duck, Bloom thought. He's pretty convincing in his nonpartisanship. Vote for the Republican or the Democrat, he doesn't care which. Bullshit. He knows damn well that anyone who takes his advice about Wendell is going to march out and follow the Republican nominee.

"I'm reminded of something once said by a politician—by a Democrat, in fact. We will only get the kind of government we deserve. Well, the American people deserve something much better than the so-called alternative being offered by the independent candidate. Now, are there any questions?"

The camera pulled back to show the usual reporters jumping to their feet, calling out, in unison, "Mr. President!" Predictably, the first question was about the president's party. How would it react to his nonpartisan stance, to his recommendation to vote for either the Democrat or the Republican? The president's response was equally predictable. He guessed, in his inimitable, down-home fashion, that members of his party would just have to accept that this was the country's chief executive speaking, not his party's standard-bearer. There was a time to be political and a time to be appropriately neutral.

Bloom felt that he might actually miss the old man after January. As much as he disagreed, sometimes vehemently, with virtually everything he had done and stood for, he admired the president's showmanship, his ability to reach out to a nationwide television audience and do the kind of job that let everyone go to bed feeling a little better about things over which they had no control. He had it, this man with the broad, naive grin—that rare quality that could have made a president like Jimmy Carter revered, rather than forgotten, by the American people, without having done one single thing differently while in office. That, Bloom mused, was both the most beautiful and the most insidious thing about politics.

Bloom turned off the television set and paced about his hotel suite. He wondered if the president's attack on the immigration commercial would hurt Wendell. He had felt it would not, but now, after having seen the president in action, Bloom challenged his own appraisal. Maybe, he thought, voters would feel a sense of guilt over the president's charge of racism. Or they might, instead, realize the hypocrisy of a president who actually had turned back the clock on the progress that had been made in civil rights prior to his term in office.

Bloom tried to turn his attention to his current project: a series of three television commercials that were to air in the final two weeks of the campaign. The immigration commercial would break the next morning, regardless of the president's denunciation of it. To date, six other spots, plus ten radio commercials, had been the media mainstay of the national campaign. In most of the fifty states, specially produced or adapted commercials had been running locally. Local adaptions had also been planned for the immigration commercial. In New York, for example, a naturalized Italian immigrant and an elderly Jewish man from Russia would be intercut into the commercial, telling viewers that they had struggled for years to gain citizenship through hard work and study; now their symbol of hope, the Statue of Liberty, was becoming a crumbling monument to politicians' lack of understanding of changing times and circumstances.

Bloom thought about the work he still had to do. It was six-thirty in the evening. He had not made plans for dinner, hoping Jeanette would finish with her work early enough to join him for a brief break. He had been doing most of his writing in his hotel suite lately, finding the campaign office too noisy, with too many interruptions. He sat down at the typewriter and stared for a few moments at the blank sheet of white paper. Finally, he began typing.

VIDEO:

A man who looks like a tour guide, or an archaeologist, is pointing to the torn, tattered remains of a picture of an elephant. He is speaking to a group of interested people. The setting is futuristic, indicating a time that is years from now.

AUDIO:

GUIDE: Now, can anyone tell me what this is?

STUDENT: A dinosaur?

GUIDE: Close. It's the symbol of the old Republican Party.

Guide moves over to another tattered picture, this one of a donkey.

GUIDE: And this was the symbol of the other so-called major party.

ANOTHER STUDENT: A jackass, right? (laughter) What did these parties do?

GUIDE: Supposedly, they provided people the tools with which to effect change, to solve problems. But they failed when they couldn't keep up with the times.

STUDENT: When did they die out?

GUIDE: In the late nineteen-eighties.

Camera pulls back to show the rest of the tattered posters, side by side; one says VOTE REPUBLICAN, the other, VOTE DEMOCRATIC. An electronic effect comes in and wipes them both off, spelling out the slogan: VOTE FOR WENDELL/LEWIS. AMERICA'S RE-DECLARATION OF INDEPENDENCE.

ANNCR: Time has run out on the old political parties. But it's only beginning for a new, independent America. Vote Wendell/Lewis.

Bloom took the paper out of the typewriter and

reread it, holding his pen at the ready to edit. He read the copy aloud and timed it with his runner's stopwatch. It was, as usual, about six seconds too long. He began his familiar surgical work, picking up a word or two here, trimming down a phrase there.

He realized the commercial was a bit on the syrupy side. But it was what everyone had concluded was needed—a positive statement about the new independent ticket out of a negative statement about the old political system. It was also quite typical for any campaign, which had been on the attack with negative messages, to show some nervousness about being too hard-hitting, too strident and, therefore, running the risk of turning off voters. Bloom had seen it happen time and again. This time, he did not resist the effort to put out some positive messages in the closing days of the campaign. Like chicken soup, he thought, it might not cure anything, but it certainly couldn't hurt.

Bloom's thoughts were interrupted by a knock at the door. He tucked in his shirt and smoothed his hair, in anticipation of a surprise visit by Jeanette. The surprise, however, was quite different from what he had hoped for.

"I hope I'm not disturbing you," said Stephen Wendell, standing in the open doorway, smiling politely. Behind him were two Secret Service agents. "May I come in?" asked the candidate. Bloom was so stunned, he could only nod at first.

"Perhaps I *did* disturb you," said Wendell.

"No, not at all. I'm just surprised to see you here, Governor. Please come in." Bloom stepped aside to let Wendell enter. The Secret Service men remained in the hallway.

"Sorry about the condition of things here," said Bloom, noticing how much of a mess there was in the living room of his suite.

"Don't apologize. It looks to me like you've been hard at work. If things were too orderly, I'd have something to worry about," said Wendell, who seemed to be in a positive enough frame of mind, considering there were fewer than twenty-one days remaining in his bid for the presidency, and still several percentage points separating him from his opponents.

Bloom cleared off the sofa and offered his guest a seat. He also offered him something to drink. Wendell accepted the seat, but not the drink. He explained he had to deliver a speech at the Washington Press Club, and he could ill afford to have any alcohol before facing the scrutiny of the national press corps.

"I wanted to deliver your latest fee payment, Jerome. I believe it's due tomorrow."

Bloom had forgotten that another $250,000 payment was due him the next morning. It was not as though he needed it to cover his mortgage or car payment. Wendell pulled a white envelope from his pocket, with MR. JEROME BLOOM typed on the front, and handed it to him. Bloom took it and, for an instant, was not sure what to do with it. He was still not accustomed to seeing checks for a quarter of a million dollars with his name on them. He reached down and slid it into his black canvas briefcase, which was conveniently leaning against his chair.

"Thank you, Governor. You really didn't have to

deliver it tonight, though." Bloom knew full well that Wendell knew—full well—that he didn't need to make the personal delivery. But he felt awkward and didn't know what else to say.

"Jerome, I wanted to have a little chat with you as we approach the homestretch in this effort of ours."

"Fine. It's been a while since we've had a chance to talk." Bloom could not help but wonder if something had gone wrong, if Wendell had become displeased with his work. Or maybe he wanted to rethink some of the commercials.

Wendell seemed to have read Bloom's thoughts. "First of all, I want to assure you that I'm very pleased with the work you're doing for us. It's first-rate. In fact, it not only lives up to my expectations, but it has, at times, exceeded them. I appreciate both your talent and the diligence with which you're working."

The words relaxed Bloom and lowered his natural defenses, which went up whenever a client wanted to have a chat with him. "Thank you, Governor, I appreciate that. As you can imagine, we don't always know just how well we're doing in this business. It's hard to measure our performance."

"Well, rest assured, the performance is measuring up quite nicely. Jeanette Wells can attest to that. I hope you're staying in close touch with her."

Bloom wondered if Wendell could see his face flush. "Yes," he replied, "her polling seems to indicate we're getting through." He could not help but see a mental picture of Jeanette, her blouse unbuttoned, her hair in disarray, when they had made hasty love before her meeting with Davis.

"Actually, what I wanted to discuss, Jerome, is your view of my candidacy."

Bloom's mind raced for some clue of what Wendell was after. "From every indication I can see, it's succeeding. If we do things right, you're going to make it, I'm convinced."

"I appreciate the reinforcement," said Wendell. "But I'm referring to your view of what I'm saying to the American people, more than your assessment of my chances for success."

"I'm not sure I understand," said Bloom.

"One thing I've discovered about you, more than anything else, during this campaign, is that you're a true ideologue. You measure people by where they position themselves on issues and concepts. You judge them according to a moral compass, and how unswervingly they follow its points. Am I correct?"

Bloom thought a moment or two before answering. "I suppose you are, Governor. But I'm the first to admit that I'm not exactly Mahatma Gandhi, spinning my own clothes. You're paying me a million dollars for what I do."

"That does not necessarily make you less of an ideologue. I'm convinced you would not have accepted my offer had you not found sufficient moral justification for doing so and, therefore, for my candidacy."

"Well, I have to be honest with you. It wasn't easy to arrive there. Maybe I'm still too much of a knee-jerk liberal. The black-and-white answers of the sixties never left my system, apparently. A dear friend of mine recently told me so." Wendell cocked his ear curiously. "Your running mate," Bloom added.

"In any event, I'm glad you arrived where you

did. And, as I said, I'm curious about your view of my candidacy as it now stands. Have I delivered what I promised you when we first met?"

Bloom laughed, looking toward his briefcase. "You pay your bills right on time. Early, in fact."

"I'm talking about the things I said in regard to the course this country must take. I told you the Republicans and Democrats had become irrelevant. And I promised you we would offer something better, something more in tune with the times. Am I doing that?"

"According to the research I'm seeing, the people believe you are."

"And do you include Jerry Bloom in your research?" It was the first time Wendell had called him anything but Jerome.

Bloom nodded as he thought about his answer, looking down at his feet. "Yes, I do include myself now. At first, though, I had a hard time believing you, and, therefore, an equally hard time justifying taking your money. But what you're saying to the people is making sense. I still won't try to hide my disagreement with a big part of your immigration position."

"I know that commercial you did got you rather pissed-off with me." That was the second surprise in Wendell's choice of language.

"No, I was pissed at myself for doing it. I can't forget my background."

"Nor can I," said Wendell. "Your parents—and mine as well—believed America's gates must be opened as wide as possible. But those were the days of Ellis Island, which no longer exists."

"That's right," said Bloom. "But El Salvador does. Along with the rest of South and Central America."

"You're quite right, Jerome." Bloom must have touched a nerve. It was back to the formal first name. "And I don't have an answer that will satisfy you on that question. No, I don't want to shut out people who are fleeing from despotism. But neither do I want to see our own citizens, our minorities that have waited so long for equal opportunity, cheated of their chance. Do you have any idea how many jobs are lost to technology and to foreign competition in this country each year? And they're not going to be replaced. The pie is shrinking, dammit, and our citizens are being forced to settle for smaller slices, rather than more pies. How can we force it to shrink even further by bringing in millions more people in the next five years?"

"I guess I don't have the answer, either," Bloom admitted.

"We at least agree on our mutual inabilities then," said Wendell. "But I still can't convince you that my position is based on a sense of humanity, can I?"

"That's not important—convincing me. We've got to convince the electorate. That's all that counts now."

"I'm sorry, but I disagree with you." Bloom stared at this complex, if not inscrutable man who sat across from him, this man who would be president. Why was he even bothering to take the time to debate with Bloom?

"Yes, I want very badly to be president. In fact, I want it more than I've ever wanted anything. But if I become a president who does not make a difference, who leaves office, or dies, having made no greater mark in the world than occupying the Oval Office, then I will have failed. And I do not want to fail. Can you understand that?"

Jesus, Bloom thought, cynically, this guy wants everything. It's not good enough getting elected president, he wants to be an effective one. That's not the way we play the game.

"Sure, I can understand it, Governor," Bloom finally answered. "But I wasn't prepared to hear that from you."

"Why? Is it because I'm a Texan? Or because I'm no longer a Democrat?"

"Maybe it's because of some of the people who've been drawn to your campaign." Bloom focused his mind's eye on the face of Harrison Davis.

Again, Wendell seemed to be reading his mind. "My campaign manager, for one, am I right?"

"Well, I do have some difficulty with Davis. I know he's a friend of many years, and he's devoted himself to your political career. But I can't help feeling uncomfortable with him. I won't let it get in the way of my work, though, I can assure you."

"It has been said, more than once, that Harrison Davis is my dark side. It sounds rather ominous, if not melodramatic. How do you react to that?"

"He does tend to be more calculating, more capable of going for the jugular than you seem to be," said Bloom.

"And that's an important part of his value, in addition to his loyalty, don't you agree?"

"Sure. I guess every campaign needs one good son-of-a-bitch. And if it can't be the candidate, it had better be the campaign manager."

"I should be offended at your underestimation of

me; I've prided myself in my ability to be one mean son-of-a-bitch." Wendell smiled.

"I'm sure you have some real potential," Bloom quipped.

"There's something else troubling me, Jerry," said Wendell, his voice becoming lower. "There seem to be things going on in the campaign that are being kept from me."

"It's not uncommon at all," said Bloom. "It's part of our job, those of us on staff, to protect you from a lot of things that go on."

"But I find that terribly patronizing. I'm quite able to deal with things that are not entirely pleasant."

"I'm sure you are. But we have to consider your effectiveness at all times. If you become too close to a particular problem—like a staff disagreement or a flap over the writing of a position paper—it could begin to have an effect on your ability to always be up. For example, you're probably all primed for your appearance before some of the hardest-nosed critics on earth—the national press—an hour from now. If you were to suddenly become angered or depressed over something that's happened in the campaign, you might not be up to form. And believe me, you'll need to be up tonight."

"I suppose that's sound advice. But I'm not troubled by being kept from involvement in petty campaign squabbles. I'm talking more about things like negotiations with contributors, about commitments being made on my behalf, without my knowledge. I don't want to sound paranoid, but it troubles me to think that people might be coming into my campaign, people with money or special interests, without my full knowledge."

"I can't see that happening, Governor. You keep a very tight rein on this campaign."

"I'm not so sure I do."

"But if you don't, Davis certainly does. You have absolutely nothing to worry about."

Wendell said nothing. He merely stared at Bloom. Something about the way he stared concerned Bloom.

Wendell abruptly changed his mood. He slapped his hands on his thighs and said, "Well, I've got to get over to that wolves' den and, as you say, be 'up to form.'"

"I'm sure you will be," Bloom assured him, rising with him.

"How's your wife bearing up under all this?" Wendell asked.

"I'm not quite sure," Bloom answered. "Why?"

"This business we're in is very hard on marriages. You're kept away from home far too much. And when you are home, generally, it's only your body that's there."

"It's part of the price we pay for our addiction," said Bloom.

"Perhaps that's one of the reasons I'm well suited for the political life. My marriage never would have withstood all this, I'm afraid. She was a very strong woman, my wife, Emily. But she would not have liked this whole business any more than I imagine your wife does." It was the first time Bloom had heard Wendell, or anyone else, for that matter, refer to his late wife, who had died in a terrible automobile accident, caused by a drunken driver, during Wendell's first term as governor. There had been no children. If successful in his campaign, Wendell would go to the White House both a widower and childless.

"Thank you for your thoughts, Jerry," said Wendell, as he turned to leave. He stopped for a moment, and said, "Your wife's name is Anne, isn't it? Say hello to her for me." And what appeared to be a sadder man than Bloom had noticed previously turned and left the hotel suite.

The reporters in attendance at Wendell's appearance before the Washington Press Club must have liked what they saw and heard. The candidate received what could be described as rave reviews. He was cited for his charm, his dry sense of humor, his refreshing grasp of the facts and of history. Two syndicated columnists wrote about the marked difference between the open and frank Stephen Wendell and the man he was trying to succeed in the White House. Wrote one writer, David Randeford, of the *Chicago Tribune,* Washington Bureau:

Like him or not, this is a man to be taken quite seriously. He might, just possibly, turn American political history upside down and achieve the impossible. He could, given just a couple of more propitious breaks, be elected president. And then what? For one thing, we might see a whole lot of special interests wondering what hit them, come January, even the powerful National Association of Teachers, which frantically rushed to endorse Wendell when their favorite congressperson, Hattie Lewis, climbed aboard. But the NAT is going to be in for a bigger surprise than a Wendell upset, if he succeeds. What they're most likely to discover is that to endorse the man, to give him the credibility of their support, along with their money, is not to buy a piece of him.

This new political phenomenon, who talks in relatively simplistic political terms, like AMERICA'S REDECLARATION OF INDEPENDENCE, is a complex man, with a political philosophy that is somewhere between eclectic and ecumenical. He borrows from some nice old notions, like new- and fair-idealism, and updates them with contemporary ideas like high-tech economics. He can put a liberal zealot in the same bed with a conservative pragmatist with the real chance that they'll fall in love once they get a little accustomed to each other.

Tom Wolfe understood where our new age of technology was taking us, when he came up with the notion of "The Right Stuff" and, thus, introduced us to a new style of American heroism, which doesn't fit the pretechnocratic, more romantic notions that canonized our earlier heroes. Franklin Delano Roosevelt conquered infantile paralysis, but that disease doesn't even exist any longer. Patton and Eisenhower prevailed in a kind of warfare that will never be waged again. The Project Mercury astronauts did not become the kind of heroes who inspire statues of themselves to be built. Perhaps that is because we do not yet understand what it is they conquered.

Stephen Wendell is, in a manner of speaking, a political astronaut. He grew up putting on his pants every morning just like the rest of us. But along the way he discovered some exciting new challenges, fraught with some very real dangers, in a world that changes with the speed of mercury. Whether he will meet the challenges and overcome some of the dangers remains to be seen. But he is at least going out there armed with some fairly right stuff.

Of course, the reviews were not unanimously favorable. Grant Chase, on another of his evening commentaries, managed to sting both Wendell and Bloom at the same time.

As we come down the homestretch in this extraordinary political campaign, the man who was, at best, a dark horse at the starting gate, is charging like fury toward what could be the most important upset in history. Stephen Wendell is remarkable in his ability to appeal to a broad cross section of American voters. But even more remarkable is the way in which people are buying what he's selling. This man has been made a package of breakfast cereal by his high-powered media consultants. He is being marketed with some of the slickest tricks to come off Madison Avenue, with style that's as zippy as a hamburger-stand jingle, and with substance to match it. In the remaining two weeks before election day, I would not be the least surprised to hear a Stephen Wendell jingle, telling America, in four-four time, that we all deserve a break today, with Wendell and Lewis.

The controversial television commercial on the immigration issue, which has been attacked by the president as foul play, is more of an affront to intelligence than it is a threat to fairness. The theme of a "redeclaration of independence" is as meaningful as "snap, crackle and pop."

Not that he has asked me for advice, but if he would, I'd offer the following suggestion to Stephen Wendell: You started with an intriguing idea—an alternative to the two major parties' candidates and platforms. But you're ending up giving us more of an echo than a choice, to coin a phrase turned by an earlier political maverick, Barry Goldwater. When you tell us you want to offer us something better than the old special-interest politics, please don't turn around and simply put together a new coalition of those interests, be they black voters, schoolteachers, or labor unions.

Cheap shot, thought Bloom. The NAT came to Wendell because he and Hattie made sense to them, not because he made any promises. And what the hell are blacks supposed to do, turn against Hattie and support the candidates who turned against them?

"Give the voters some credit, Governor Wendell," Chase concluded. "They're not going to cast their votes the way they buy their hamburgers. They're going to think about issues. They're going to look for some substance. If you don't give some of both, people might just ask what it is that's so independent about a candidate who depends so much on slick media hype.

"This is Grant Chase."

Chase got through to Bloom, who had always admired the dean of television commentators, who now had appointed himself a self-styled critic of political media. Bloom found Chase a hypocrite; after all, wasn't his own network, with all its self-promotion and ratings-hunger, selling its own newscasts just like hamburger chains and breakfast cereals? But no matter how angered Bloom became at Chase, he was still hurt by his criticism. Of all the qualities Bloom had acquired in his career, a thick skin was definitely not among them.

15

ON THE THIRD MONDAY IN October, Bloom arose early, at four-thirty on a chill Washington morning, to take a long run along the Potomac River. It was going to be an important day. At seven, he was to have breakfast with David Braun. By nine, he had to be on location with his film crew to shoot a new television commercial, in the heart of Washington's most depressed neighborhood, less than a mile from Capitol Hill.

The breakfast with Senator Braun was an event to which Bloom did not look forward. It would be the first time they had spoken since Bloom had told Braun of his decision to handle the Wendell campaign and, therefore, be unavailable to work any longer on Braun's reelection bid. The senator had been kind to Bloom, reassuring him that he wouldn't want to stand in the way of Bloom's opportunity of a lifetime. "You have no choice, Jerry," Braun had said. But Bloom still was not sure his friend had been truthful. He was sure only that he had been a friend.

"You look like you're holding up all right," Braun said to Bloom as they sat in the atrium restaurant on the lobby level of the Hyatt.

"I feel like I've lost ten pounds and gained twenty years," said Bloom. "It seems like you've had some time in the sun."

"Not really. My film people got me to bake in one of those coffinlike things a few times so I'd look like a healthy Californian on camera."

Bloom tried to conceal his discomfort. He had missed his old friend. But this was a sad occasion, especially in light of the information Bloom had just received about the Braun campaign—that it was not faring well. Braun's conservative opponent was gaining rapidly, and some observers were predicting defeat at the polls for the popular Californian. And, of course, Bloom was already beginning to take on responsibility for what might happen to David Braun's campaign.

"How are things looking?" Bloom asked.

"Not too terrific. But I'm still ahead by six points. If we can keep the undecideds breaking even, we're fine. Of course, this guy's a real son-of-a-bitch. He's got the whole religious right marching against me, calling me a baby-killer, and an atheist, because of my school prayer stance—you know the routine. What's frightening, though, is that people are buying a lot of that stuff."

"I understand they're spending a fortune against you," said Bloom.

"It'll probably come in at about ten million."

"Where the hell is it going to stop? Ten-million-dollar Senate campaigns. It's crazy."

"Hey, friend, that's paltry compared to what you folks are spending."

Bloom felt defensive. "You're right. It's interesting—I don't look at the presidential race as an exercise in excessive spending. And that's wrong, I know. We tend to excuse the price tag, I guess, because it's the heavyweight championship."

"And that puts me in an exhibition match, right?"

"Okay, enough with the needle. You're right. All the campaigns are spending too goddamn much. I remember what Gary Hart once said, during his second Senate race. He told a *Wall Street Journal* reporter that campaign spending had become an obscenity."

"And he was speaking as a winner, not as a sore loser," said Braun. "One of these days, we'll all acknowledge that the whole damn business has gone too far. And maybe we'll exercise some common sense and put some real limits on campaign spending. Maybe we'll resort to public funding for *all* races, not just the presidency. Of course, I'm not trying to put you out of business," Braun chuckled.

"I know. But I think maybe *I* am," said Bloom. "This one's my last hurrah."

"There you go. The biannual lie. Every other November you tell me and anyone else who'll listen that you're getting out of politics. But I know you better. You're hooked, like the rest of us. Sure, you want to make movies, write books, whatever. We all do. But this stuff's in your system. There's one other problem, too."

"And what's that?"

"You're good at it. Maybe the best. And that's not

a time to quit something. You can make a difference. You can put what you know, and what you create, to good use, for good causes." He paused, looking down at his cold scrambled eggs. "For good people."

"You don't think much of Stephen Wendell, do you?"

"The truth is, Jerry, no, I don't think a hell of a lot of the man. But I respect him. I think he really means it when he says he wants to make a difference, that he wants to give us a real alternative. The guy's got conviction, as much as any of us. But I don't like the idea of blaming everything that's gone wrong in this country on the political parties. Sure, we screw up now and then. But I still believe that the Democrats screw up less than the Republicans, and that we can be a successful route of access to our own government."

"You don't agree that the parties are losing their relevance?"

"Sure they are. But so is every other institution. Our schools are becoming irrelevant all the time. So are our professions. The damn car you drive. Everything loses its relevance faster these days; the times and problems are changing more quickly than ever before. But that doesn't mean we tear down our schools or do away with law and medicine. We try and keep them changing enough to regain their relevance."

"That's a nice idea, in the abstract," said Bloom. "But it doesn't work too well for a guy who's lost his job in a factory, or for his parents, who've lost their Medicare benefits. The political parties just give them double talk. And broken promises. Look at the platforms of both parties this year. They both miss the real problems by a mile."

"Sounds to me like your client has gotten through to you."

"What's more important, he's getting through to voters."

"I know," said Braun. "And maybe history will one day prove him right. But that's not going to stop me from supporting that irrelevant party of mine and its candidates."

"Is there anything I can do to help?" Bloom asked, trying to get off the subject of Wendell.

"With my campaign? Well, if you can think of a way to get those crazies off my back, I'd be forever grateful. But I don't think anyone can do that."

"You're on their list of fourteen, I understand," Bloom said.

"That's right. I've made it to the big time. Four-teen Senators who've been targeted by the New Conservative Coalition."

"That's where the spending is really getting out of hand—the PACs." Bloom was referring to the politi-cal action committees, most of which had acro-nyms, like NewCon, the coalition that had targeted Braun.

"Tell me about it. Here, look at this garbage." Braun fished out a thick white envelope from his suit coat pocket, and put it down on the table. Bloom's eye caught the return name and address: CITIZENS FOR FISCAL RESPONSIBILITY, 1500 CON-NECTICUT AVENUE, WASHINGTON, D.C. He picked up the envelope, feeling apprehensive about what he suspected was inside. His fear was justified when he caught the first sentence of the computer-typed letter: *When you got into financial trouble last year, where was your United States Senator, David Braun?* It was the same letter—the same invasion of privacy—Jeanette had shown him, the one the Wendell campaign was using nationally. Bloom tried to control the anger rising inside him, along with what little food he had eaten. He felt himself break out in a cold sweat as he tried to think of how—or whether—to tell his friend what he knew about the letter.

"What's wrong, Jerry?"

"David, I've seen that letter before."

"You mean you got one? Wow, they must have gotten a good list to mail."

"No, I saw a draft of it, before it was ever mailed."

Braun looked troubled, confused. "What are you saying? You saw this letter before it went out? Who in hell showed it to you?"

"Someone you don't know."

"I should hope I wouldn't know anyone on that goddamn committee. The question is, how do *you* know someone on it?"

"I don't," said Bloom. "The letter was first sent out on behalf of Stephen Wendell. I thought it was a cheap shot, if not illegal, at the time. But I had no idea it would be going out in Senate campaigns, too. Against targeted incumbents."

"So Wendell is also out to get me defeated," Braun said. "It doesn't surprise me."

"It doesn't make sense. Why would he get involved in a Senate race?"

"Well, try this one. If all fourteen of the targeted liberals in the Senate get beaten, conservatives could get a hell of a lot done. Look at the new immigration bill they're pushing—along with your client. They could muster enough votes to pass it handily with fourteen additional seats."

"It wouldn't be worth the money and the effort for Wendell to try and pull off a stunt like that," Bloom answered.

"I'm not so sure. But listen to another scenario. Let's say Wendell comes close enough, not to win, but to deny either of the other two candidates a majority. Then what happens?"

"It goes into the House, obviously."

"Right. And what about the vice-presidency?"

"What about it? I don't know. It goes along with him." Bloom paused. "Doesn't it?"

"You must not have paid attention somewhere in your civics classes, Jerry. If the presidential campaign results in less than a majority, only the president is elected in the House. The vice-president is elected by the Senate."

Bloom searched his mind for some sort of sense he could make out of what he was hearing. "In other words, if Wendell wins, there's no guarantee Hattie wins with him."

"Precisely," said Braun. "No guarantee at all. And guess what a conservative majority in the Senate would do to a black, liberal woman who wants to be vice-president? *And* president of the Senate?"

"But wait a minute. The *sitting* Senate votes in November. Not the new Senate, in January. Right?"

"Wrong again. And these guys want to be sure they can run again. So, if they get a message from back home that the voters don't want Hattie Lewis as their vice-president, I think their wishes are going to be honored."

Bloom couldn't get to Jeanette's office, one floor above the Wendell campaign headquarters on Massachusetts Avenue, fast enough. The cab seemed to take forever to travel the fifteen blocks from the Hyatt. He would have walked, but it was raining hard. He had called Jeanette from the hotel lobby as soon as he and Braun had finished breakfast. He took the stairs up to the fourth floor, where Jeanette waited. He knew he must have looked strange, dripping wet from the rain and panting from the run up four flights.

"My God, look at you," said Jeanette, looking quite dry, very pretty, and certainly not out of breath.

"It's raining. And I'm in a hurry."

"I can tell," she said, looking at her watch. "Aren't you due on location?"

"Not for half an hour. Come on, let's take a walk."

"A walk? It's raining." She looked at his wet hair.

"I know that, thank you. But we have to talk."

"What's wrong with you?"

"I don't know yet. But something is," he said impatiently. "Look, I'm not kidding. We have to talk about something. Please."

Jeanette shrugged. "Okay. We'll talk." She went to a closet.

"Where are you going?"

She stopped. "I'm getting an umbrella, if, of course, you can give me the time." She opened the closet door and reached in. Out came a rolled-up black umbrella. "There. Now, that wasn't too much of a delay, I hope."

Bloom had no time for small talk. "Come on." He took her elbow lightly and held the door to the hallway open for her. Jeanette rolled her eyes and walked briskly with Bloom down the stairway and out to the rain-drenched street.

Washington in the rain was similar to New York in the rain. It somehow seemed more inviting than it did in drier weather. Things tended to glisten and shine when wet, looking bright, rather than gray, new, rather than overworn. Bloom compared it to the car commercial look. City streets were always hosed down to create a glossier, richer environment for the cars being hawked.

They stood under a building's protective entranceway. The rain showed no sign of stopping. "All right, now what? Or where?" Jeanette asked Bloom.

Bloom searched up and down the street. He saw a restaurant, more of a luncheonette, where he had once had lunch with Jeanette. "There," he said, pointing to it, "let's have coffee."

"I don't drink coffee," she answered.

"But we have to get out of the rain."

They ran the short distance to the restaurant door under the cover of Jeanette's umbrella, only to see the sign that said CLOSED. Jeanette turned to look at Bloom sympathetically, as if to ask what odd move he might make next. Bloom provided her with the answer by waving at a taxi standing at the curb. He pointed to it and nudged Jeanette in its direction.

271

He opened the rear door and shouted into it. "You available?"

The dark-complected driver, probably a Pakistani, simply nodded. Bloom held the door open for Jeanette and took her umbrella when she got in. He fought with it, cursing, until he finally managed to collapse it, and climbed in the taxi.

"Where you going?" asked the driver in a thick accent.

Jeanette turned to Bloom. "I can hardly wait to hear, myself," she said.

Bloom thought a moment. "Can you just drive us around here for a while?"

The driver looked alarmed, as though expecting some sort of trouble. "I cannot do that, mister."

"Why? I'm paying the fare."

"You got to go somewhere. Look," he said pointing to the zone map on the back of the seat. "Everything is in zone. I go round and round, I stay in one zone. Cost me money. No, you got to go somewhere."

"All right." He thought quickly. "Take me to National Airport. Happy?"

"The airport?" asked Jeanette, almost laughing at him.

The driver shook his head. "Airport." He turned. "You got baggage?"

"No. No baggage. Just take me there." He knew it was a fifteen-minute ride.

"What airline?" asked the puzzled driver, edging the cab out into traffic.

"I'll pick one when we get there, okay?"

The driver repeated what Bloom had said, not entirely under his breath, and Bloom breathed a deep sigh, now turning to Jeanette. "I'm sure you think I've totally lost it," he said to her. "I may be close to that point, but I'm not quite there yet."

"What's all this about, Jerry? We can't talk in my office. Whatever it is can't wait." She looked into his eyes, and a slight smile appeared on her face. "Oh, my God," she said, smiling more broadly. "Is this a marriage proposal?"

At another time, under other circumstances, Bloom would have enjoyed Jeanette's playfulness. Today, he found it irritating. "What the hell is this campaign trying to do to David Braun?"

Jeanette's brow became furrowed. "What are you talking about?"

"Remember the letter you showed me last month—the one that went out to people in financial trouble?"

"Yes, I remember. Why?"

Bloom pulled from his suit coat the envelope Braun had given him. "Here's an extra copy."

Jeanette curiously took the letter and opened it. She read it in silence. "Well," she finally said, "I gather you think I had something to do with this."

"Did you know about it?"

"Now wait just a moment." She was angry. "Before you piss me off any further with your prosecutor's style, I happen to like, and support, David Braun. And it may surprise you to learn I don't make it a practice to try and injure people I like and support."

"I'm sorry. I didn't intend to be accusatory. I'm upset. I just met with David for the first time since I got out of his campaign. And I feel like shit about what's happening to him, what I did to him."

"You didn't send out that mailing."

"I abandoned him," said Bloom.

"That's your particular, guilt-ridden view. As I recall, he counseled you to take the Wendell assignment."

Jeanette's reassurances were not helping. "All right, that's another discussion. In the meantime, I've got to know how this letter got into the campaign to defeat David Braun. Wendell has gone too far," said Bloom.

"*If* he's involved."

"How could he not be involved?"

"Quite easily," said Jeanette. "Weren't you yourself telling me recently of your talk with Wendell about the need for campaign people to keep certain things from the candidate, to protect him?"

"But we're talking about dirty tricks."

"That's right. The kind of dirty tricks that I don't believe Stephen Wendell would have any part of. It's not his style."

"Until this morning, I would have agreed with you."

"You're making judgments again," said Jeanette.

"Well, then, who else is responsible for this kind of thing?"

"For starters, what about our campaign director?"

"Davis wouldn't do something like this without consulting Wendell."

"Why not?"

"For one thing, he couldn't keep it a secret. If you and I know about the connection, the press can sure as hell find out about it."

"But Davis could build in a cover. Example: The PAC working against Braun could simply claim it

274

saw a good idea in our letter, copied it, and got its own list."

"And you think the public will buy that fairy tale?" asked Bloom.

"They've bought a lot worse. Like El Salvador."

Bloom thought about Wendell's question: Do you think I have a dark side in Harrison Davis? He also added up some of the things that had been bothering him about the campaign—particularly those pieces that had fallen into place a bit too fortuitously. The Blandemann drug problem, followed by the Blandemann withdrawal, followed by the Lewis replacement. Bingo. Six points gained overnight. The bizarre mugging incident. The kind of newsbreak a media adviser wouldn't dare even dream about. Presto. Fifty million people learn about it on the evening news. Add another four points. Bloom knew he must be becoming paranoid again. Too little sleep. Too much stress. He knew the signs.

"Jerry." Jeanette interrupted Bloom's racing search for some answers. "I think you ought to confront Wendell. Or Harrison."

"And you think I'll get straight answers?"

"Maybe you won't. But you have a right to ask for them."

"How the hell did this business get to this point?" Bloom asked rhetorically. "Christ, it's supposed to be the way we help people make the choices that will give them good government. But now it's the way we manipulate them into the choices we make for them. We're not serving free choice. We're preempting it."

"You don't think it's possible you're overreacting?"

"I wish I did. I might sleep better. It's going too damn far."

"Maybe it is. But that doesn't make Stephen Wendell less deserving of election, does it?"

Bloom stared silently out of the rain-mottled window.

"Come on, Jerry. Wendell could be as much a victim as David Braun."

"I hope you're right. If you're not, God help all of us."

"What airline, mister?" The cab had slowed to a crawl along the approach road to the airport.

"I forgot my baggage," said Bloom. "Take me back to the city, please."

The driver hit the brakes, nearly causing a collision from behind. "I ask you if you have baggage, you say 'No baggage.' I ask you what airline, you say 'I don't know what airline.' Mister, you got money? I can go to police."

"Relax." He reached into his pocket and fished out a twenty-dollar bill, shoving it toward the perplexed driver. "Here's my money. Now, just turn around and take us back. Please."

"It's not that much money. I don't have change."

"Well, I'm a big tipper, goddammit. Okay? Give me a break, will you, pal?"

The driver mumbled something, this time not in English, and resumed driving, until he found a chance to turn around and head back toward the city. Bloom had him drive to the Hyatt, where he could pick up his rental car. He would be twenty minutes late to the filming location. But in this weather, the outdoor commercial, to be filmed in front of a deserted apartment building, would have to be postponed until the rain cleared.

Jeanette set about her mission of discovery with zeal. She had promised Bloom to find out just how much, if anything, of what he suspected was true. It was a combination of her zeal and her word to Bloom that led her close to something she at first refused to believe.

It started with a blinking red light. And her act was entirely innocent. She was in Davis's inner office, waiting for him to return from a brief meeting with Wendell in the campaign headquarters' conference room. The red light on Davis's telephone answering machine was blinking. She knew Davis only used the machine at night, to answer calls on his private, direct phone line. As she waited, pacing impatiently, for Davis to return, she reached down to turn off the machine, which, she surmised, he had inadvertently left on from the previous night. She thought she had turned the switch to the off position. But, instead, she moved it to playback. Before she could go back and turn the machine off, she was stopped by a man's voice. The man spoke with a Texas drawl.

"Yeah, this is Peterson. I paid a visit to our friend in Colorado, and I'm having trouble sleeping. Gimme a call just as quick as you can, at the ranch."

At first the message sounded routine enough. But something troubled Jeanette. She couldn't quite make a connection between the name Peterson and *the ranch*. Whose ranch? Wendell's? But then, something clicked when her mind raced over the miscellaneous data she had processed and stored in her memory since working on the campaign. *Peterson. Clarence Peterson. Wealthy rancher.* She recalled reading something in a profile of Wendell. It had appeared in *Time* magazine. When he was a first-year law student, the story had said, Wendell confronted a powerful Texas rancher, named Clarence Peterson, on behalf of migrant workers. Would his past now come back to haunt him? the story had asked. It most likely would, it had answered, since Peterson had said publicly that he had a long enough memory to do whatever he could to impede the Wendell campaign. When you raise money in Texas for a political campaign, you don't want enemies like Clarence Peterson, which is precisely what Stephen Wendell has.

Then why, Jeanette asked herself, was Peterson calling Wendell's campaign manager on his private line? It didn't sound like a call from an enemy. Not at all.

When Jeanette finished the presentation of her latest polling update to Davis, she excused herself and left the headquarters office. Back at her apartment, it took only thirty minutes, and two long distance phone calls, to learn of an alarming connection between Peterson and a man named Kern. Her source was a network radio reporter, an old college friend, who covered national politics.

Jeanette knew Bloom would be working in his hotel suite, so she took a cab to the Hyatt.

"What do you know about Clarence Peterson?" she asked Bloom, who had come out of the shower, dripping wet and with a towel wrapped around his waist, to answer Jeanette's knock at the door.

"I'd hoped you came rushing over here because you needed my body or something. But I don't know an awful lot about Clarence Peterson, other than what I've read—that he's loaded. One of the richest men in America, I guess. And he plays around with a lot of ultraright-wing oil guys."

"You also know about Wendell's confrontation with Peterson years ago, at his ranch? It was during the migrant workers' strike that he led."

"Sure. It was Wendell's first big political score," said Bloom.

"Well, the strike ended up costing Peterson a great deal of money and prestige. Also, Peterson had been considering a political career, but when he was portrayed as a greedy landowner, who abused immigrants, that drew his aspirations to a sudden halt."

"And he owed it all to Stephen Wendell, right?" asked Bloom.

Jeanette nodded. "But now, after all these years of supposedly being out to get Wendell, he seems to be somehow involved in his campaign."

"Well," said Bloom, "maybe the man has mellowed over the years, or come around and realized where the real action is, although I can't imagine him sinking a lot of dollars into a campaign for Wendell. The two guys are a hundred and eighty degrees apart philosophically. Peterson would fund a campaign for Attila the Hun maybe, but not for Stephen Wendell."

"Let me ask you one more question," said

Jeanette. "Do you know anything about a former army man by the name of Thomas Kern?"

Bloom sat down on the bed and began to think. The name sounded familiar to him. "Kern. Yeah, I know that name. But why? Wait a minute. Kern— Jesus, yes. He's that strange one who tried to form some kind of elite citizen reserve unit—a National Guard kind of group, only trained in terrorist operations. He's kind of scary, if you take him seriously. What about him?"

"I read a story about a speech he made in California a couple of weeks ago. It was an attack against David Braun, and in support of his opponent."

"That doesn't surprise me," said Bloom. "I certainly wouldn't expect a nut like Kern to do anything *but* oppose David."

"Well, here's another little surprise for you," said Jeanette. "Kern and Peterson are partners in a huge oil company that does a lot of importing of oil that's bought on the spot market in the Middle East."

"I thought Peterson is a domestic driller."

"He is. But he's also into buying imported oil. Most of it comes from the overproduction reserves some of the OPEC nations are trying to hold back."

"And you think Peterson is involved in the campaign, and maybe even his crazed friend, Kern?"

"I don't know," said Jeanette, obviously more troubled about what she was learning than she was proud of her ability to piece things together. "I feel like I pulled a loose thread off a sweater and it keeps on coming out and unraveling."

"You know, David is convinced Wendell is trying to stack the Senate, and therefore is involved in the effort to beat him in California," said Bloom.

Jeanette thought for a moment. "Well, when you think about it, David Braun in the Senate certainly doesn't help Wendell get where he's going. But, I just don't see it as the kind of thing he'd do. It's not only unscrupulous, it would be against the law if Wendell participated in another federal race."

"But then there's that prince among men, Harrison Davis. I wouldn't put anything past him."

"Do you think he'd get involved in something like that on his own, without telling Wendell?"

"Yes, I do. Interestingly enough, I have a feeling Wendell thinks he would, too."

"But they've been close friends for thirty-five years," said Jeanette.

"Don't forget, this is politics. The biggest of big-time politics. That's where people stop worrying about things like friendship and morality. New values are discovered, like power and greed, remember?"

"This is getting frightening. We've got to find out just what's going on," said Jeanette.

Bloom looked down at the carpet, saying nothing. A feeling of panic again washed over him. Election day was less than a week away. The American people were about to make the most important decision they'd be faced with probably for years to come. Bloom was deeply involved in the process that would lead to that decision, which should have made him feel good about himself and his ability to make a difference. But, as that strange piece of thread Jeanette had begun to pull started to look like it might continue to unravel, Bloom had a terrible feeling that he had gotten into something very different from what he'd expected. Bloom tried to shift gears, to avoid the unpleasant prospects they were discussing. He jumped to his feet, and as he did so, the towel he had wrapped around himself fell to the floor, leaving him standing naked in front of Jeanette.

Jeanette smiled. "Your offers are getting more unusual all the time. I thought you were going to propose marriage in the cab the other day. Now it looks like you're offering me a wet body."

"Maybe if we got under the covers for a while, we'd both feel a little better about things."

"I don't want you to think you're unimportant to me," said Jeanette, the smile gone now. She stepped closer to him and placed both her hands on his face. "I want to be with you, right now. I need some love from you. But we also have to find out what's happening. For David Braun's sake. For your sake."

Bloom looked into her eyes. "You're wonderful," he said. Jeanette smiled at him, but then a look of concern returned.

"In any event, I think the notion of confronting Davis isn't a very good idea," said Jeanette. "I hope we're really seeing things that don't exist. But just in case we're not, the worst thing we could do right now is to let Davis know that we think something isn't right."

"I agree. It's beginning to sound too much like cloak and dagger. You just never think any of that exists except in novels."

Jeanette kissed him softly on the lips. "I'm due back at headquarters in about an hour. But first I want to go over to the *Post* and look through some clip files. I'm curious about the oil partnership Kern and Peterson are involved in. Do you remember the hearings David Braun tried to conduct into American oilmen repurchasing Arab crude oil?"

"Sure. He took a lot of heat from the oil industry, and was applauded by Jewish leaders, who saw a threat to Israel in the repurchase business, with possible new alliances between the U.S. and Arab countries."

"Well," said Jeanette, "maybe there's a pattern here, and maybe not. I might just start sounding like you, suspecting politicians of having questionable motives."

"Hang around enough of them long enough and you just might," he said.

"Where will you be later today?"

"I'm supposed to do a run-through for a series of wrap-ups with the candidate. But I don't know. I want to find out what's going on, too. I think maybe I ought to have a talk with Hattie, but trying to get her attention has become impossible."

"Thank God she's with us. If anything really bad is going on, it's at least not at the candidate level," said Jeanette.

"I don't think Stephen Wendell would break the law. And I sure as hell know Hattie wouldn't."

Jeanette left, with one last, quick embrace, and walked the short distance to the *Washington Post* building, where she went directly to the microfilm department and began her tedious search of newspaper feature stories about oil repurchases from the Middle East.

Bloom placed a call to Hattie Lewis, who, he was told, was in Boston, addressing a convention of Women in Business. Leaving a message, he decided to do some writing for last-minute radio commercials. As he passed the television set, he flicked it on, hoping to catch the network news. The familiar-sounding voice of a narrator startled him. In an instant he realized his own television commercial for Stephen Wendell was airing. It was running nationwide, and its purpose was to drive home the threat to future employment posed by unrestrained immigration. Producing commercials had always been exciting work for Bloom. But most exciting of all was seeing them broadcast on television, hoping they were not only well-produced, but were having an impact. It was always that particular bottom line that finally spelled the difference between a good commercial and a bad one—how much effect did it have on people who saw it, on people whose minds could possibly be changed?

The commercial opened with a long line of children, some of them infants in strollers and baby carriages, others age three to twelve, many of them looking bored or preoccupied. As the camera pulled back, with the announcer's voice over the action, it was revealed that the children were in a long line at a state unemployment office. At the head of the long line, a sign proclaimed: UNEMPLOYMENT BENEFITS. FORM LINE HERE.

The announcer asked, "Do you realize that as our country grows, the number of available jobs shrinks? With each passing year, America will have more people competing for fewer jobs. Do you think it makes sense to throw our doors open wide to workers from other countries when we can't provide jobs for ourselves? You want the best for your children. Vote for Stephen Wendell, an independent president for America."

Bloom stopped and stared at the television screen as the commercial faded. He asked himself the same question he frequently asked. Does this one go too far? Or is it on the mark? It was an imprecise business, this whole political media process, and the line between penetrating, effective advertising and heavy-handed emotionalism was becoming razor-fine. The trick was to tread that line, trying always to come down on the effective side of it. But given the pressures of the campaign and the discoveries that Bloom and Jeanette were beginning to make, walking the line was becoming more difficult than ever. Now, Bloom was not sure whether he had produced a commercial that would be scorned and mocked by the public and the press or one that would have an explosive effect on voters. This particular effort could just as easily fall into one category as the other.

16

JEANETTE WAS GETTING ACCUS-
tomed to the microfilm machine
after two hours of going
through every newspaper story she could find that
had a reference to either Clarence Peterson or
Thomas Kern. At this point, she had found only two
clippings mentioning Peterson; one was in a story
that looked like it had been excerpted from the *New
York Times* piece. The other was an article about
right-wing politics. In the latter story, Peterson was
featured rather prominently. A photograph of him,
taken on his ranch two years earlier, also appeared.
Thomas Kern's name had come up in four different
stories. The first was about his retirement from the
army, and focused on the controversy that had sur-
rounded his military career, primarily because of
his strong ultraconservative political views. The
other stories dealt, as did the one on Peterson, with
right-wing political movements. In the most recent
one, there was a large photo showing Kern addressing a rally held by the Society for Fair Play for
South Africa. The caption said: THOMAS KERN, WHO

OFTEN FIGURES IN RIGHT-WING POLITICAL AC-
TIVITIES, ADDRESSES A RALLY ATTENDED BY MEM-
BERS OF SEVERAL GROUPS SUPPORTING FRIENDLIER
SOUTH AFRICAN POLICIES. THE SOCIETY HAS BEEN
BRANDED IN SOME CIRCLES AS A FRONT FOR RADICAL
CONSERVATIVE GROUPS.

Jeanette squinted to see some of the faces in the picture. An alarm went off somewhere within her when she saw a man standing next to Kern, looking out over the crowd. Jeanette pressed the close-up switch on the microfilm machine and centered the image. There was little doubt in her mind as to his identity. She continued to study the face. She was virtually certain it was Aram Saraf, the Palestinian terrorist who had been suspected of masterminding at least two bombings of American embassies in the Middle East, as well as the capturing of twenty-three American hostages, who were eventually exchanged for forty terrorist prisoners being held in a London prison. The photograph had been taken one year earlier, before Saraf had been named as a suspect in various terrorist incidents. It had been reported that he was still traveling freely in the United States, although he probably was being investigated by the FBI. Jeanette had vivid recollections of Saraf, whom she had met four years earlier, when Jeff Wells had interviewed him for a film on Israel and its enemies. Saraf had frightened her with his intensity and militant posture.

Jeanette continued her search for any additional stories about the two men, but found nothing. She returned the files, then went to the back issue desk and bought a photostatic copy of the page on which the last story about Kern had appeared, together with the photograph of both Kern and Saraf. She tucked it into her purse and left the building, flagging down a taxi, which she took to the Rayburn office building of the House of Representatives. She took the elevator to the third floor, then walked briskly down the hall to the two large walnut doors bearing the seal of the State of Arizona and a sign that read REPRESENTATIVE HATTIE LEWIS.

It was a typical congressional suite. A large photograph of Hattie, her arms raised in a victory gesture on the steps of the Arizona State Capitol, hung over the reception desk. The furniture was governmental in its unimaginative colors and textures. The seats were dark red imitation leather; the walls were paneled in the same walnut as the front doors. The green carpet seemed to be the same found in virtually every office in Washington that didn't have linoleum or tile on its floors.

The receptionist, a young Oriental woman, smiled warmly and asked if she could help.

"Is Don Brody in?"

"May I tell him your name, please?"

"I'm Jeanette Wells. Don and I are old friends," Jeanette replied, trying not to show her impatience to see Brody, whom she had known since her early days of political activism. They had dated a few times before she'd met Jeff. Their friendship had been a surprise to Bloom, who knew Brody, too.

The receptionist hung up the telephone and smiled again at Jeanette. "Don will be with you in just a few moments, Miss Wells. Would you like to have a seat?"

"Yes, thank you." But Jeanette continued to stand, lost in thought. The door leading off the reception area opened, and Don's smiling, almost mischievous-looking face appeared. He still looked very much like a sixties activist. He wore round, gold-rimmed eyeglasses and a full beard, which was sufficiently neat in its trim, however, to avoid a look of vagrancy. He also wore a blue chambray work shirt, a tan knit tie, khaki cotton trousers, and leather deck shoes. He stood barely five-foot-six-inches. Everything about his appearance and his manner created the impression of someone whom most people would want to know more about.

"How you doing, kiddo?" asked Brody, smiling through his beard and winking one eye, as he had always done.

Jeanette felt good just seeing him again. "Nice to see you, Don. Sorry I didn't call first." She went to him and gave him the kind of hug, touching her cheek to his, that was common with most of Jeanette's associates from the old days of politics and filmmaking.

"No problem," said Brody. "Hey, I feel kind of honored, actually. I mean, just four days till election day, and you've got time to pay a pal a visit. Everything must be done and you guys are headed for inauguration, huh?"

"I don't suppose the boss is around," said Jeanette.

"The truth is, she hasn't been in the office in thirty days. So we've all been catching up on things like letters to constituents while she's out trying to bring the vice-presidency home."

"Do you have a couple of minutes to talk?" asked Jeanette.

"Sure. Want to go back to my office?"

Jeanette nodded, and Brody opened the door for her, following her to his small office, which was merely a corner of a large room, partitioned off by floor-to-ceiling bookcases; these held endless rows and stacks of government documents and books on the law, on history, and on the workings of the Congress of the United States.

"Well, how does it feel to be working on the big one?" Brody asked.

"Most of the time it's mind-boggling to think I could be involved at this level. Some of the time, though, it's enough to make me wonder why I ever wanted to leave the sanity and the security of normal market research."

"I'm sure you did it for the very same principles by which the rest of us have always been guided here in Washington—power and greed, right?" said a smiling Brody.

"Of course. At least I haven't slipped to the level of people who do it because they want to make a difference."

Jeanette looked down at the purse on her lap. She was trying to joke with her old friend, but it was not coming easily. He seemed to notice.

"You look like there's something fairly large on your mind."

"There is," said Jeanette. She reached into her purse and pulled out the copy of the newspaper story and the photograph. She handed it to Brody.

"See anybody you know there?" she asked.

Brody studied the picture for a few moments and shrugged. "Just Dr. Strangelove, that whacko colonel who was drummed out of the military." Brody read the caption below the picture and said, "It's too bad, the way he attached himself to legitimate organizations, like the immigration reform folks. It hurts us, the way he uses their legitimacy."

Jeanette pointed to a section of the picture. "How about that man, the dark one next to Kern. Recognize him?"

Brody shook his head.

"I'm positive that's Aram Saraf."

Brody raised an eyebrow. "The Palestinian? Out in public?"

"This was taken before he went underground."

"What the hell is he doing with Kern?"

"That's what I'd like to know," said Jeanette. "I'm getting a terrible feeling—and I hope to God I'm wrong—that there's some kind of connection between the Wendell campaign and Kern. And now I'm even beginning to wonder if that connection even extends to Saraf."

"I think maybe you're not getting enough rest," said Brody. "Wendell and Hattie don't hang around in circles like that. Give us a break."

"Like I said, I hope to God I'm wrong."

"Tell me, what led you to think there was a connection?" asked Brody.

"Can we take a walk?" Jeanette was fidgeting again.

"Want to go down to the big greasy spoon in the basement?"

"That's fine. I'll buy you a cup of coffee."

"Oh, no, you won't," said Brody. "That shit is still as bad as ever. But I'll take a 7-Up."

Jeanette and Brody rode the elevator to the basement level of the Rayburn building. The cavernous cafeteria had all the warmth of a military mess hall.

Everything was either made of plastic laminate or stainless steel. The long line of steam tables contained various daily specials, most of which were hard to distinguish from one another. The taco special looked very much like the lasagna, which strongly resembled the goulash.

The two friends each got a soft drink and went to a far corner of the room and sat at a table off by itself. It was comforting to Jeanette to see her old friend again, his presence giving her a moment's relaxation. However, it didn't lessen the urgency of her mission. She felt there was too little time left to find out what, if anything, was at the bottom of the connection she had accidentally uncovered.

Jeanette began by explaining the letter Senator Braun had received. She discussed Bloom's reaction to the letter, mentioning his anger at his first awareness of the earlier letter that went out on behalf of the Wendell campaign. She traced her involvement in the research efforts, and also in the target-mailing projects. She referred to Bloom several times, perhaps not realizing the fondness with which she spoke of him.

"You seem to be as interested in Jerry Bloom as in Wendell or Hattie," said Brody. "Should I be making anything of this?"

"I don't imagine I can hide that very well. Yes, you could make something of it. I've become close to Jerry."

"He's married, isn't he?"

Jeanette said nothing. She nodded slowly.

"I'm not going to give you lectures, but this whole business of politics has a way of spawning relationships that otherwise might not happen. It's like traveling with a rock-and-roll band. We get put into close situations with one another on buses, in hotels, in crowded cars. We get up at five in the morning together; we go to sleep at two in the morning. And pretty soon we start doing *that* together. It just happens. But you always have to wonder about the day after election day. Those Wednesday-morning blues, when the concert tour's over, and there are no more hotels and buses."

"I understand that," said Jeanette. "But my concern now is about what's going on in this campaign, and what it all can do to Jerry Bloom."

"Hey, he's a big boy. He can take care of himself."

"I had a lot to do with his decision to handle this campaign."

"Well, so did Hattie. So did the fattest fee ever paid a media consultant. Look, this guy did it for several reasons, most important of which, I would imagine, is that nice round number—a seven figure one."

"But he was torn over the decision. His wife was violently opposed to his doing the campaign. He, himself, had some real problems of conscience. It was wrenching for him to desert the Democratic party. Bloom was a loyal member, and it furnished him a living all those years. He also has a problem with what has turned out to be Wendell's best issue, immigration. Bloom's parents came here from Europe just a couple of steps ahead of Hitler. A lot of his cousins and aunts and uncles didn't make it out of there in time and died in the camps. Now Bloom is asked to work for a guy who seems to be saying we should seal the borders."

"Okay. So he once had conviction. How did *you* manage to change his mind?"

Jeanette looked down at her folded hands. She didn't need to answer. Brody seemed embarrassed.

"Sorry," he said.

"It's okay. Look, I first wanted Jerry Bloom in this campaign, because I wanted to see Stephen Wendell become president. And later, I wanted to see Hattie Lewis become vice-president. It's the most important mission I've ever been on in my life. For some reasons I won't ever be able to explain adequately to anyone . . . it also has something to do with Jeff and what was taken away from him, what he didn't get to finish giving to the world. Yes, I wanted Bloom to change his mind and join us. I believed—and still do—that he's able, more than anyone else, to make the kind of difference that can give the Wendell ticket a chance at success. Sure, there are film and advertising people in this country just as smart, as gifted, as Jerry Bloom. But Jerry has that certain indefinable quality called instinct. He knows exactly when to do what everyone else in the business would never do, and how to turn it into an unexpected success. I've seen his commercials get ridiculed one day by the national pundits and, the next day, be responsible for a gain of two or three percentage points in the polls. Do you know how many people are represented by just *one* percentage point in a national poll? About a million. Think about it. Somebody sits down at a typewriter and writes thirty seconds of seemingly simplistic dialogue, attaches some images to it, and by so doing, changes the minds of one million supposedly thinking, intelligent people."

"Okay, I'm not arguing. Obviously, I think he's pretty damned good, too. Look what he did for Hattie. She's appreciative. I'm appreciative. We all are. And I'm also damn glad he's handling this campaign. I don't happen to agree with you, that he can make that much of a difference. I guess I don't *want* advertising to do that. It offends me. But it's good having him here, just in case he *can* make the difference. This is the best shot Hattie is ever going to get at going all the way. And, judging from what I read this morning, there's a hell of a good chance we're going to make it. Harris says we're three to four points away from getting into a three-way deadlock. If the undecideds continue to seesaw back and forth between the other two guys, you know what's going to happen on Tuesday, don't you?"

"It could go to the House."

"And what happens if it goes to the House?" asked Brody. "Do you think there's any chance we can pull it off there?"

"Not only is there a chance," said Jeanette. "I'd put my money on Wendell to take it. Look, it's not the way a lot of people think it is when it goes into the House. Party loyalties are important. But some of them could go out the window for a lot of representatives once Tuesday has passed. They've all had to scramble for their own reelections. Conservative southerners can't accept Hart. He's not in the "club." Wendell is. They've gotten a message from the folks back home. Now they can sit down to some hardheaded bargaining. And Wendell has been preparing for that all along. I'm telling you, he can take it if he can get it thrown to the House. And you know as well as I do, those House members like to deal with "a good old boy," which Wendell is, and which Gary Hart is not. You also have to remember Wendell is still a Democrat to a lot of people."

"You mean he's actually been plotting to take it in the House?"

"I'm not sure I like the word *plotting*," said Jeanette. "Maybe he's simply been smart enough to anticipate what his one opportunity really is. And don't forget, each state gets just one vote. Little Wyoming gets an equal voice with big New York. It's a very different game."

"What about the Senate?" asked Brody. "That's where we have to do our worrying. Can Hattie carry it?"

"Well, I think she could. The Senate is looking like it's pretty fond of Stephen Wendell."

"But that's not my question," said Brody. "They don't get to vote on Wendell. Just the vice-president. And that's gotten to be a pretty conservative bunch of folks over there. How do you think they're going to react to a black woman for vice-president?"

Jeanette thought back to the conversation she had had with Bloom, in which he had related Braun's questions about the Senate, his doubts about that body's willingness to go for Hattie Lewis as vice-president. Again, she was uncomfortable as she thought of the Peterson and Kern connections. Now, there was the possible Saraf connection, a plot to defeat Braun, perhaps, and, finally, the notion of the United States Senate being stacked against Hattie Lewis.

"Well," said Brody. "I still have my doubts about this Senate thing. I sure as hell would rather leave it up to the people right now, rather than up to the hundred members of that useless private club."

"But I don't see any way the people are going to do it. We just don't seem like we're going to be able to make fifty-one percent."

"Well, maybe Washington's hottest polling expert will be off," said Brody. "In fact, I'm going to be hoping you're a dismal failure, at least with this set of numbers."

"Hey, I'm with you. I'd love to be wrong Tuesday and see us with fifty-one percent."

"You know," reflected Brody, "I sometimes wonder if there really is such a thing as majority rule anymore."

Brody looked around the cafeteria, as though not wanting to be heard. "Well, if what you suspect *is* happening, Congress might not be planning to do very much to ensure majority rule."

"Careful, you could end up as paranoid as I'm getting," Jeanette said.

"What do you want me to do?" asked Brody.

"We need to find out if there's anything to this connection, whether Saraf is involved. If it's true that there's some kind of conspiracy to defeat people like Braun, to grease the Senate, for example, we've got to know about it. There could be laws being broken. What about money? If people like Kern and Peterson are involved, that means big money. The wrong kind of money. What would Arab terrorists gain by getting into the action?"

"Hey, that's a lot of questions at one time. And you're beginning to sound like someone out of a Ludlum novel. This is the real world. Do you really think things like this can happen here?"

"You, yourself, reminded me that politics isn't the real world. Yes, I'm afraid any of it could happen."

"I'll see what I can find out. What about Hattie? Do you want me to talk to her?"

"No. God, she's got so much on her mind now. Four days until the biggest moment of her life. I don't think there's anything she could possibly do to shed any light on this. Obviously, if there *is* something going on, she wouldn't know the first thing about it."

"What about this guy you're working for, Harrison Davis?" asked Brody.

"You know, Jerry's raising the same question. He just isn't comfortable with Davis. He never was. But, on the other hand, we both realize Davis is Wendell's lifelong friend. If he's up to anything, he's doing it without the candidate's knowledge; we're convinced. What we don't know is how he could get away with it."

"Well, he could get away with it. But only to a point. Sooner or later, it's got to catch up. The question is, does it catch up too late?"

"How do you think you can find out anything about Aram Saraf?" asked Jeanette.

"I've got a friend at Justice."

"I'll bet you do," Jeanette said knowingly.

"No big deal. Just a smart young lady I've known over the years. And I'm not going to ask her to do anything illegal. I'll just try and get a quick rundown on what the department knows about Saraf."

"And Peterson and Kern? Do you think you can find out anything about what they're up to?"

"Maybe. A guy I know is writing a book on the far right in America. He's been doing a lot of digging into Texas characters. You may know him. Peter Bergman. He wrote that exposé last year about abortion-clinic violence. He's good. If anybody knows what's going on down in Texas with the loony-tunes, Peter does."

"Do you think you can get something quickly?"

Brody looked at his watch. "How's this afternoon?"

"You're terrific. Thank you."

"Hey, nothing to it. We may have ourselves another Watergate."

"But this time it could be one of us, instead of Richard Nixon."

"Or a whole bunch of us," said Brody. He was beginning to look worried, which was very unusual for this generally calm, virtually unflappable young man.

Bloom decided to take a five-mile run in an attempt to clear his head. He hoped to sort out some of the worries that both puzzled and troubled him, and he pushed himself hard as he approached the stark, black monolith that was the understated memorial to Americans killed in the Vietnam war. It was an unusually warm day for the last week of October. The skies were bright and clear and, had it not been for the Friday morning rush-hour traffic in Washington, it would have felt like a pleasant run in the countryside of the Los Angeles hills. The lawn in the park was still bright green, and the fragrance of lingering summer flowers and fresh-cut grass hung pleasantly in the air. Bloom saw the sea of names, etched, black on black, into the shiny stone walls, coming into view. He ran on the grass, along the asphalt path that followed the monument walls. He had always found the monument appropriate to the war it memorialized. It was completely devoid of pomp, of heraldry, of pride. It reflected a sad time in America's modern history, one whose deeds should not be memorialized, but whose unfortunate participants should. And the black stone walls, set low and unobtrusively in the ground, did just that.

This early morning break from the final days of the campaign should have been exhilarating. The last weekend before November's first Tuesday was usually a welcome time for Bloom. There was very little that could be done with media at that late date, unless some last-minute response to an issue or a charge needed to be made with a fast, videotape commercial. Otherwise, everything that could have been done had been done. The final weekend could be spent winding down, preparing for the twelve hours of waiting for a hundred million people to decide who would be president of the United States. But today the tension was far from winding down. Bloom's heart sank in anticipation of what he might find out and at his helplessness, at being unable to do anything about it at this late hour.

The campaign had been a very demanding one, as all campaigns are. But surprisingly, Bloom had found the pace to be less frenetic than smaller ones, such as Senate or gubernatorial campaigns. Focusing on one candidate, nationally, instead of six or seven individuals scattered across the country seemed to simplify things, even though the scale was vastly greater. Also, the organization was so well structured and managed that there was very little of the stopping and restarting typical of state-wide races. The machinery for a presidential campaign was so large, it was a foregone conclusion that it could not easily be moved and shifted. A television commercial might take only a few days to produce, but it would also take several days to traffic prints of it to stations across the country. It was unlike the old days for Bloom, when he could film a commercial one morning, supervise its editing that night, carry it across town the next morning to have dubs made, personally deliver them to four television stations by four in the afternoon, and see it run at six.

Bloom let his mind drift back to those earlier days, when his responsibilities were so much smaller, when life was simpler, more in keeping with what he had imagined it would be. Those were days when presidential politics was something to observe from a distance. Helping people get to the Senate or the House, making a difference in a governor's race or a mayoralty campaign—that was what he would do with his life until, of course, some good fortune and some gained wisdom would allow him to write a screenplay that would be produced or a book that would be published.

He reflected back on scenes, on events, on conversations from those simpler times. The warm sun reminded him of the warmth he had felt some ten years earlier, when he and Anne had driven to a deserted stretch of beach in northern Baja California for a day of picnicking, walking on the sand, plus an unplanned and totally fulfilling seduction of one another. They had finished a bottle of wine and were sitting on a blanket, holding hands, watching the late afternoon sun perform its colorful magic on the sky over the Pacific. They toyed with one another, petting and giggling. Anne whispered things in Bloom's ear, things that aroused him to a level of passion to which no other woman had been able before or since. She needed to be reassured that no one could see them, as Bloom began to open her blouse and as he fumbled for the metal buttons on her jeans. And then they made love, each giving equally to the other.

"My God, someone may see us like this," Anne had said, as she neared her climax.

"Jesus, I hope so," said Bloom, laughing, moving with her. "We can't keep something like this from the world. It wouldn't be fair."

Afterward, they had talked about the future. About Bloom's decision the previous day to turn down a handsome fee to handle the campaign of a popular senator from Oregon because "something's flaky about that guy." He had a difficult time explaining it to anyone, especially Anne, but it was the only way he could operate his business.

"There goes our vacation in Switzerland," Anne had joked with him. "Guess we'll have to settle for some more picnics."

"I don't want a felon or a flake on my record," he explained to her on that marvelous day as they sipped from another bottle of May wine and watched a blood-red sun finally drop into the ocean.

"But how can you tell if your candidates will always be pure?"

"You can't. But anyone who worked for Richard Nixon should have seen it coming, don't you agree?"

That's it, dammit. You should have seen it coming. Or did the pile of money block your vision? And Bloom picked up his pace as he neared the bridge over the Potomac.

"But Nixon was the exception," Anne continued, in Bloom's memory. "You can't write bond on all your clients."

"No, but I have only one reputation."

That had been a time in their marriage when they'd had endless questions to ask one another, endless stories to share. Marriages, even close ones, often lapse into long, comfortable silences, but theirs had not. Bloom had related a story that day on the beach, to illustrate his point.

"Did you ever hear of Pierre the builder? He complained, 'I build the biggest bridge in the world, and am I known as Pierre the bridge-builder? No. I build the longest tunnel in the world. Am I called Pierre the tunnel-builder? No. I build the biggest airport in the world. Am I known as Pierre the airport-builder? No. I commit one act of sodomy, and I'm known as Pierre Le Cocksucker!'"

"Funny," said Anne, with a wink. "What does that make me?"

"A very beautiful woman," said Bloom, stroking her back gently. "And my wife, I'm happy to say."

Bloom reluctantly wrenched his mind back to the present. He had to take some action and he had to do it soon. But *what* action, based on *what* information, he couldn't say. His emotions were churning within him. His warm recollections of Anne were challenged by his equally warm memories of Jeanette. The catalyst was guilt. And added to the confusion was the feeling of something ominous, something beyond control, eclipsing everything else.

Fight or flight. What's it going to be? he asked himself, as he felt the tingling in his hands and feet, the sensation of the hair on the back of his neck standing out.

When Bloom opened the door of his hotel suite, he saw a manila envelope on the floor. It had been slid beneath the door. His initials, J.B., were scrawled across the front in red felt-tip pen. He knew it came from Jeanette.

Inside was a copy of a newspaper story and a photo of Kern and Saraf. Jeanette had circled both the men's faces in red. Clipped to the copy was a handwritten note: *The dark man is definitely Aram Saraf. What are he and Kern doing together? Trying to find out. Will call later. Miss you.*

Bloom knew exactly who Aram Saraf was. He had heard of the threat the Palestinian posed to Israel, to Jews everywhere, and to any nations that supported Israel. It seemed to Bloom that every new danger signal was leading to another, more alarming one. First Senator Braun was targeted by the right wing, with some connection to the Wendell campaign. Then the right wing was connected to the Palestinians, who, in turn, were connected to the militant fringe, which was connected back to the campaign. From Peterson to Saraf to Kern and back to Wendell. What kind of circle was being formed? Bloom wanted to talk with someone. But who? Jeanette was out somewhere. Anne? Sure, she's just waiting to have a friendly chat. David Braun? He's hurting enough right now, thank you. Bloom got his wallet, pulled out a small white card, and read a phone number next to the initials H.L. He dialed Hattie Lewis's unlisted home phone, but got only a recording of her voice, saying she was sorry she was unavailable and reciting the usual message one finds on an answering machine. Of course she wouldn't be at her home in Washington. With four days remaining in the campaign, she was completing, along with Wendell, the last-minute crisscrossing of the country, shoring up strength where it was known to exist, seeking out support where it might still be found.

The telephone rang just as Bloom was about to take off his running clothes. It was probably the last voice Bloom wanted to hear. "Jerome? Harrison Davis. I'd like to speak with you right away."

"I'm meeting with the radio coordinators in an hour," said Bloom. The campaign had "found" an additional $500,000 with which they could shore up nationwide radio appeals from Wendell to uncommitted voters on Monday. It was one of the few eleventh-hour strategies the campaign had decided upon. Just where the money had come from had not been explained yet.

"I know about your meeting. I've taken the liberty of postponing it for an hour. I'd like to meet you outside the office. This is a matter that requires confidentiality, and I'm sure you know how uncertain security can be during these final days."

Now what? "All right. Where?"

"Do you know where the Vietnam Memorial is?" The coincidence was crazy. "Yes."

"Good. There's a walkway nearby, and a Park Service information booth. Meet me there in thirty minutes."

"Fine. Do I need to prepare?"

"No. I just wish to have a brief discussion with you."

"I'll see you then," said Bloom. His mind swirled in the circle of unlikely people who continued to haunt him. Now, in the middle of it, he saw the calm, if not smug face of Harrison Davis.

It was easy for Bloom to pick out Davis, who was slowly walking near the Park Service booth. He wore the same dark, three-piece business suit and the same gray fedora. He was broad enough across the midsection to resemble Alfred Hitchcock in profile. But that was where the comparison ended. There was not so much as a hint of humor in his face. His eyes seemed always to be trying to penetrate, rather than merely seeing something, which was how he fixed his gaze on Bloom.

"Jerome, I've run across some news that disturbs me deeply, especially with the election just a few days away." He paused, watching Bloom's reaction. "It concerns Jeanette and, therefore, it has to do with you."

"I hope we're not going to be talking about my private life," said Bloom.

"Only as it relates to this campaign and directly affects it. It's quite clear that you and Jeanette are involved in a—" he searched for a word. "Shall we say, a relationship?"

"We spend some time together."

"I'm sure you do. And it's not any of our concern

as to what that relationship has to do with your private affairs, or with your marriage."

"I would hope not."

"The point is, Jerome, that Jeanette has gone on some sort of investigative journey, in these closing and critical hours of our campaign. She apparently feels that something is amiss—that there are some improprieties or irregularities. Unfortunately, she has not come to me, nor to anyone else in the campaign, to discuss her suspicions. With one exception, of course. She has come to you. Am I correct?"

Bloom quickly tried to assess how much Davis knew versus how much he was trying to guess. "I know she's upset about some things that have happened lately in the campaign."

"Come on, Jerome, I don't have time to fence with you. She is more than merely upset. You know it. And I know you know it."

"Now, wait a minute." Bloom was angry enough to drop his guard. "My nerves are getting pretty frayed at the edges. I've seen some things lately that I don't like. So has Jeanette. I'll be happy to tell you about the things I've come across. As for Jeanette, you're going to have to ask her yourself. And I hope you'll do it with a lighter hand."

"I'd be pleased to discuss it if I could locate her. She was due at a meeting two hours ago, an important meeting, and she never appeared. We've still not heard from her."

That worried Bloom. Not because she'd missed a meeting, but because it was totally unlike her not to appear where she was expected. That just didn't happen.

"Well, I don't know where she is right now, but I'm sure she had a valid reason for not showing up."

"Oh, I have no doubt she felt she had a good reason. But I must find out the details of these bizarre notions she has about the campaign. Did you know she went to see a young man by the name of Brody, a Donald Brody, in Hattie Lewis's office?"

"No, I didn't know that." But Bloom did know that Jeanette and Brody were old and close friends. It was something she hadn't told Bloom until recently. He had been surprised, because he, too, had known and liked Brody for years. They had, in fact, worked closely on Hattie's congressional campaigns.

"Well, she met with this Brody and somehow convinced him there were some sort of wrongdoings in and around the campaign. Very unfortunate. Now Brody is conducting an investigation of his own. And I can't tell you how damaging that can be at this point. Both of the political parties, and most of the press in this country, would love the opportunity to hurl some outrageous accusations at the governor during this last weekend. The timing would be just right for them; we would not have enough time to appropriately answer the charges."

It was so easy for perpetrators to act like victims when confronted, Bloom thought. "I really don't think there's a plot afoot to discredit the candidate," he said.

"But you are ready to accept that *we* have some sort of plot we've constructed."

"I didn't say that. But let me ask you something. What does our organization have to do with Senator Braun's campaign in California?"

308

Davis didn't react, other than to narrow his eyes. "What are we doing? Nothing. Don't you think we have enough on our hands without getting into Senate campaigns?"

"I definitely *do* think so. But apparently someone in this campaign disagrees with me. Why did the same letter that went out from us to people in financial trouble go out to voters in California, calling for the defeat of David Braun?"

"You're obviously referring to the mailing by the independent PAC people. And when I say independent, I mean it—a group that operates independently of us, and of any other campaign."

"On the record, they do. In fact, if they don't, they're guilty of election-law violations, along with the candidate with whom they're in concert."

"Thank you for the information. I'm quite familiar with election laws, however."

"And you're saying it's only coincidence? That this campaign isn't trying to stack the Senate?"

"Just what are you talking about now?"

"I'm talking about the notion that maybe Stephen Wendell wants to be ready for an election decision in Congress."

"But the presidency is decided in the House in the event that no candidate gets a majority." His tone was most patronizing.

"And I thank *you* for the information, of which I'm quite aware. But the Senate could be greased to our advantage, too, couldn't it?"

"To Hattie Lewis's advantage. Not the governor's."

Bloom felt frustrated. The need to swing the closely divided Senate made more sense when

Braun made a case for the idea. "But that's where the governor needs help with his immigration bills."

"Perhaps he does. But that's much farther down the road than we can possibly deal with now. If you told me a presidential candidate was working to create a friendly environment in the House, I might at least say your tale has some plausibility. But the Senate? Come now, Jerome, that doesn't make any sense. Of course, if Hattie were to do some homework there, that, too, might have a shred of plausibility."

Bloom realized how absurd that idea was. Hattie Lewis trying to stack the Senate, where her fate would be decided? Come on, Bloom. However, for just one fleeting moment, he acknowledged to himself that Davis was right, that there was at least more believability to that kind of scenario.

"What about Clarence Peterson?" Bloom asked.

"Clarence Peterson? He's a very wealthy man who has borne a grudge against the governor for a number of years."

"Yes, I'm familiar with the migrant worker story. But what has Peterson got to do with this campaign?"

"He, himself, has said, more than once, that he would do what he could to block Stephen Wendell's political career."

"But I'd still like to know what he has to do with the campaign."

The two men looked into each other's eyes. Davis showed no sign of weakening, and Bloom had no inclination to back away. Finally, Davis spoke, in a lower, controlled voice. "I want to make myself abundantly clear. You and Jeanette are posing a se-

310

rious threat to this campaign, an effort to which people have dedicated themselves completely, one to which people have given a great deal of effort and money. It is not a lark. It is a real effort, with a definite chance of success, to change the course of American history. I will not tolerate any attempt to undermine or subvert that mission. You are tampering with something enormous. I must urge you to stop doing so immediately, and to see that Jeanette stops as well."

Bloom glared at Davis even more intensely. "I have a real problem with threats, even when they come from someone who thinks he's going to sit at the feet of the new emperor. So, I'd suggest you back off and ease up. If I believe someone's screwing the system, or the people, or, worse, breaking the law on behalf of a political campaign, I'm going to blow the whistle as loudly as I can."

"And that, I presume, is *your* threat?"

"I think you read me correctly."

"I'll consider myself forewarned." Davis reached into an inside pocket in his suit coat. For an instant, Bloom was alarmed, perhaps because he expected to see something preposterous, like a gun. Instead, Davis fished out a white business envelope and handed it to Bloom.

"It would be pointless to dismiss you now," said Davis, "since this is your last fee payment. On time."

Bloom paused before reaching for the envelope. The last 250,000 pieces of silver.

"I suppose my refusing this would be as pointless as your dismissing me."

"I think it would be. Jerome, you've done a remarkable job for us. You made a genuine difference. And it appears that we may very well win, although I don't have the benefit of Jeanette's polling data for today." Davis was not hiding the contempt for Jeanette in his voice. "If we do win the presidency, it would be a shame to see the achievement you've made become obscured by this misunderstanding. If we succeed, and if you are still with us, your future is secure. In fact, it is limitless. I hope you'll keep that in mind."

"I'll try to," said Bloom, anxious to leave and find Jeanette. He found it strange that he should now have been at this same spot, the Vietnam Memorial, twice within two hours. Davis asked Bloom to go over some of the last-minute radio arrangements before leaving, which he did. There was no further reference to Jeanette, and Davis's tone returned to its usual businesslike formality as he recited a list of cities across the country, telling Jerome what dollar amount would be spent on last-minute radio in each. His mind functioned like a computer, Bloom thought, as he scrambled to take notes on what Davis had committed to memory.

Ten minutes later, Davis looked at his watch and said he had to be going back to the campaign offices. And he made only one last reference to Jeanette before they parted.

Bloom nodded and said he would get together with the radio people in the afternoon. Walking back to his hotel, he looked in every direction along the way, as if actually thinking he might run into Jeanette. But he knew she wouldn't be out taking a sunny stroll on this warm October morning.

Clarence Peterson's voice gave away the stress he was under as he spoke quietly into the telephone from the study of his ranch outside Austin.

"I'm telling you, Saraf, she's figured out too damn much already."

"You don't think she is calling your bluff?" asked Aram Saraf, from the living room of Thomas Kern's ranch house in Colorado.

"It doesn't sound like a bluff to me. She said she knows of the connection between you, the Colonel, and me, and of our involvement in the Wendell campaign. She said if I don't talk to her, she'll take the story to the goddamn *Washington Post*."

"This is the time to be calm and careful. We are very close now."

"But this whole thing has become a different story. You guys are talking about putting a hit out on somebody—not just somebody, the vice——"

Saraf sprang like a switchblade knife, cutting off Peterson. "Do not say anything more! Do you understand?"

"Nobody's tapping my damn telephone. All right, have it your way. But we're going to have to deal with this woman."

"We will," said Saraf, much softer now. "We will."

17

"IT'S BEEN A LONG TIME," BLOOM said to Don Brody, shaking his hand, impressed with Brody's ability to retain the same youthful appearance he had always had. "You look like you're still ready for the next march on Washington."

"We don't do those anymore," said Brody, smiling only slightly.

They were in Brody's car, a somewhat bruised and dirty Volvo station wagon, predictably enough. Brody had called Bloom early Saturday morning, telling him he had to talk with him about Jeanette and what she was learning about the Wendell campaign. His request was for Bloom to drive to Georgetown, park his rented car, and wait to be picked up.

"Sorry about all the cloak and dagger," said Brody, as he turned his car into the traffic. "But I have a feeling you're probably being tailed now."

"You think it's all that serious?"

"I'm afraid so. Jeanette's discovered a damn big

time bomb. And she may be setting it off prematurely."

"Where is she now?" asked Bloom.

Brody shook his head and sighed. "I don't know. All I can tell you is, she's safe. Somewhere out of town. Do you know where she was yesterday?"

"No. And it made me kind of crazy."

"Austin, Texas."

"What? Come on. Austin? What the hell would she go there for? She was supposed to be in Washington. At meetings. Davis was expecting her. So was I."

"You know who Clarence Peterson is?"

Bloom felt that uncomfortable twinge run through him again.

"Yes. All of a sudden, his name is coming up regularly. He's in Austin?"

"Yes. And so was Jeanette. For just a few hours, I guess."

"What was she doing? Confronting him?" Bloom chuckled nervously.

"That's exactly what she was doing. I guess she went down there with the stuff she found in the newspaper files, and with what I dug up for her."

"And what was that—the stuff you dug up?"

"It's all in here," said Brody, reaching down on the seat between them and under some newspapers, for a large red-and-white envelope from National Express Couriers. He handed it to Bloom. The shipping label had Brody's name on it.

"What is it?" Bloom asked.

"It's an audio cassette that Jeanette made last night in Austin. And I think she included some of the things she's gathered, like pictures and newspaper stories and canceled checks. Anyway, she called me and told me this package was coming. I just picked it up at the airport. She didn't want to chance sending it to your hotel. She thinks you—and she—are being followed. Maybe they're even tampering with your mail and messages at your hotel."

"Does Hattie know what's going on?" Bloom wished he could open the envelope and play the tape right there.

Brody, without turning his head, said, "She's heard the whole story from Jeanette. They had a forty-minute phone conversation last night."

"And?"

"And Hattie told Jeanette to lay low for a while. In fact, she made arrangements for a place for her to go and stay, probably until after Tuesday. Hattie feels there isn't conclusive proof of anything yet, but she thinks there might just be enough to make her want to protect Jeanette. Even though Hattie's inclined to disbelieve most of the story, she doesn't want Jeanette taking any unnecessary risks."

"She won't tell you where Jeanette is staying?"

Brody shrugged. "She didn't offer the information, which is her way of telling me she doesn't want me to know. I'm sure she doesn't want anyone knowing."

"What do we do now?" asked Bloom, wondering if he could summon the control he was going to need to see this bizarre affair through without doing anything precipitous or foolish.

"The only thing that Hattie has told me about her talk with Jeanette is that she didn't learn anything that would warrant bringing in the cops or the feds. If she, or anyone else, were to make this thing public, who knows what the hell would happen, with the election seventy-two hours away. It's the proverbial loose cannon on the deck. No one knows what it will hit when it goes off. If we were to break the story, and disavow whatever these creeps are up to, maybe it wouldn't hurt us. Maybe it would help us. Who knows? I think what we'd see is sheer chaos on Tuesday. I mean, we're talking major disruption of the whole damn system. Can you imagine what would have happened if Nixon had gotten caught with the altered tapes the weekend before the election? Only this one may be even bigger and more ominous than that. At least, that's what Jeanette thinks."

"So we just sit on it?" asked an irritated Bloom.

"I don't know what we do. The crazy thing is, the ball might just end up in your court. Jeanette's given her evidence, or at least her notions of evidence, to you. She obviously wants you to make some judgment about it, and about what to do." He reflected for a few moments. "You know, it's crazy. Who would have thought the media flack would end up being the chief investigator, and the special prosecutor, too? I hope they're paying you enough of a fee to justify the extra assignments."

Bloom said nothing. He had a curious fantasy, however. He wondered if something inside him could actually burst, like a balloon inflated beyond its capacity, if the stress level exceeded what the body could withstand. He rolled down the window a few inches, to breathe some outside air in an effort to overcome the feeling that everything, even the old station wagon, was closing in on him.

Bloom was clearly in a hurry when he arrived back at his hotel, clutching the envelope from Jeanette in his hand. As soon as he was in his suite, he got his portable tape recorder out and tore open the envelope. Inside was a black plastic box, containing the single audio cassette. The label was blank. Also in the envelope were several newspaper stories, with Jeanette's familiar red circling and underlining on them, plus photos and memos. There was a brief, handwritten note as well. It said, simply, *Jerry: The story's on the tape. I hope we both see a brighter day soon. Lovingly, J.*

Bloom inserted the cassette into the small machine, sat down in the desk chair, pressed the play button, and waited for Jeanette's voice.

It's very late. And I'm very tired ... very frightened as well. I want you to know that I wish I were with you now, that I need very much to be with you. But these extraordinary events that have happened don't allow that. I wanted to make this tape because I felt you should hear from me what I'm about to say, rather than read it. There's something about the way we've communicated, talking endlessly with one another, that is so genuine, so meaningful, that I find it important for you to hear my voice.

I'll begin with a confession of my own. As magical as our relationship has become, it was begun, not as you suspected, out of a happy coincidence, a chance meeting on an airplane. Jerry, I was on that airplane for a purpose. I knew about your visit to Dallas from Phoenix, when all this began for you. I volunteered to do whatever I could to help convince you to join the campaign. I arranged to be on the same flight for which Davis got you a ticket, presuming you would respond to the offer.

Bloom stood up, angered, suddenly humiliated, at what was unfolding. "No, God, not Jeanette, too," he said aloud to himself. She continued:

Why would I do such a thing? For a reason that I think only a Jerry Bloom could understand, if you're willing to. I believed in Stephen Wendell. And even after what I've learned now, I still believe in him, and in what he's trying to do for this country of ours. I also did it because I always have, and always will, believe in what my husband, Jeff, did and stood for. Stephen Wendell made certain that Jeff's work will reach the audiences for which he created it. The Institute is terribly important to me, and I'm grateful to the governor for helping it. But there's still another reason why I did what I chose to do: I have within me an irresistible desire to see some justice—or call it revenge, if you will—come out of the tragedy that took Jeff. As committed as I have been in the past to the very same things to which you are, I feel a need for—in fact, I demand—a change in the way this country deals with its immigration problems. The people who killed Jeff were in the

319

country illegally. Like the Marielitos Castro sent us in the seventies, they were not the downtrodden seeking asylum from totalitarians; they were the ruthless and the criminal, seeking the freedom to roam America's streets and to steal, to kill or do whatever they chose to do. We have not had strong enough political leadership in this country to deal with that problem, not until Stephen Wendell came along. An eye for an eye? Perhaps. And if so, I don't apologize for it. My pain over the loss of Jeff will not allow me to.

What else did I do to you out of my commitment and, therefore, dishonestly? Well, I suppose you could say that I seduced you, just as I think several of us did, to get you to join us. Hattie did, as did Davis—and the candidate himself. The difference is, they seduced you intellectually or monetarily. I did it literally. I invited you to make love to me because I thought it would draw you closer to me and, therefore, to what is so important to me.

Bloom looked out at the quiet street below, and over toward the Capitol. He could see the dome, shining bright, looking clean and untarnished by all things that went on beneath and around it. His eyes were welling with tears. His emotions were confused.

The predictable happened, however. I soon discovered that I wanted you for other, more selfish reasons. Yes, I fell in love with you. I hope that there will be within you some wish to at least talk to me again, to let me regain what I have now taken from you: your confidence in me. But we shall have to wait and see.

Now, I want to tell you what I have learned in these past few days, and what I feel I have sufficiently documented only today. Again, I felt this tape was the best way to tell you about it, since I cannot be there with you, and since a letter would also involve some risk of interception. Sorry if I seem too melodramatic, but I'm very frightened.

Clarence Peterson, Thomas Kern, and Aram Saraf are deeply involved in this campaign. Their motive is to affect the outcome of Tuesday's election, with Stephen Wendell the winner. They are helping insure their chances by also participating in several House campaigns. But, and very much to my horror, they have other goals, incredible goals. It is their plan to be certain that if Stephen Wendell takes office as president, Hattie Lewis will never be sworn in as vice-president. A bizarre, yet quite plausible plot has been devised to kill Hattie before she can take office in January, if she is elected. That plot would only be implemented if Hattie cannot first be blocked in the Senate. And that is the only way in which we can win. A majority win for Wendell is not possible now. I'm sure you're finding this as preposterous, as hard to believe as I first did. But I'm convinced it's true.

Even without the plot against Hattie, these people have entered into conspiracy and collusion, and broken a host of federal election laws.

Several so-called PACs have been established, solely for the purpose of laundering illegal campaign funding, which comes from such sources as three different oil-producing countries in the Mideast, Palestinian terrorist groups, and wealthy oilmen here in the United States, who have given hundreds of thousands of dollars more than the law allows, by funneling it through phony fronts.

Clarence Peterson, who is in way over his head, and who wants no part of the plot against Hattie, admitted virtually all of this. He, of course, will not confess any of it to authorities, but he agreed to tell me his story in exchange for the time I have agreed to give him before taking it to the police or FBI. I need the time to discuss this with you, and with Hattie, before I try to take it any further. And the question still remains of withholding what I've discovered until after Tuesday. There are enormous implications, most of which I cannot yet sort through. I need your help and counsel.

It began last December, when Clarence Peterson and Aram Saraf met to discuss their mutual interests, particularly in finding a way to profit from an artificial inflation of oil prices, a goal that could end up giving Peterson and fellow oilmen millions, if not billions, in new-found profits. Saraf, at the same time, wanted to find ways to force this country to change its policies on Israel, so that he and his associates could operate more freely as they try to destroy the Jewish state. . . .

322

And Jeanette continued to unfold her story, step-by-step, with details, with names and places. She went on for another twenty minutes, quoting verbatim from her conversation with Peterson and using as support excerpts from newspaper stories she had collected, stories that at least verified connections between the three principal conspirators, and memos from Don Brody's contact in the Justice Department.

When she was through with her presentation, Jeanette left Bloom with one last thought:

If I never see you again, I hope and pray it is not because you will not allow it. I love you. And I ask your forgiveness, my beloved.

Bloom picked up the tape recorder and turned it off. He let his body fall limp on the sofa, then he picked up a pillow and placed it over his face. To keep the world from his view. And to keep his tears from the world.

18

THE SIRENS OF RACING FIRE EN-
gines broke an otherwise quiet
and peaceful Saturday night in
northeast Denver. It was just after midnight when
the first truck pulled up in front of the Eternal
Light Baptist Church and Brotherhood, at the corner of Martin Luther King Boulevard and Maple Avenue. The large frame structure, with its pictur-
esque white steeple, was already engulfed in orange
flames. It was some time before firemen could get
sufficient control of the blaze to go inside the building, which had partly collapsed as its supporting
beams were eaten through by the fire.

At three in the morning, the Reverend Abraham
Lewis, father of Congresswoman Hattie Lewis and
pastor of the church, was interviewed by a reporter
from KCNC, the local NBC affiliate.

Lewis, a big, handsome man with distinguished
gray hair, was dressed in an overcoat thrown over
his nightclothes. He had been awakened by the sirens and had run the three blocks to his church, arriving as the flames were already shooting skyward.

"Reverend Lewis," said the young woman reporter, "we're told there was one person in the church, and that that person did not get out. Is that true, sir?"

Lewis nodded sadly. He spoke so softly, he could barely be heard. "Yes. We had a visitor staying with us, in our guest apartment. She was trapped. She died of smoke inhalation, I'm told."

"Can you tell us who the victim was?" the reporter asked sympathetically.

"She was an old friend and associate of my daughter's." Lewis stared down at the ground, shaking his head. "Her name was Jeanette Wells."

It was eight-thirty in the morning on Sunday when Bloom received the call from Hattie.

"I have some very bad news that I find difficult to tell you," said Hattie, her voice under as much control as possible. "Jeanette died during the night." That sort of news seemed to come without fanfare, so matter-of-factly to Bloom. It was the same way he had been told, by phone, that his father had died. And, a few years later, when his brother had been struck dead by a heart attack. That, too, came to him by phone. In one brief sentence.

"How?"

"She was staying at my father's church, in Denver. I arranged for her to go there until Tuesday. It seemed like such a safe place to be. A church. One that we built as a memorial to love and to brotherhood, on the boulevard that carries Martin Luther King's name. That's where she died. I don't know what else to say, Jerry."

"Did someone do this, I mean, intentionally? Did someone kill her, Hattie?"

"I don't know. She was the only person in the church. There's no sign of arson at this point—they say it was faulty wiring."

"I can't accept coincidence any longer when something happens to anyone involved in this campaign," said Bloom. "No, if it was faulty wiring, then someone made it faulty, did it methodically and efficiently. That's what I think we're up against."

"Were you in love with Jeanette?" Hattie asked.

"Does it really make any difference? Does anything, anymore?"

"Yes. Things still do. Somehow, we've got to move past this horrible tragedy, Jerry. I no more feel like making a speech tonight than you feel like going out dancing. But I've got to do it. Just two more days and we will have done what all of us have believed needs doing, or we will have given our goddamnedest effort to do it."

"Jeanette believed in it," said Bloom. "Right up until she breathed her last breath."

"And do you?"

"I don't know what I believe in right now. It costs too much to believe."

"What are you going to do now?"

"I don't know. I think I'll go to Los Angeles."

"That's where I'm calling from. I'm going to finish here tomorrow night. At the Ambassador."

"I'd like to see the children. And Anne. It's been a while."

"Give them my love, will you, media man?"

"Yeah."

"And Jerry—I'm hurting for you, real bad."

Bloom arrived in Los Angeles on Sunday evening. He didn't go home to Pacific Palisades. Instead, he went to the Ambassador Hotel, where he was able to get a room for two nights. He would be staying until election day. The hotel had actually been fully booked, but his position with the Wendell/Lewis campaign, which had several rooms reserved, got him in.

He didn't call home until Monday morning, after sleeping through most of the night, with the help of two Dalmanes. He was still groggy when his wake-up call came at six-thirty. After breakfast, which he didn't actually eat, but merely stared at, he walked around the busy downtown area, then went back to his room, where he read more accounts of the death of Jeanette Wells. He also read that most polling experts were now predicting the presidential race would, in fact, be put into the House, with no candidate gaining a majority.

Anne was cordial on the telephone, and sympathetic at the news of Jeanette's death. She almost seemed to know that there had been some association between them. They talked for several minutes, mostly about the children, both of whom were in school and looking forward to the following day, which would be both a school holiday and a chance to see how their famous father had succeeded at making political history.

Bloom didn't, as he had planned, go to visit his family. Anne didn't invite him. And when he thought about it, why should she have? It was still his home. Wives don't invite husbands, generally, to their own homes. Husbands just appear there. But not Bloom. Not today. So he never broached the subject. And he spent the remainder of the day preparing for something he had been planning, since Sunday, in the Ambassador Hotel, on the eve of the election. He only told Anne, "You and the kids might be interested in what's going to be on television tonight. At six o'clock."

"Why?" Anne asked.

"It's not another Wendell commercial, I promise. It's a message. From me. To you, and the children. And to a couple hundred million other people."

"What on earth are you up to?"

"I guess you'll have to watch to find out, won't you?"

"Jerry?" Her voice was affectionate.

"Yes?"

"When will you see the kids?"

"I hope tomorrow. If I'm around."

"Are you leaving town again?"

"No."

"Well, good luck tonight."

"With the Wendell campaign?"

"With whatever it is you're doing at six."

"Thanks. I may just knock 'em dead."

Jerry Bloom had never held a press conference. He was quite familiar, however, with the process and procedure. He had coached others on how to look, how to speak, what gestures to use, what traps to avoid. After all those years of working behind the lights and the cameras, it was now to be his turn to be out front.

Bloom contacted, in the early afternoon, all three major television networks, as well as the independent and cable groups, the radio press corps in Los Angeles, and the major newspapers and wire services. The television networks were contacted with phone calls to key people, such as assignment editors in the news departments. Radio and newspaper reporters were sent copies of a telegram:

At six P.M. today, I will hold a press conference for the purpose of breaking a news story that will have an unprecedented impact on tomorrow's presidential election. It is a very serious story, with very serious implications for our democratic process. It involves improprieties and illegalities at the highest levels, and its magnitude would make Watergate appear to have been a minor misdemeanor.

Jerome Bloom
Media consultant to
Stephen Wendell,
Hattie Lewis

The invitations must have worked, Bloom realized, as he watched the television crews arrive—from all the networks—followed by radio and print media representatives. When an old friend from ABC asked him what the hell was up, Bloom politely said it would be the biggest story of the campaign, and he would have to wait with the rest. Another reporter asked Bloom, rather directly, if the press conference was some form of media hype, designed to bring out the press on election eve for an insignificant story. Bloom simply replied that the reporter was welcome to skip the conference and watch the story on the other networks as they broke into regular programming with bulletins. The reporter said nothing more, then went into the ballroom to wait for things to begin.

At five minutes before six, Hattie Lewis appeared in the hallway outside the ballroom. She went to Bloom, smiled politely, and motioned for him to step over to a more private spot, where they could talk.

"I haven't been in this hotel since Bobby was shot. Did you know it happened here?" she asked.

"Yes, I guess I did."

"I just talked to the governor. I waited, as you asked me to, until after five to tell him what's happened. Jerry, the poor man is shattered. He, of course, denies any knowledge whatsoever of anything that Jeanette claims took place. He swears he's never met, or even heard of, Aram Saraf. He knows Peterson and Kern and despises them both."

"Do you believe him?" asked Bloom, looking around, checking his watch.

"Yes, I do. Do you know, he heard that Kern sent him a thousand dollars six months ago? He demanded to see the check and tore it up into little pieces, bellowing an order that no money was to be accepted from Kern or anyone like him. Jerry, the man is decent and honest. Ambitious? Hell, yes. So am I. So are you. But he's got a vision for this country that I share. Don't tear it down, baby, please."

"It's not my intention to tear down anything, Hattie. As bad as I want to see you go to the top of the mountain, we've got to get this out for the people to see. Let them decide what gets torn down and who pays for what's happened. Sorry, but I'm on," he said. "I love you, lady." He quickly kissed Hattie on the cheek and entered the ballroom, trying to keep everything in control, from his anxiety to his bladder.

He walked, as confidently as he could, to the podium, which had a cluster of microphones attached to it. He opened his black attaché case, took out the portable tape recorder, and placed it on the podium. He checked his watch. Exactly six. He cleared his throat. He watched the red lights on the television cameras come on. Each cameraman gave a subtle signal, from a nod to a pointing finger, to indicate that they were rolling. With that as his cue, Jerry Bloom began speaking to millions of Americans and, for all he knew, to audiences in other countries as well.

"Good evening. My name is Jerome Bloom. I serve as director of communications for Stephen Wendell and Hattie Lewis in their campaign for president and vice-president. My responsibility is for the television, radio, and newspaper promotion.

"I've asked to talk briefly to the American people tonight about events that have been uncovered recently in this presidential campaign, and that threaten the very system that allows us, each four years, to freely and democratically elect a president.

"Early Sunday morning a young woman died in a fire in Denver, Colorado. Her name was Jeanette Wells. She served as director of research and polling for the Wendell campaign. I am convinced that her death was not an accident, but a successful attempt to silence her, lest she tell the nation what I am about to tell you."

Bloom paused long enough to take a deep breath and let it out. He noticed the previously skeptical reporter was furiously taking notes and whispering to his cameraman.

"This is the voice of Jeanette Wells, recorded just hours before she died, in Austin, Texas." He turned the recorder on, and Jeanette's voice came through it and into the room, into the microphones.

Clarence Peterson, Thomas Kern, and Aram Saraf are deeply involved in this campaign, it began, and continued to reveal the details of the plot Jeanette had uncovered and pieced together. Bloom watched the reporters and cameramen as they showed their awe at what they were hearing, which was unusual for hardened members of the press, who ordinarily cultivated a jaded approach to politics. The tape ran for another ten minutes, naming names, citing dates and places. Then, Bloom turned off the recorder and resumed.

"I believe that Jeanette Wells uncovered the truth. What I do not know is who was involved at the level of campaign management. Nor can I say— as Jeanette did not—that Stephen Wendell had any knowledge of any of these events. But I do raise the question: Is the captain responsible for the wrongs that occur on his team?—a question once asked rhetorically, and ironically, by Richard Nixon. It is up to the people to judge that issue. My responsibility tonight is to warn every American who will vote tomorrow that the Wendell candidacy got where it is today, in part, with the help of unscrupulous people, motivated by greed and hate, to influence—and even control—the highest office in the land. For a higher profit on a barrel of oil, for a chance to spread racism and destroy the state of Israel, this handful of people has jeopardized the candidacy of a man I have grown to admire and respect.

"Among the several lessons to be learned from this dark experience is that the entire process of electoral politics has become sullied by excess. What was intended to be a process of debate and judicious selection of government has become a war of the dollars, a battle of the television commercials, a money game that has taken politics out of the hands of the people and placed it in the fists of special interests. It is not a question of who has the best credentials, but, simply, who has the largest television budget."

Bloom pointed to a stack of white, 9″ × 12″ envelopes on a table beside the podium. "I have prepared for members of the press a collection of documentations of the charges Ms. Wells made in her tape. They include articles from newspapers, photographs of the alleged conspirators, and even canceled checks that represent money illegally laundered into the campaign.

"The campaign manager for the Wendell/Lewis candidacy, Mr. Harrison Davis, when confronted with these charges, chose not to discuss them with me, but, rather, to threaten me and imply that Ms. Wells would suffer grave consequences if she pursued the matter—which, sadly enough, she did. I asked Mr. Davis to appear here this evening, and he declined. Both his silence and his absence will have to speak for themselves.

"That is all I have to say, except to once again appeal to the voters of this country to think carefully about your choice tomorrow. And please remember, as you heard tonight, the charges include conspiracy to commit murder, even to assassinate the vice-president of the United States, as incredible as it sounds. I'm sorry, but I did not feel it would be appropriate to take questions from the press. My purpose was to make an announcement and to sound a warning, nothing more, nothing less. Besides, I feel questions at this time, just thirteen hours before the polls open, would be directed most appropriately to the candidates. I hope they will make themselves available. And I hope that this cherished, free system of ours will prevail against those who would try to subvert it or take control of it. God help us all if we cannot stop democracy's adversaries. Thank you, and good night."

It took Bloom several minutes to work his way through the mayhem that erupted in the ballroom when he finished. Reporters shouted questions at him, many of them with anger in their voices, demanding more information. Cameras were shoved in his face, along with microphones. He must have said, "Sorry, no, I'm sorry," at least a hundred times as he fought his way out of the room.

A crowd had gathered in the hallway. More reporters and more cameras, along with the curious. Bloom searched the mass of unknown faces for Hattie. He couldn't locate her. He continued to work his way through the crowd, toward the stairway. Out of the corner of his eye, he saw a figure lunging toward him. In a millisecond an image registered: dark skin, dark hair, sneer, suit, tie, shiny metal object—gun? Something shouted, in Arabic? And then came the explosion. And the sharp pain. The room spun, with Bloom at its vortex.

Screams of panic came from all sides as people

moved away, trying to escape what might happen next. The dark man was still holding the gun, and two large men, Secret Service agents, were immediately on him, trying to wrestle the weapon away. The attacker's arm was held upward, and another shot reported from his gun, going into the ceiling.

As the assailant managed to lower his arm again, the revolver still clenched in his hand, two more shots were heard. They came from the gun of a third Secret Service agent, firing from just three feet away. The man shouted something in Arabic again, and slumped to the floor, the two agents still on him. Blood oozed out onto his white shirt. He had been mortally wounded in the chest.

Bloom lay on the carpet, still conscious. He finally saw the face of Hattie Lewis, as she kneeled beside him. She looked into his eyes and then cradled his head in her arms, against her bosom. She rocked to and fro slightly, saying, "It's okay, baby, it's okay. Hang on."

The taste was bitter in Bloom's mouth. The sounds of voices were echoed. He fought losing consciousness as best he could. He saw the color of blood on Hattie's white silk blouse. He worried for her. But it was not hers. A hand shoved a microphone in front of Hattie's face. "Congresswoman, Congresswoman Lewis!" a reporter shouted.

Hattie slowly stood up. She took the microphone from the reporter's hand. Suddenly there were television cameras being thrust toward her. Small spotlights came on. Hattie looked down at Bloom. who had a dazed look on his face. The crowd had moved back. Only a doctor, who had been in the crowd, remained near him. And Hattie began to speak.

"I am Hattie Lewis," she said, her voice sounding as though it would break at any moment. Tears were streaming down her cheeks. "I must talk to the American people. Please." And the screaming seemed to stop. The room became much less noisy. "Millions of people have just witnessed, once again, an act of violence, an attempt to murder a man who spoke out against what he saw as an injustice. It was not so long ago when we saw, with collective horror, other such acts of violence. They were against John Kennedy, against his brother Robert— here, in this hotel . . . against Martin Luther King. Will it never stop?" She raised her voice. "My God, will it never stop!" she shouted.

"I am outraged," she said, her voice booming across the room. "I am outraged that someone would do this to this man, my friend, who only spoke out against what he saw as a threat to us all.

"And I am outraged that people would conspire to interfere with our precious elective process. I promise you, whether elected or not—and Stephen Wendell will join me in promising you—that we will not rest until every charge leveled tonight is either proved or disproved, until every conspirator is brought to justice, no matter who he or she may be."

She looked down at the red stain on her blouse. Her voice now lowered. "This is the blood of an innocent man, a decent man. It was spilled by yet another in what seems to be an endless line of assassins, ready to use hatred and violence to silence truth. But it will not be silenced. There are not enough guns, enough assassins, to silence those of us who demand that justice be done.

"Tomorrow, the jury of all this—this insanity—will make its decision. Millions of you will issue judgment with your votes. Please keep the faith in our system, in the decency of people who want only to serve it and to protect it. Your judgment, your vote, has never meant more than it will mean tomorrow."

Jerry Bloom couldn't hear what Hattie was saying above him. He could see her tears, however. But his focus was failing. Now he could only see the faces up close to him. And the badges on the uniforms. He felt himself floating downward.

So this is what it's like, getting shot by someone who wants you dead.

"*Salaam*," said Aram Saraf into the telephone, calling from New York.

"*Salaam*. Allah be praised," said Hattie Lewis, from Los Angeles.

"Are we to be victorious tomorrow?" he asked.

"It's hard to tell. I think we have a chance. A good one."

"You were superb on television."

No response.

"Is Bloom dead?"

"He's hanging on. They have him in surgery now."

"Unfortunate. My courier was sloppy. He did not deserve to meet Allah after performing so poorly."

"There was no need to do that."

"I'm sorry, my sister, but you are wrong. He would never relent in his efforts. He is committed to his causes as we are to ours."

Hattie thought for a moment. "Did you arrange things in Colorado?"

"It was unfortunate, what happened to the church."

"To a friend. I will not forgive you."

"No matter. But I must remind you, friendships do not deter us from our sacred missions."

"I need no reminders from you." And she hung up the telephone.

It was close to midnight when a Secret Service agent knocked on Hattie's door and announced that Harrison Davis would like to see her. She said he could come in.

"How are you, Hattie?"

"Oh, I'll be all right. It's been one hell of an evening."

"Well, tell me," said Davis, taking a chair, although it had not been offered, "how do you assess things for tomorrow?"

"We can make it." She stared hard at him. "You knew what they were going to do to Jeanette, didn't you?"

Davis turned his head, as though he were about to scold her, in a now-now attitude.

"Well, I'm sure you'll deny it. But I think you approved of what they did."

Davis said nothing. He tried to stare Hattie down.

"You may have even known about that insane plot to kill me."

Again, Davis said nothing. But it seemed that just the slightest hint of a smile began to show at the corners of his mouth.

Davis finally spoke. "Hattie, my dear, the game is

about to end, victoriously, I hope. If you can prevail in the Senate, you'll be filling the second highest office in the land. What a marvelous feat for your people."

"*Which* people?" she asked. Now it was her turn to smile slightly, while Davis's mouth fell back, grim again.

"What do you mean?"

"I simply asked which people this would be so marvelous for. My fellow blacks?" She paused. "Or my fellow Muslims?"

Davis's mouth fell open, as though he had been struck by something incredibly powerful. He seemed to quickly add up elements to a preposterous conclusion. "I'm not sure whether to believe you," he finally said.

"It's your choice."

"What's your plan now?" Davis asked warily.

"First of all, to make sure Kern and Peterson—and especially Saraf—are brought to justice. As swiftly as possible."

"Your fellow Muslim?" he asked facetiously.

"He is a fanatic. He has to be eliminated."

Davis smiled again. "You never were with them, were you?"

"Only enough to gain their confidence."

"*And* their money, which helped us get where we are tonight, so very close to victory."

"They also have no way of knowing that I'll be president within, oh, is it about nine months he has left?"

Davis was stunned again.

"That's right. There are *two* people who know about Stephen's cancer. You and I. He apparently felt it wise to confide in just one other person what he has succeeded in keeping from everyone else. I know the whole story. How he had that severe attack of hepatitis ten years ago, and how it led to his cancer. He even called from Sloan-Kettering, to tell me it was hopeless."

Davis seemed unable to say anything.

"And that's why I think you *did* know about the plan to take me out. You knew I'd be president before the year was out, and a lot of your friends wouldn't like that. But you see, that's what makes Stephen Wendell the man he is. Do you know the kind of legacy he wants to leave behind next year? Not just that he went from a dirt farm in Texas to the White House. No, there's one other thing: He wants to be the man who put a black woman in the Oval Office. Now that's making history."

"I think I'm ready to believe you," Davis said.

"And I hope you're ready to serve me, as your president. Now I really need to rest up. It's going to be a big day tomorrow."

Grant Chase appeared to have aged. His makeup did not hide the fatigue in his face. "Good morning," he said to millions of Americans, as stunned as he was by the events of the previous night.

"The polls are now opening across America. In the next twelve hours, voters will try to make some sense out of the incredible events that have led up to this historic election. No matter what the outcome, this system of ours will never be the same again. It has been changed by what we witnessed last night, and by the events that led to the spectacular disclosures by Jerome Bloom and to the terrifying attempt on his life.

"At this moment, it appears that Bloom will survive the attack, and have the chance to pursue the truth behind his allegations. What he did last night was heroic; only time will tell whether what he did prior to last night was less than heroic. For it is the very craft he practices—media promotion—that has contributed so much to the excesses of political campaigning. But he did sound a warning for us all, a warning to look very closely at alternatives to the way in which we choose our leaders.

"Now comes the question of who shall emerge victorious from this chaotic affair. As the polls open, Stephen Wendell and Hattie Lewis are in the lead, by as many as five points over the other candidates. It is very likely none of the three tickets will be able to achieve a majority. In that case, no winner will be declared tonight. The contest will then have to go to the houses of Congress for a decision, where there is every reason to believe there is an encouraging and growing base of support for the Wendell candidacy. Or, at least, there was, prior to last night. How much that has changed, and will continue to change, is anyone's guess. The Bloom affair could pull votes away from Wendell in just hours. On the other hand, Hattie Lewis's brief, but dramatic speech had to add support for her ticket. It all depends on what the American voter is prepared to believe and willing to accept.

"It is so very sad to see how vulnerable our system is to tampering. But, somehow, we will prevail, a bit wiser for it all, we would hope. We are a sturdy people, something for which we can be thankful to-day, as we are put to this test.

"As for trying to predict today's outcome, I will have to join my colleagues, who seem unanimous in concluding that this presidential election is simply too close to call."

Get the Inside Story—
It's Stranger than Fiction!

THE MAN WHO KILLED BOYS:
THE STORY OF JOHN WAYNE GACY, JR.
by Clifford L. Linedecker

As horrifying as *Helter Skelter*, this reveals the hidden horror amid the daily lives of ordinary people. "A sensational crime story that evokes both curiosity and revulsion." —*Chicago Tribune* With 8 pages of photos.

_____ 90232-8 $3.95 U.S. _____ 90233-6 $4.95 Can.

LOVERS, KILLERS, HUSBANDS, WIVES
by Martin Blinder, M.D.

These blood-chilling true stories are case studies in the intimate passion of murder—from the most shocking files of a top legal psychiatrist.

_____ 90219-0 $3.95 U.S. _____ 90220-4 $4.95 Can.

TOO SECRET, TOO LONG
by Chapman Pincher

The astonishing and infuriating story of the man who was called "the spy of the century" and the woman who controlled him. "Remarkable..." —*Newsweek* With 8 pages of photos.

_____ 90375-8 $4.95 U.S.

SIDNEY REILLY by Michael Kettle

This true story of the world's greatest spy is the first account based on wholly authentic sources—with 8 pages of extraordinary photos.

_____ 90321-9 $3.95 U.S. _____ 90322-7 $4.95 Can.

THE LAST ENEMY by Richard Hillary

The devastating memoir of a dashing pilot who, after he is shot down and horribly burned, learns the true meaning of courage. "A deeply affecting account of courage in fighting the enemy and in fighting oneself." —*Publishers Weekly*

_____ 90215-8 $3.95 U.S.

NOW AVAILABLE AT
YOUR BOOKSTORE!